I0572786

UNSECRET ORIGIN

ERIC ICARUS — BOOK TWO

UNSECRET ORIGIN

ERIC ICARUS — BOOK TWO

JON MCBRINE

Copyright © 2026 Jon McBrine
Unsecret Origin: Eric Icarus - Book Two
All rights reserved
jonmcbrine.com
info@jonmcbrine.com
The characters and events portrayed in this book are fictitious. Any similarity to real persons, living or dead, is coincidental and not intended by the author.
No part of this book may be reproduced, or stored in a retrieval system, or transmitted in any form or by any means, electronic, mechanical, photocopying, recording, or otherwise, without express written permission of the publisher.
ISBN 979-8-9985156-3-7
Cover and interior art design by Jon McBrine

CONTENTS

UNSECRET ORIGIN

ERIC ICA... BOOK TWO

ERIC BOXWORTH
SKETCHBOOK
[PRIVATE]
JAYCEE MADDOX
(POWERHOUSE)
DAVID BOXWORTH
(DAD)
ERIC ICARUS
(ME)

Chapter One: *AERIAL*

ERIC

"**P**OWER!"
David's voice bounced off the hangar's steel walls. Eric floated near the rafters, looking down at his father from behind crisscrossed bars.

"Strength! Dominance!" David said into his headset microphone. "You want an unstoppable force on the battlefield? Gentlemen and ladies, you're all about to be very happy warmongers!"

Eric descended, hovering at a toe-to-eye level with David.

"These are army guys and scientists," Eric said. "They don't want to listen to your carnival barker spiel."

"My son has decided to grace us with his presence," David said, brushing the tips of Eric's blue boots away. "Eric Boxworth, everybody! He wasn't here for this but still thinks he knows everything!"

Men and women in dark green military uniforms and slick business suits assembled in a shadowy area of the vast floor. They stared in silence a few feet from the wide stage David stood on. The officers and Wall Street-types appeared motionless—they didn't even blink.

Eric gave them a funny look as he positioned himself above center stage. The overhead lamps provided a clear view of his two-tone blue superhero costume. Eric's double-S Super Society insignia belt buckle glistened, stealing the spotlight from David.

David tapped his foot, waiting for the attention to return to him. Instead, he received eerie silence. The unmoving audience remained shrouded; they stood where the lamps' light faded. Eric gazed at the blurry blackness around them.

"Is this how all your big presentations go?" Eric asked.

"You forgetting something, chief?" David said, side-eyeing his son.

Feeling weightless, Eric lifted a few inches while patting the smooth leather of his tunic.

"Um," he said, curling his lip. "I don't think so."

David walked to stage left, disappearing into the darkness at the edge of the platform. David's black V-neck blended him out of sight immediately. He re-emerged with a blue steel backpack. Holding its truncated, flat angular wings, David tossed the pack to Eric as if it were hollow. The backpack struck Eric's chest, knocking the wind out of him as if it were filled with rocks. The impact sent Eric flying over the soundless audience. Eric waved his arms to steady his buoyant body. The faceless people under his feet remained stiff as statues.

Eric strapped on the weighty backpack, and it sank him like an anchor. He landed on the concrete floor, surrounded by the amorphous figures.

"Before we were so colorfully interrupted," David said, his voice booming from hidden speakers. "I believe we were all here to see the premier weapon in modern warfare."

Eric grunted and heaved himself above the heads and shoulders that blocked his view. The girders and pillars faded to nothingness, taking away any semblance of a hangar bay. David's shiny black loafers practically slid across the stage, clearing the way for a strange fluttering behind him. The wavy abyss materialized into a thick black curtain. A neon green light shined through a thin sliver in the folds.

"Oh no," Eric said in a quiet breath.

Heavy, slow thumps followed by mechanical whirring sounds emitted from behind the curtain.

"Folks, you commissioned me to build a tank on legs to resolve conflicts," David said from stage right. "Instead, I created a metal beast that wins wars."

The dark curtain opened, pouring in blinking blue and green lights. Eric squinted, struggling to see the imposing figure walking up the stage. David faced his audience with a beaming grin.

"It is my absolute pleasure to introduce you to the pinnacle of cybernetic battlefield weaponry—Dreadnaught!"

Lamps above and below pointed at the seven-foot-tall hulking robot. Its stiff footsteps carried it to the middle of the stage. Ominous music blared from the speakers, and the lights switched to a deep red to match the dirge.

"This isn't simply an automated super soldier," David said over the death-march song. "This is a message. This armored titan doesn't just win decisive victories—its mere presence prevents future attacks."

Thrusters on the hefty boots complemented a wide, smooth jetpack on the robot's back. Sleek cannons mounted on the gauntlets, along with its smooth, thick chest plate, made it look even more intimidating. Gunmetal gray paint coated the armor casing, highlighted by dark red accents in stripes, arrows, and other outlining dots.

"Slap on some red, white, and blue paint, and everyone will know who's boss," David said.

A spark flashed from Dreadnaught's chartreuse visor, and long silver cannons popped from its back. Skinny turrets and fat barrels jutted from its thick metal legs. Laser scopes shot up from its wrist gauntlets. Dreadnaught's chest plate fell open, revealing an inner chamber full of short green missiles. Its knee casings flew out, projecting spinning saw blades.

"You don't want to mess with those pizza cutters!" David said, chuckling.

More guns sprang out from Dreadnaught's outer shell, with broad blades flaring like silver wings. Needles spiked out across Dreadnaught's big body, then its blank green face retracted into itself. A fireball erupted from the empty head, illuminating the space in brilliant light.

"Whoa!" Eric yelled, covering his face with his arm.

The people in the crowd offered no reaction to the dissipating blaze. The fire's radiance exposed hazy blobs where their faces would be. Puzzled, Eric inspected his forearm—gripping his sleeve and the thick blue band around his wrist, he felt no heat.

David strutted to center stage and stood by his creation.

"You wanted me to build you terror incarnate?"

Dreadnaught's jade-colored faceplate slid up, resetting to its original form. It glowed a piercingly bright, pulsating light.

"I am Dreadnaught," the robot bellowed in a monotone voice. "I exist to destroy!"

"Do I deliver, or what?" David said, smiling with

his tongue poking his cheek.

"I can't watch anymore of this," Eric whispered.

Eric turned to find an exit, brushing through the featureless people. He ascended to find a sea of nothingness awaiting him. The collection of twenty members of the crowd grew to hundreds, lining back into infinity. Eric flew as fast as he could over the endless rows of blank people but found no way out. A glimmer streaked in the corner of his eye. Eric careened to where he spotted the twinkling, but it vanished.

"That backpack got real light, didn't it?" David said from somewhere.

Eric's brown hair remained unkempt, yet no wind flowed through it. Despite increasing his velocity, he felt no gravitational forces.

"Am I even moving?"

"Were there a million literal nobodies here?" David's disembodied voice said. "Did somebody forget to pay the electric bill? Did you fly around in circles accomplishing diddly squat?"

"Shut up," Eric said, grumbling.

"Hey, you're the one piecing this together from the little snippets you've heard. We're just going off your playbook."

The yellowish spark flickered from the shadows, then the stage formed around it. David waited, checking his non-existent wristwatch. Dreadnaught attempted to cross its arms, but the bulk of its artillery made it cumbersome, and it retreated its limbs to its sides.

"I exist to destroy, not to wait!" Dreadnaught stated.

"Tell that to the aerial architect," David said, scoffing.

Eric pushed himself farther, but the stage stayed

a mere glimpse on the horizon. The shining energy shaped itself into a humanoid figure at the side of the black platform. The golden glowing rescinded until it became an orb atop the featureless person's head. Eric strained but did not get any nearer. The ball of light dimmed with a reddish tint and morphed into something, but Eric couldn't tell what.

To his relief, Eric approached the stage, which appeared as a drifting black square in an eternity of liquid darkness. The rose gold-colored energy shifted into something familiar.

"Hair?" Eric said, crinkling his nose.

Strawberry blonde locks hung from the top of the translucent mannequin body. An unseen entity etched eyes, a nose, and lips into the head, fleshing it out and giving it color. Eric boosted himself like a human torpedo, desperate to see the forming face up close. A black mustache seemed to teleport from thin air, and a body assembled around it.

"Baron Maddox!"

"It's 'Mister Maddox' to you," Baron said, leering.

Baron stuck out against the darkness in his pristine white suit. Eric halted, stopping an inch from colliding with Baron's matching ivory tie. He towered over Eric—an undetectable light source gleamed across Baron's slicked-back hair like a halo. Eric sniffed the air, earning a confused cocked eyebrow from Baron.

"You usually wear some kind of cologne," Eric said, flaring his nostrils. "Some expensive stench. But I don't smell anything."

"It doesn't compare to your putrid Phoenix Swagger body spray poison, eh? How do you expect my daughter to ever like someone as foolish as you, boy?"

Baron crossed his arms.

"Enough of this nonsense! I only permitted two

Boxworths to attend today," Baron said. "And you, young Eric, are not one of them!"

Eric planted his feet on the void, which thankfully—and impossibly—supported his feet.

"It's Eric 'Icarus!'"

Baron narrowed his eyes, getting in Eric's face.

"You are what I made you!" Baron said.

"You didn't give me my power!"

"Nor did I give you your weakness."

Electrifying pain surged throughout Eric's body as he collapsed onto the floor.

"You go too long without being afloat, and you suffer unbearable agony," Baron said, pulling a mask from behind him. "As if gravity itself is punishing you for defying it."

Baron slipped the mask of Truther onto his head. The blonde sewn-in wig curved in a bouffant wave. A thick golden "T" visor covered most of his face, but Baron's intense glare somehow remained. Scientists in lab coats scurried about in the background, hustling and bustling in and out of the shadows. Baron frowned under his cowl; despite wearing his superhero mask, he emanated villainous rage.

"I gave you your costume," Baron said. "I made you a member of the Super Society."

Eric writhed in anguish as the invisible force seized his nerves.

"I provided your father an opportunity to create a massive power battery," Baron said. "A career-saving invention. I gave him purpose again!"

"Hey, can I get paid for that?" David said from behind them. "Preferably before I turn into a shadow person or whatever this place will do to me."

"Not now, David," Baron said, glancing over his shoulder.

He returned the cold, blank stare of his T-shaped visor to Eric. The wide bottom of the "T" extended downward, covering his mustache.

"Eric, I supplied your decoy backpack," Baron said. "The world thinks it is an anti-gravity device. No one suspects your natural gift of flight. You haven't been locked in a government lab or studied like a caged animal! No one has dissected you to get to the root of your power—all because of me!"

Eric curled, holding himself, riding out the searing storm overtaking his insides.

"Gahhhhh!" he screamed.

The floor melted, opening a rippling wormhole underneath Eric. The circular mouth swallowed his body, then dropped him into a swirl of colors and images moving too rapidly to discern.

"Whaaaaatt isssss happenniiinnnngggg?!"

A spiraling nexus whirled at the end of the crazy tunnel. Eric's heart thumped through his chest when he recognized the spinning blades of the *Pegasus*, the Super Society's helicopter. Eric dropped closer to the blades, and the tunnel shrunk, closing him in tighter. Eric panicked, unable to will himself away from getting ground into little pieces of meat.

He phased through, feeling nothing. Eric plopped through a ceiling and then landed in a chair. He blinked and felt a slick desk in front of him.

"Eric? Aren't you permanently absent?" Valerie said from the front of the classroom. "What are you doing here?"

Astonished to see his science teacher, Eric gawked at her, mouth agape. Scratches and squiggly chalk lines covered the blackboard behind her.

"Ms. Cooper?"

Melvin sat next to Eric, wearing his Supercut

costume. The pointy end of his mask wiggled in fuming anger.

"Truther is insane for recruiting you!" he said, snarling.

A few rows ahead, Tiffany whipped her fiery red hair, revealing her orange and pink mask—her colors as the crime-fighter Extra.

"I was the new 'it' girl," she said. "Then you came along and stole my thunder!"

A tapping on his shoulder rattled Eric. He swiveled to see Yvette in her Go-Go outfit. Her brow scrunched under her silver visor.

"You're a liability to the team, Icarus!" she scolded. "You're too inexperienced! You'll get us all killed!"

"I'm only on the team to hide my secret power!" Eric said.

He tried to stand, but the chair seemed to have a hold on him. He shimmied but did not raise a millimeter.

"Mr. Maddox said if I pose as a superhero, no one will suspect my flying ability is real!" Eric blathered, sensing nervous sweat dripping down his forehead—yet could not feel its coldness. "He told me that everyone loves the Super Society! I wear this backpack, and I can float all day! Where's Jayc—?"

"You can float on down to detention," Valerie said, stretching her mouth to an unnatural width. "Final warning!"

"But I didn't do anything!" Eric pleaded. "I just want to go home!"

"You got to be home, remember, honey?" Eric's mother said, soothing and creeping in from the corners of the room.

Desks, chairs, and chalkboard erasers evaporated into dusty wisps. The other kids dematerialized, and

Valerie liquified and then drained into darkness. Eric sat on nothing, then stood upright. An eternity of emptiness surrounded him. Eric found himself on the stage alone yet felt a ghost in the air.

"What're you still doing here?" Eliza asked from behind him. "I thought you wanted to spend the day goofing off? Eating ice cream for dinner, reading comic books?"

"Wha—no!" Eric said, turning.

His mother stood a few feet from him, dressed in the cardinal-red cardigan and gray slacks he remembered her wearing so often. Stunned, Eric lost his voice and could hardly blink as the hangar's walls reappeared around them. People in lab coats marched in from Eric's periphery, writing on clipboards and tapping on tablets.

"Eliza?" David said, his voice bouncing and reverberating from what sounded like sporadically placed speakers. "Please move to the visitors' area. We will begin soon."

Banks of boxy power generators popped up on the floor, and the steel girders and support beams returned. Serious-looking people paced behind large observation windows at the rear of the spacious room. Eric backed away, nearly tripping over a bundle of multi-colored cords snaking across the floor. He levitated and spun to see a vast night sky through a huge open hatch. A massive white moon hung among the blinking stars.

"You made such a stink about wanting to be home by yourself," Eliza said, standing in the eye of the reality developing around her. "Eric, you whined and whined until I finally gave in and decided to leave."

"Mom! You gotta get out of here!"

"Am I interrupting your video game whatevers?

Sorry, sweetie, but you wanted me here at your dad's big demonstration. You wanted me out of the way."

Ceiling-mounted lamps directed streams of light to something behind Eliza. She did not move, silhouetted and growing darker.

"Please, Mom, it's not safe!"

"Oh, you don't need a sitter," she said. "You're ten. You're a big boy now."

BLAM! BLAM! BLAM!

Blinding energy exploded from behind Eliza. Her face deformed into pure shock, widening her eyes and unhinging her jaw. Slow-motion white bolts crackled and surged across her skin. Eliza's body raised and soared at an angle, swooping across the open bay.

"I exist to destroy!" Dreadnaught roared.

Dreadnaught marched up the stage, firing its arsenal of cannons at where Eliza flew.

"No!" Eric shouted.

He took off, flying after his mother throughout the expanse. A bent piece of shrapnel stabbed Eliza's side. Eric yelped as she wordlessly let momentum carry her. Before they could cross the threshold and escape to the void outside, Eliza stopped cold. The night produced a tall steel door that slammed shut, confining Eliza into a cylindrical pod. Her terror-stricken face glared at Eric from behind a glass pane. Eric pounded on the thick metal door, then slid his hands across its curved surface.

"How's this thing open?!"

"You can't open it, Eric," Eliza said, muffled from inside the chamber.

"I'm gonna save you!"

"Oh, honey," she said, shaking her head. "Baron Maddox saved me. But, sweetie, you're fourteen now—look at this as a lesson in responsibility."

Clank clank clank. Eric looked down to see a gray robotic dog bang its chrome snout onto the pod's base.

"Did someone say 'responsibility?'" the automated animal said in a voice that sounded like David talking through a tin can.

"Responsi-Bulldog?" Eric said, pursing his lips, utterly baffled.

"I have been programmed to teach Eric the value of hard work. Woof. Woof."

Dreadnaught unloaded a barrage of crimson lasers, blasting the generators. The batteries ignited, erupting into a maelstrom of lightning. The shockwave crashed into Eric, sending him back to black nothingness.

The dream dissolved into a surreal reality.

"Is he awake?" Eric heard Eliza ask from what sounded like a galaxy away.

Eric willed his heavy eyelids to crack open. Through a haze, afterimages of his mother faced him.

"You need your rest, sweetheart," she said before stepping away.

"M-moooooom," Eric said with a gelatinous tongue and saggy cheeks.

"As far you can tell in your current state, she may as well be your real mother," Baron said.

Baron's shadowed face appeared behind the windowpane. His breath fogged the glass.

"Not that you'll remember any of this," Baron said, his voice piping in and out like faulty headphones. "The sedatives can sometimes take an extra minute with certain people. You're more strong-willed than I expected, young Mr. Icarus."

Bobbing like bait in a river, Eric sensed the close quarters of the pod. The drive to move abandoned him, so he surrendered to remaining trapped in the cramped shell.

"Your resilience will serve me well," Baron said. "But defiance? That will get you in trouble."

Baron exhaled a steady sigh, clouding the glass in a gray mist.

"Go back to sleep," Baron said. "This earth won't be the same when you wake up—it will be mine. I'll show you the true way to use your abilities. With them, I will control an entire population. I'll reign, beloved and unopposed."

The fog faded, revealing Baron's cold stare.

"I'll gut your mother and take her gifts. And I'll have dominion over the sky."

Eric sealed his eyes, and his mind traveled to a colorless abyss. Baron's voice entered his ears like a slithering worm.

"Then I'll drain you of every ounce of superpower in your blood."

Chapter Two: *PITCH*

JAYCEE

"**C**OME ON, FLOOR IT!"

A cacophony of honking and revving engines blared around Jaycee.

"Can't this thing move any faster?!" she said over a pop song played at full volume from the next car.

"Faster? We're bumper-to-bumper!" Kev said, barely heard over a slew of profanities from another motorist. "I didn't think game day traffic would be this bad—especially for a Tuesday!"

Jaycee brushed a blonde lock from her forehead as she stood, her calves pressed against the warm passenger seat. With the milk-white roof retracted, she got a clearer view of the four lanes full of frustrated drivers trapped in their vehicles. The skyline of New St. Cloud City hung on the horizon, seeming more like a portrait of skyscrapers rather than an attainable destination. She glanced down at Kev's antsy fingers tapping at the steering wheel.

"I'm starting to think this isn't a study session," he said with a nervous laugh. "...And I'm just now realizing that your mom didn't let you leave campus. And I'm the accomplice to this school-skipping scheme."

"She pays you to tutor me, and today's lesson just so happens to be..."

The car inched forward, then stopped. Jaycee clenched onto the metal frame of the windshield to steady herself. The honey-colored steel was hot from the midday sun. She quickly withdrew her hand.

"...how to go nowhere fast."

She pressed her lips on her heat-stung fingers while surveying her exit strategies. Jaycee squinted, scanning past the dizzying sunlight. Metro Memorial Stadium sat less than a mile ahead of them, but with the bottlenecking cluster of cars blocking every entrance, it may as well have been on Mars. Jaycee rubbed her finger on her pink-and-white striped shirt; then, her nose perked up. Her nostrils welcomed the aroma of bratwursts and popcorn wafting through the air, covering the pungent smell of exhaust fumes.

Sunbeams glistened across the amphitheater-style windows lining the curved stadium. The stone-colored exterior made the gargantuan building look like a fancy institution. A shimmering crisscross of metal beams ran along the rim of the upper deck. The season began a week prior, and hopeful excitement was on every fan's face. People of all ages traveled in herds across walkways and sectioned-off streets to reach lengthy box office lines. Jaycee was so close and yet so far away.

"Ugh! This traffic is literally the worst!" Jaycee huffed. "It'll take forever to get inside!"

"I didn't realize you were such a baseball fan," Kev said, puffing his chest out as if Jaycee hadn't noticed his "DAWSON UNIVERSITY ATHLETICS DEPT." t-shirt.

Jaycee also noticed how the tight top stretched over his well-sculpted chest—not that she'd ever admit that to him. Nor would she confess to stealing more than a glance at Kev's neatly trimmed black curly hair, which complemented his handsome features. Despite his biceps that were far more sinewy than any sixteen-year-old should possess, Jaycee's mind drifted to another boy.

What's the point of having a friend who can fly if he's nowhere to be found? Jaycee thought, curling her lip. *Apparently, Eric Icarus' other superpower is vanishing right when things get hard.*

She diverted her attention to the white double-S logo on her phone. She tapped on the icon, launching a three-dimensional map of the area. A blinking red arrow pointed at the ballpark. "Super Society TROUBLE ALERT" sprawled across the top of the screen, followed by "BOMB THREAT in stadium: team is in position, DO NOT ALERT the public."

"Oh, uh, baseball? Yeah, I'm a diehard Majors fan," Jaycee said while twisting her palm away from Kev in a weak attempt to conceal her phone.

A new message popped up: "All active Super Society members have received their orders. Powerhouse is not cleared for action. Repeat: Powerhouse is not authorized for active duty."

"Getting in the game will be tough, though," Jaycee said.

I still have access to the Super Society app; that counts for something, right? she thought. *Or maybe they just forgot to delete me—or forgot about me entirely...*

"Can't afford tickets? I hear that," Kev said, leaning back in the driver's seat. "It's the same story with my folks. They think I don't need extra money just because I got a track scholarship. I can't imagine what it must be like for your dad to be a gazillionaire and cut you off—"

"Wait," Jaycee blurted, plopping back down next to him.

The hot leather seat seared her legs. Jaycee squirmed, adjusting her denim shorts while keeping her narrowed eyes on Kev.

"How do you know—I mean, what're you talking about?"

Kev breathed through his teeth.

"Tiffany had mentioned something about Mr. Maddox in a text..." he said, grimacing. "And how he is, er, giving up custody of you..."

"Why would she tell you—hold up, you're texting Tiffany now?"

"We kinda connected at the dance the other night, and—"

"You know what, never mind," Jaycee said, pocketing her phone.

Gotta focus on the mission! she ordered herself. *No allowance, no problem. This is superhero business! I don't care what Dad says—Powerhouse is saving the day!*

She wanted to tell Kev that her father was not only a famous tech tycoon but also the crime-fighter known as Truther, leader of the Super Society. Keeping track of secret identities wasn't fun but lying about a double life had only gotten easier with time—a fact she wondered how proud of she should be. Jaycee reached over and grabbed her pink and blue bookbag. The hefty bag sank onto her lap.

"How many books do you have in there?" Kev said, spiking an eyebrow.

"Can't leave home without the classics, right?"

She felt the grooved imprint of a metal disc underneath the smooth texture of her bag. The car crawled another inch.

Snails must be laughing at us.

Sweat beaded down Jaycee's forehead. They were on the eve of summer break, but it felt like late August, and it was only getting hotter.

Jaycee peeked at the track running parallel to the street. A green trolley emerged from around a bend. It carried a gaggle of fans under its ivory-painted roof. Men and women hung from the side of the cable car, each wearing matching Majors jerseys. As they got closer, Jaycee spotted the letters "VIP" on the lanyards dangling from their necks.

"Consider the day saved," she whispered.

Jaycee flung her bookbag over her shoulder as she stood. Kev wiped his perspiring forehead with his forearm. He blinked away droplets of sweat, then did a double take. Jaycee climbed into the backseat.

"What're you doing?"

"Gonna go find a place with working air conditioning," Jaycee said, positioning her sneaker onto the top of the backseat door.

"I won't have money to fix my car's AC if my tutees bail!"

Jaycee landed on the street.

"Don't worry!" she said as she ran in front of the motionless sedan next to them. "But, Kev, just try to get out of here as soon as you can!"

"That sounds like a 'worry' thing!"

The trolley edged nearer.

Pick up the pace, Powerhouse! Jaycee commanded herself.

She hopped and climbed onto the hood of the neighboring car, earning an angry honk. Jaycee skipped onto the hood of a blue pickup truck in the next lane. As the infuriated driver shouted from behind his windshield, Jaycee hit the pavement feet-first. The trolley rode alongside the stalled traffic, passing Jaycee. She sprinted across the sidewalk and onto the track, trailing the transport. If it moved any faster, Jaycee would need her superhero speedster teammate Go-Go's accelerator armor attachments.

That, she thought, *and a way to even contact the Super Society. I'm blocked from sending messages on the app—I can only receive trouble alerts telling me to sit by and do nothing. Jeez, I'm sidelined for, like, a day, and then everyone ghosts me!*

A few fans hanging from the sides of the trolley creased their brows under their ball caps. Others laughed in disbelief. Jaycee tugged at the strap of her bookbag, wondering if her equipment had always felt so heavy. Adrenaline turbocharged her muscles, and within seconds, Jaycee caught up to the rear of the streetcar. She grabbed hold of a silver handlebar stretched across the back, pulling herself closer to a surprised family of Majors' faithful.

A hail of cheers and jeers poured over Jaycee as she found footing on the bumper.

"Whoa!"

"Holy crap! Tell me somebody is filming this!"

"Excuse me, miss, this ride is for VIP guests only!"

"You wouldn't happen to have an extra ticket, would you?" Jaycee said with an unconvincing smirk while keeping an eye on the approaching ballpark entrance.

Lengthy lines snaked away from a row of ticket booths. Clumps of people crowded around the rows of glass doors at the park's base. The trolley rolled by them and headed for a closed-off gate beside the waiting commoners.

"Hey, no scalpers allowed here!" a deep voice said from behind the irked fans facing Jaycee.

People in the middle of the trolley parted, giving way for a pair of aviators and a thick mustache to come to the rear.

"No free rides," the stocky, mustachioed man said as he stepped up to the silver guardrail.

Jaycee saw her surprised reflection in his shiny sunglasses. The guy's lanyard had a tag with "security" on it. His buzz cut, white polo, and black slacks made him look like an official fun-killer.

The trolley pulled nearer to the VIP-only gate. A white-haired man monitored the glass entryway. His neon-yellow shirt had the words "EVENT STAFF" written across the front. The older man sported a slight hunch and a paunch, but Jaycee knew he'd be trouble.

"No ticket, no ride," the security guy said, scrunching his face in a mean frown. "If you're trying to sneak your way into the game, then I gotta report you!"

Jaycee whipped out her phone to read a new notification: "Enemy has been spotted. Extra and Supercut, secure the perimeter. Keep the supervillain away from civilians!"

Just a little farther… Jaycee thought, counting the seconds until she would be close enough to the entrance. *I'm really gonna have to kick it into high gear if I want to outrun these very important pains in my—!*

"Hey, are you listening to me?!" the security guy said, snapping Jaycee back to reality. "I said, if you don't have a ticket, then you gotta—!"

"Make a run for it!" Jaycee finished for him before hopping off the trolley.

She hightailed it to the gate. Her ponytail whipped the back of her head with every hurried step. Jaycee saw the trolley parking. The lone event staffer at the VIP entrance gate extended a hand to stop her, slowing

Jaycee to a jog. His loose-fitting sleeves wavered as he advanced.

"Ticket, miss?" he said with a crooked smile, visibly perplexed by what he saw.

More trouble alerts rumbled the phone in Jaycee's pocket.

"I don't have time for this!" Jaycee said.

She huffed, blowing a loose blonde strand from her forehead.

"I didn't want to pull this card," Jaycee said, twisting her lips as if she was going to puke up her lunch. "My father is Baron Maddox. Head honcho of Pantheon Solutions. He owns the ballpark. Now, can I just get in already?!"

"Baron Maddox?" the staffer said, scratching his wrinkled temple. "No, he owns the football stadium across town."

"Wait, he does?" Jaycee said as her eyes bounced around, mentally searching through her jumbled memory banks. "Dang, he does, doesn't he?"

"I got to let these folks in," the staffer said. "Best you be getting on, now, miss."

The white-haired man unlocked the glass door. Across from them, the VIPs marched down a crosswalk with the security guy leading the charge.

"You're gonna spend the game in our holding facility!" the security guy shouted. "I'm sure your parents will love hearing about—!"

"Hey, look, it's the teenage superhero sensation Powerhouse!" Jaycee yelled, pointing to the lines of waiting fans.

Gasps and cheers erupted from the VIPs. The staffer's crow's feet deepened as he squinted. The security guy lowered his shades, curious to catch a glimpse of the celebrity hero.

Now or never! Jaycee thought.

She raced into the open doorway, unseen by the dumbfounded staffer or the confused VIPs.

"Okay, Jaycee, damage control," she said as she ran down a corridor with concrete bricks lining the walls. "That little stunt will probably get me in deeper crud with Dad."

As she turned a corner, Jaycee looked behind her to ensure she wasn't being followed.

"But I'm helping the team—saving people!" Jaycee said, nearing the end of the long hallway. "Besides, what can Dad do that's worse than ditching me? And he wouldn't risk telling Mom I'm Powerhouse. So, I'm in the clear!"

Images of her alter ego flashed in Jaycee's mind. She refocused as she approached a display of Majors t-shirts and caps. Jaycee retreated to the opposite side of the hall, peeking from around the corner. Programs, posters, and baseball card packs littered a wide merchandise table. A woman with a kind, round face and curly brown hair hung a shirt on the top rack. She wore a Majors jersey under a bundle of lanyards and buttons.

Jaycee's phone buzzed. The latest Super Society notification read, "Intel reports the bomber is approaching the premium box seats. Truther and Go-Go are en route to the VIP lounge. DO NOT ALERT THE PUBLIC!"

The merch woman faced Jaycee's direction to arrange a few items on her table. Jaycee recoiled, flattening herself against the warm wall. She prayed they did not notice her.

"Using my stealthy, ninja-like prowess would be much easier if this merch-lady turned around or something!" Jaycee whispered. "And, of-freaking-course, the bad guy would be headed where the VIPs are going!"

Across from the merch table, a small crew of vendors dropped hotdogs on a metal rack and sprinkled salt on pretzels. They'd be the first to welcome hungry fans who would soon enter this stadium section.

Those fans will be here any second! Jaycee thought.

Marching footsteps reverberated throughout the concrete hall. Jaycee sighed in relief when the merch woman bent down to dig through a crate. After a few big, quiet steps past the oblivious woman, Jaycee slid behind the display wall. She crouched between stacks of cardboard boxes.

"Finally, some privacy!" she said under her breath.

Unzipping her bookbag revealed her superhero costume inside. Muscle memory guided her quick change: Jaycee threw off her school clothes and shimmied into the form-fitting, blue and yellow Powerhouse uniform. Jaycee pulled the mask over her face, covering her eyes with rounded, yellow-tinted domes. Her jaw fidgeted, adjusting to having the cowl only conceal the top portion of her head. She tugged at her ponytail and brushed the hair sticking out of the top of the mask.

Jaycee retrieved the final pieces to complete her ensemble—two metal discs, one gold, and the other silver. Snapping them onto her shoulders initiated a linking sequence.

Okay, armor, do your thing!

Piece by piece, curved silver steel rings ejected from the discs and coiled down her left arm. Her right arm followed suit, shimmering in gold. Chrome casings over her knuckles lit up, flashing yellow until switching to solid neon green, signaling the enhancers were at full power. Jaycee smiled as the hot rush of super-strength coursed through her muscle fibers.

She spied an elevator at the end of the hallway. A sign beside it was labeled, "To Skybox."

Jaycee side-eyed the food vendors across from her, who appeared too busy slathering butter on pretzels to notice her. The delicious smell caused Jaycee's stomach to grumble, drowned out only by the sound of the VIPs storming up the corridor. Jaycee peeked around the merch wall—the woman still rummaged, face buried in a crate. Jaycee hurried over to the elevator and tapped the "up" button, and the glossy door retracted. A moment later, the lift pulled upward.

Jaycee chalked it up to sheer luck that no one else waited in the spacious elevator. A glance at the ceiling panels proved enough for Jaycee to spot the little corner-mounted surveillance camera.

Well, it's not like the stadium security doesn't already know the Super Society is here, right?

She withdrew her phone from the side pocket of her pants, then leaned, letting her armored arm *clank* against the metal wall. Jaycee's steel-encased thumbs hovered over the screen as special sensors in her glove accessed the trouble alerts. She was careful not to touch the glass as to avoid risking cracking it with her supercharged, armored fingertips. A tapping motion activated the messages app.

"'Intel reports the bomber has entered the skybox,'" Jaycee read aloud. "'Civilians and stadium personnel have been cleared. Extra and Supercut will stand guard. No one enters. Truther and Go-Go will engage the target. Identity of the bomber has not been confirmed—be ready for anything, heroes.'"

She swiped the notification away.

"Mystery villain, eh? Nothing I can't handle."

Jaycee stared at the backlit row of numbers next to the "up" button on the panel. Despite willing it, the elevator did not move any faster. Jaycee switched to her personal messages. She looked at the name "Eric Boxworth" and sighed—no new texts.

"I hate that Dad is just giving me up like this," Jaycee said, talking at the phone. "Tiffany, Yvette, Melvin—they're just following Dad's orders, so I understand why they wouldn't reach out."

Jaycee placed the phone back into her pocket and blew a deep, sad breath.

"But you, Eric—you running off without saying goodbye, that I don't get."

Ding! The elevator came to a stop, and the door slid open. Jaycee stepped into a wide hallway with painted murals of all-star baseball players on the walls. She saw no one, but voices came from around the corner ahead of her.

"Not that I'm complaining about getting out of fifth period Biology," Tiffany said in her familiar snarky tone, "but guard duty is soooo unworthy of my talents. But I suppose someone has to make sure you don't wander off after the first shiny object you see—no offense, but yes, offense, Supercut."

"Um, I think none taken?" Melvin answered, his gruff voice sounding unsure.

"This must be the place," Jaycee muttered.

Jaycee took slow steps, planting her blue boots firmly on the slick floor.

If I'm going to do anything superhero-y today, I have to first get past the tattletale twins, Jaycee thought. *Dad must see that Powerhouse shouldn't be benched, which means I have to go big or literally go home—permanently.*

"Ya know, Extra," Melvin said, his voice growing

louder the closer Jaycee approached the corner. "You could always just make duplicates of yerself. Leave one of your copies here, then take off somewhere if you want to leave so badly. But I think you can't stand being away from me."

"You know that's not how my gear works—"

Zap!

Tiffany's body flew past Jaycee's face. Spine-shaking volts of electricity convulsed across Tiffany's exposed midriff. Jittering white electricity crackled over her orange utility belt. Dazed, Tiffany crumpled to the floor, collapsing past the corner. Her slim body lay still a few feet from Jaycee.

"Extra!" Melvin cried.

The pointy yellow boots of Melvin's costume squeaked as he ran to the unmoving girl. He did a double take, stunned to see his superhero teammate—and fellow high school classmate—Jaycee.

"Jay—Powerhouse?!" he blurted, kneeling by Tiffany. "What're you doing here?!"

"Saving your butts!"

Melvin's hairy arm yanked on the silver disc on Jaycee's armored shoulder. She backpedaled from the edge of the corner.

"You can't go in there!"

"Why not?" Jaycee said, almost yelling.

"Keep yer voice down!" Melvin whispered, hushing her. "The super-baddie in the next room has an itchy bomb-finger! He sees you, and it could jolt him into going ka-boom!"

They froze when a haunting cackle entered their ears—it was how a snake would laugh.

"Take you out of the ball game, pick you out from the crowd! I'll shock you with my electric attack, and I promise you won't ever come back!"

Spending lonely school nights studying Super Society case files easily made Jaycee recognize the sinister singer's voice.

"Shock Jock..." Jaycee said in a small voice as if speaking a cursed name aloud.

She brushed Melvin off her, taking careful steps beyond the corner. A yard or so ahead of her, two wide, clear doors were propped open. Cushy seats waited inside the swanky lounge, along with a row of baseball diamond-shaped trays and a humongous glass window overlooking the field—the hum of Shock Jock's electrified weapon buzzed in the air.

A white cloak whooshed into view, immediately followed by the broad frame of Truther. His black boots stuck out from beneath the majestic cape.

"How about a little one-on-one?" Truther challenged, rebalancing his footing a bit, providing a clearer picture of him.

Dad...!

A gray plastic cart rested by the open door. Jaycee hurried and ducked behind it. She looked through the middle rung of the cart above a stack of white serving trays.

The golden T-shaped visor covering Truther's eyes, nose, and upper lip must have been in overdrive. Jaycee intuited that the scanners within Truther's mask didn't detect her because they were focused on the threat. Jaycee edged the rolling cart nearer, unable to see anything beyond her team leader's imposing figure.

"How about I hit you outta the park?" the voice of Shock Jock countered, snickering.

A peek behind her showed Jaycee that Melvin wasn't leaving Tiffany's side. His face told her he hated the idea of Jaycee moving an inch closer.

Shock Jock stepped into view, standing across

from Truther a few feet from the entranceway. He quickly stroked his pointy caramel-colored goatee, then playfully dangled his electric chrome bat. Shock Jock took his time approaching, casually adjusting his reflective shades.

"Whattaya waitin' for?" Shock Jock said. "Play clock is runnin' out!"

He held up his club and let it flash with bright, wriggling bolts of electrical energy. Jaycee crouched lower behind the cart. While Shock Jock and Truther remained locked in a lethal staring contest, Jaycee's mind raced, picking apart the potential weak spots of this athletic antagonist. Jaycee noted Shock Jock's exposed neck nestled beneath and between his large metal shoulder and chest pads.

Truther's wrist-mounted T-gauntlets primed with a blue flare. He aimed them at the insulated outfit Shock Jock wore, which resembled a perverse parody of a baseball player's uniform. The cruel competitor's sinister sniggering infected Jaycee's ears.

"Surrender, Shock Jock," Truther demanded in his augmented voice, deeper than the natural voice of the man behind the mask.

Dad can be scary when he's angry as just Baron Maddox, Jaycee thought. *But leave him trapped in a room with a guy known for attacking people in large gatherings; well, Truther doesn't get much scarier than this.*

Shock Jock slid over to match Truther's position as if in some ritualistic dance. Jaycee held her breath, hoping the villain didn't spot her. Shock Jock paused.

"Well, who do we have here?"

Jaycee's heart stopped.

Shock Jock peered over his shoulder. A blurry purple haze materialized behind him. Yvette formed in full costume as Go-Go. Her puffy afro wiggled as her speedster body halted.

"Not so fast, Go-Go," Shock Jock said, looking back at Truther. "You'll never find the bomb I planted—that is, if you even live long enough to look. If I press this button, then it's game over!"

He nodded to the black cylindrical device he held in his free hand. His gloved finger caressed a pill-shaped yellow button.

"You Super Society suckers think you're big and bad just 'cause you stopped my associate, Time Thief?" Shock Jock said. "He was just a casualty of war. And believe me, this is a war against you delusional do-gooders! You won't stop all of us united! The Guerrillas will win!"

"Gorillas?" Yvette remarked. "Like, apes?"

"No, like guerrilla warfare!" Shock Jock snapped. "What's so hard to understand about that?!"

An arch of lightning sparked from his bat, shining across the silvery surface of Yvette's wraparound visor.

"You'd be willing to sacrifice yourself, Shock Jock?" Truther said. "A glory hound like you?"

Shock Jock took a batting stance, careful not to drop his detonator. The voltage pulsated from his silver slugger with a loud hum.

"Good point, Truther," he said. "Maybe instead, I'll settle for taking you out of the game for good!"

Jaycee placed her hand on the floor, ready to pounce. Yvette moved from behind Shock Jock, but his glare froze her in place.

"Calling an audible," Shock Jock said. "Double play!"

He swung for the fences, but a barrage of neon-blue lasers pitched from Truther's wrist-gauntlet rocked him. Crackling with electric power, the bat absorbed the blast. Unfazed, Shock Jock smirked.

"Good hustle, but I'm afraid you just struck out—"

"Go time!" Jaycee said, pushing the cart away with super strength.

The plastic pushcart shot like a missile, crashing into the chair between Shock Jock and Truther. Jaycee bolted toward Shock Jock, bombarding the bat-man. She clutched tightly with her steel hands, using her powerful momentum to force the villain forward. They headed straight for the giant window.

SMASH!

Glass shattered, splintering into a furious flurry of flying shards—the rush of falling overwhelmed Jaycee. Grabbing hold of Shock Jock's geared-up body provided her only sense of reality. Awestruck faces of fans below warped in her speeding vision. Jaycee and the villain plunged into the ocean of seats beneath them.

An invisible force carried them over the aisles of chairs, steps, and guard railing. Somewhere between the mad mixture of blustering air and crowd noise, Jaycee heard Shock Jock gurgle something. Jaycee's power-enhanced arms squeezed tight and weren't letting go.

Shock Jock landed on his back. The sudden collision with the green turf rattled Jaycee's bones, sending her rolling next to a mound of dirt. Her eyelids fluttered until the world made sense again. A pair of cleats stood atop a heap of tan-colored clay and sand. Jaycee lifted her head to see a man silhouetted by the sun. Squinting, she saw it was the Majors starting pitcher gawking, pushing his cap back from his head.

Drool spewed from Shock Jock's open mouth. Down for the count, steam rose from his sizzling, concussed body.

"Lucky for you, I think fast on my feet," Yvette said.

Jaycee shook her head as she took in the view from the pitcher's mound. She cupped her hand over the domes covering her eyes to gaze at the massive park. Excited fans clapped in the seats while bewildered players stared from inside the dugout. The raucous crowd noise blared, rivaled by the anthemic organ music blasting around her. High above, a twinkle of sunlight flickered—the silver Super Society helicopter, the *Pegasus*, hovered in the sky.

Security guys in white polos and black slacks jogged toward her. Yvette, in her psychedelic-patterned costume as Go-Go, waved them off.

"You carried me? Us?" Jaycee said, getting to her feet.

Yvette nodded, flashing a grin. Truther stomped over; the wavy blonde hair sticking out of his cowl bounced with every step. Sunlight sparkled over the golden T-symbol on his chest.

"Go-Go, find the bom—!" Truther said, stopping before dropping the b-word in front of hundreds of civilians. "Find the you-know-what."

"On it, boss!"

Yvette dashed away like a phantom. Jaycee patted some dirt from her pant leg, afraid to look up. When she did, she saw Truther glaring down at her. Even under the T-shaped visor, she could recognize the angry face of her father, Baron Maddox.

"Didn't I tell you to go home?" he asked.

"Oh, I thought you meant steal home! Like, it was this whole baseball-themed thing, and I just—!"

"Powerhouse," he said. "Report to HQ. Now!"

Truther turned, flipping his ivory-colored cape up, then stormed off. Jaycee gulped. She looked behind her at the pitcher. He scrunched his gaunt face, then held up his hands—one gloved in a mitt—gesturing to her that she was on her own with this one.

Chapter Three: *VERTICAL*

JAYCEE

"**W**HAT ARE YOU DOING HERE?**" Tiffany asked, sneering with a curled upper lip.

Jaycee asked herself the same question while peering through the doorway. The orderliness of Tiffany's bedroom took Jaycee by surprise, not that she knew what to expect. The idea of hanging out with Tiffany outside school or Super Society business usually curdled Jaycee's guts.

I can't remember the last time I was here, Jaycee thought. *Were the walls always this pink?*

"I'm looking for my dad," Jaycee said, stepping inside.

"Um, sure, I guess you're invited, come on in," Tiffany said, scoffing. "I'm fine, by the way. Thanks for asking."

"High voltage and nanites that freeze your body—it all comes with the superhero job, right?" Jaycee said.

In her mind, Jaycee replayed a recent encounter with another "Guerrilla," Time Thief.

Getting "frozen" by microscopic robots isn't something I want to relive anytime soon, Jaycee thought.

Jaycee eyed neatly arranged equipment on a polished white desk in a corner: a tripod, ring lamp, and a little clip-on microphone with a wound-up power cord beside it.

All the gear a social media influencer needs.

"Too bad we didn't get it all on video, huh?"

"Oh, I think plenty of people witnessed you getting chewed out by Truther," Tiffany said while approaching Jaycee.

I wonder if I should finally just tell the rest of the team that Baron Maddox is secretly Truther, Jaycee pondered. *I bet that would get Dad's attention!*

"Y'know, if you're really just hiding from Truther, don't worry," Tiffany said. "He's in his lab; where else?"

"Oh, uh, right," Jaycee said. "When the 'copter dropped us off, I guess we all scattered, and I didn't see where he went."

Ugh, of course, Dad would be in his Man Cave of Solitude.

Jaycee bent over, gawking at the scores of makeup supplies adorning Tiffany's vanity table. Pungent perfume invaded her nostrils. She lost count of the lip gloss tubes arranged on the wide surface. Jaycee considered her just-the-basics makeup set at home and felt an unwelcome twinge of envy. As she gazed upon the bombardment of glam before her, Jaycee glimpsed at herself raising her eyebrows in the mirror. Tiffany's face dropped next to Jaycee's in the reflection.

"Look, I love this newfound interest in. well…" Tiffany said, wiggling her fingers and gesturing around Jaycee. "An interest in, you know, trying in general, but I don't have time to blend your contours at the moment."

Jaycee gravitated toward Tiffany's large closet. Its open, mirrored doors unfolded, making the expansive wardrobe look that much more impressive. Tiffany hovered close by.

"You think Mr. Maddox is in there trying on my jackets?" Tiffany said.

The red-haired girl's unamused smirk stared back at Jaycee from the mirrors. Her glossy polka-dotted top glistened in the reflections.

"As far as 'daddy dearest' goes," Tiffany said, oozing with snark, "I know I'm still the newish girl on the squad, but I'm fairly certain he doesn't hang around our living quarters."

"I've looked everywhere else," Jaycee said. "Everywhere I still have access to, that is."

"Sucks we got screwed outta our rooftop base, huh?" Melvin said from the doorway.

"Melvin, what did I tell you about creepily staring into my room?" Tiffany snapped.

"The door was open," he said with a shrug. "Plus, my room is next door, and I can hear everything."

Tiffany scowled as Melvin sat near the big white bed in a plush chair. He straightened his black, dragon-themed t-shirt as he made himself comfy.

"Sure, sit down, stay a while," Tiffany said, rolling her eyes.

"Yesterday, we're told the Super Society is disbanded," Melvin said with a huff. "Today, we're called out to a mission. Like, are we still a thing, or what?"

"We aren't technically broken up," Yvette said, entering from the hallway. "Not yet anyway."

Tiffany hissed a frustrated sigh.

"Is there a sign outside my room that says, 'Losers Welcome?'"

"Mr. Maddox said we'll be relieved of our duties soon," Yvette continued, ignoring the irritated redhead.

"We're officially active until we get the final word."

"Which could be tomorrow for all we know!" Melvin said. "We aren't getting evicted or whatever, right?"

Yvette sat on the edge of the mattress.

"I'm sure you can still live here," Yvette answered with an uncertain smile.

"Not to worry, Melvin," Tiffany said, sitting beside Yvette on the bed. "We'll just crash Go-Go's dorm room."

Tiffany wrapped her arm around Yvette's shoulder.

"College parties, here we come!" Tiffany said with a wide grin. "You're moving out in a couple of days, right?"

"Well, right after the last day of school," Yvette admitted, grimacing. "So, er, yeah, I guess at the end of this week..."

"Hold up!" Jaycee blurted. "I thought you weren't going away until the fall."

Jaycee marched over to Yvette. Jaycee's ponytail quivered as she shook her head in disbelief. It had been hard to swallow when she first heard her teammate's news of going to college. This sudden bombshell placed a solid lump in Jaycee's throat. Every past taunt about taking Go-Go's position as the Super Society's second-in-command came back to bite Jaycee.

"I thought you were still gonna be around for the summer," Jaycee said. "And, you know, mentor me. I'd make a great mentee!"

Yvette grabbed her arm as if hiding the Dawson University logo on her shirt.

"I got offered this student-intern thing for their athletics program," she said. "Being one of Baron Maddox's foster kids has its perks, right? I was gonna tell you..."

"Well, it'd be nice if Mr. Maddox would tell us why any of this is happening," Melvin said, resting his bare cheek on his hairy knuckles. "Or even bothered to show his mustachioed face."

"Tell me about it," Jaycee caught herself whispering.

"Mr. Maddox is the reason we got to do any of this, right?" Yvette said.

"Kiss-up, much?" Tiffany said.

"Look," Yvette said, standing. "We can discuss everything later. We gotta get our butts back to school."

"You have to go back to class?" Jaycee said, scrunching her lips in disgust at the notion.

"Yes, fellow North New St. Cloud High School student," Melvin said with a chuckle. "We all have to go back to class."

"But, by the time we get there, there'd only be, like, maybe an hour left of school," Jaycee reasoned.

Yvette made her way to the door.

"Your first lesson as my mentee is that ditching doesn't get you into college."

"Why'd we bother coming back here then?" Jaycee asked.

Before Yvette could make another step, a pair of blondes in matching pantsuits filled the doorframe. Jaycee recognized her father's assistants, Chelsea and Dahlia. One wore her hair up, the other down— no other discernible differences left Jaycee guessing exactly who was who.

"Why come back?" Yvette said. "This is why."

"Hi, kids!" Chelsea said, beaming with a bright smile while brushing her shoulder-length hair back. "Thanks again for returning your uniforms!"

"Uniforms—like, our 'super' uniforms?" Jaycee said.

"Yep," Tiffany confirmed, hopping off the bed. "We can't get to our lockers, remember? We literally have to answer to the fashion police."

"We triple-checked our little list, and we still need the Powerhouse costume," Dahlia said, squinting with a cheery grin. "So, that's where you come in, Jennifer!"

"It's 'Jaycee,' everyone knows that," Jaycee said.

Her eyes widened, and her lips shriveled.

"And you two apparently know a lot more about our secret identities than I realized…"

Jaycee's shoulders slumped.

"And this is why Dad really wanted me here. He just wants his suit back."

"Hey, Jaycee," Yvette said. "I know that sometimes it only feels like he's our adoptive father on paper, but I've been living here in the tower for a long time now—and I'm not saying our relationship is the same as yours, but…"

Jaycee raised her head to look at Yvette, as did the others.

"Trust me," Yvette continued. "Baron Maddox is a dad first. Our dad. Despite everything, he wants to see you, not some suit of armor."

"Oooo, that's a no-can-do," Chelsea interjected. "Mr. Maddox is very busy and is not seeing any visitors!"

"Well, I was trying to have a moment, but okay," Yvette said.

Melvin got up and patted Jaycee's shoulder as he walked toward the door.

"Hey, wait!" Jaycee exclaimed. "Chelsea, um, or Dahlia! You said you only needed my uniform—that means you have Eric's, right?"

"Oh, my, no," Dahlia said. "Eric Icarus is no longer in the building."

"Eric's gone?!" Jaycee said, flabbergasted. "I just saw him here yesterday!"

"I knew Eric didn't have what it takes to hang with us," Melvin said, joining Tiffany as they gathered by Yvette.

"When did he leave?" Jaycee asked, nudging Tiffany aside.

"Obviously, he was too embarrassed by your almost-kiss at the dance," Tiffany said.

We had an argument, Jaycee recalled. *But he was apologizing after, and—ugh, this makes no flushing sense!*

"He ran—or flew—back to whatever basement he used to dwell," Tiffany added. "I only regret that I didn't ghost him first."

Something is definitely off, Jaycee thought. *The others just can't see it.*

"Your Super Society uniform is very important," Chelsea said, staring at nothing. "It's our responsibility to keep it safe in our secure storage vault."

"Here at Pantheon Solutions," Dahlia said, "protecting top-secret property is our primary priority!"

This is wasting time. I need to get out of here!

"Super interesting, but ya know what?" Jaycee said. "I left my costume in the *Pegasus* in the midlevel hangar bay!"

She pushed her way past the others. Jaycee parted Chelsea and Dahlia and entered the corridor.

"Suuuure you did," Melvin said from behind Jaycee.

"That actually isn't a lie!" Jaycee said over her shoulder.

She faced forward, rushing toward a featureless orange door.

"In fact, I'm kinda over all the lies," Jaycee said to

herself as she sped to a sprint. "Time to get the truth from Truther, once and for all!"

DAVID

His heart skipped a beat as he lost his breath. David sucked in oxygen, his head light with wonder.

"I've never met a house with its own brain before," Eliza said, grinning. "Does it have any other body parts I should know about?"

"No," David said, exhaling. "BRAIN is just an AI program I created."

"AI?"

"Artificial intelligence," David explained. "A bit of an oxymoron; true wisdom and intelligence cannot be reproduced..."

Eliza's empty brown eyes stunned him still. Her happy smile beamed, showcasing her perfect pearly whites. The overhead lamp brightened her already vibrant features, yet her unblinking face indicated there were no lights on inside.

"...only replicated," David said, finishing his thought.

His mouth hung open, uncertain of how to navigate these confusing waters. He shook himself back to reality and caressed his beloved's arms.

"Any trip back to the Boxworth Building is only temporary, Eliza," David said. "We have a second chance at life, at being a family! And thanks to my invention, we are going to be so rich we could buy the moon!"

"Does the moon have a brain, too?"

David gazed at her porcelain skin. Her strawberry blonde hair shimmered in the lamp's glow.

"Oh, who needs brains?" David said, his lips forming a slow smile.

"Ooo!" Eliza chirped. "I almost forgot! I can't leave yet. I have to store the super-dupers' costumes in the sewing room!"

"Leave? We aren't going anywhere just yet."

Eliza turned away. Her patterned skirt twirled along with her.

"Mr. Maddox doesn't want me here for when his big machine does its thing!"

"But we're, ya know," David sputtered. "Starting our second chance, purchasing satellites, and—"

She faced him as she stepped to the edge of the light's reach.

"It won't be long now, deario!" Eliza said before vanishing into the darkness.

David sighed, then looked to the cylindrical pod erected beside him. The vertical tube-like husk of steel stood in silence. He leaned closer to the window slat at eye level. Inside the metal tomb, the real Eliza rested in deep sedation. David frowned as he studied the lines etched into her face. Unlike her youthful counterpart, this Eliza had aged.

"I know I'm not brave," David said to her motionless face behind the glass. "It took every single one of my guts just to come here."

He eyed the rows of identical casket-like cases surrounding him.

"I get cleared to roam the tower, and the first thing I do is take Eliza for a romantic stroll amongst the pod people," David said, scoffing. "Real romantic, genius."

David's head lowered, avoiding facing his actual wife in her crypt.

"I know she isn't you," he said softly. "She's just some lab experiment Barry created."

A weak smirk sliced open his lips.

"Barry wouldn't be thrilled that I'm here, but I…"

He looked away.

"I wanted to tell you in person that our boy will be safe."

David stepped back, staring at his black loafers.

"If I could change what happened to you, I would," he said. "Barry secretly stole you away as you were on the brink of death, but he kept you alive. I hate him for so many things, but he preserved you long enough to do something miraculous."

David raised his head, squinting as the overhead light pierced his eyelids.

"I'll live out my final days knowing I could hardly look at you in the end," he said. "I wouldn't forgive me either, but what I lack in courage, I make up for in knowing when to seize an opportunity. Especially when it's gift-wrapped and served to me on a silver platter."

David placed his fingertips on the cool glass with his eyes shut, lowering his head.

"Eric and I will get the life we deserve."

Each step away took David in and out of darkness. David speculated why Baron designed the vast room to have such sparse illumination between each gap of overhead light. He glanced at a few plaques on the pods he passed. Each bore the name of some super-criminal apprehended by the Super Society—all in the name of justice and all in secret.

I guess that's the thing about shame, David thought. *Even if you hide it in a classified facility away from prying eyes, you still don't want to look at it more than you have to.*

Automatic doors whisked open, and David entered

a brightly lit corridor. His pupils adjusted to the bare walls beside him. He retrieved his phone from his gray slacks. After a few rings, he spoke.

"Hey, Eric," David said into the phone, approaching a featureless door. "Just in case we don't see each other right away after Barry's big brouhaha, I wanted to let you know everything is going to be fan-freaking-tastic."

He walked through another hallway. The Pantheon Solutions upside-down lightning bolt logo sprawled across the walls. David spiked his lip at the sight of it.

"I hope you don't dismiss my voicemail as simply 'not a text message' and delete it," David said. "But look, man, I just kinda want you to hear my voice. I'm sorry about putting on the Ultranaut armor. Barry reset its settings, and it reverted to its original Dreadnaught programming. And, well, we traded more than a few blows, eh? I was only trying to take you away from all this, but that was before I knew the whole story."

He entered a large conference room. David lowered his voice despite being alone.

"I didn't know Barry was going to hold you in one of those pod things. And, please, believe me, I did not know he'd been keeping your mom here all this time."

The lengthy, dark wooden meeting table stretched across the room.

"Barry will answer for everything he's done."

David spotted a big leather chair at the end of the table. A nameplate read, "Chairman."

No doubt that's Barry's seat.

"Answer to who exactly?" David said. "I'm not sure the Pantheon Board of Directors is even real. Who knows how many government agencies he's skirting."

David skittered through the nearest door in a hurry to exit the windowless room. A large, silver cutout of the Pantheon lightning logo met his eyes. David hissed in disgust as he stepped out to find himself at an elevator hub.

"Eric," he said. "I don't expect you to understand everything right now; just know I'm doing what I can for you. Just know that I lov—"

Beep!

David pulled the phone from his face. He half-hoped it wasn't him exceeding the voicemail recording limit—he thought it'd be Eric picking up instead. The screen's stagnant grid of app icons showed no such luck.

He stood at a crossroads of hallways.

"Can't get this second shot at life started without getting paid."

He pocketed his phone while noticing the odd quietness of the area.

"The rooftop is where all the action is, I suppose."

David mentally eeny-meeny-miny-moe'd the row of elevators before him. He approached the central lift.

"Eric will get over not seeing any of his little super team buddies," David said. "It'll be nice to finally drop the act of pretending not to know who their real identities are. It'll be good for Eric to get away from all the distractions."

He pressed the "up" button.

"There's only one he might get twisted up about—the nosy one. Hopefully, we can leave without ever having to see Jaycee Maddox again."

Chapter Four: *ELEVATE*

JAYCEE

J AYCEE PRESSED THE BUTTON AND felt the car lift. In less than a minute, the doors reopened. David Boxworth stepped inside.

"Ms. Maddox?" he said, standing beside her.

"'Sup, Mr. B?" she said through gritted teeth.

He grimaced right back.

"Um, going up?"

"Uh, yeah," David said, raising an eyebrow at her. "Rooftop."

The Super Society's former headquarters, Jaycee thought. *It's off-limits to the actual team, but Eric's dad can go?*

Jaycee caught a glimpse of her scrunched brow in the mirror. David noticed it, too.

One minute he's locked up in his lab for going AWOL in a killer robot suit, and now he's free as a bird! What gives?!

"Who let you out of genius jail?"

"Your father," David answered. "That's who I'm on my way to see."

"Me, too!"

"It's a restricted area," he said, inspecting his black

V-neck in the mirrored wall. "Authorized personnel only."

The doors opened, and David barged into a construction zone buzzing with workers in white jumpsuits and hardhats.

"Are you still here?" David said, looking over his shoulder at Jaycee. "Authorized personnel, remember?"

"My dad specifically requested my presence," Jaycee said with a smug smirk. "Guess I must be pretty authorized."

Hot on his trail, Jaycee stepped over tools, wires, and clunky machine parts.

Wait, this used to be the trophy room! Jaycee thought, gazing at the bare concrete walls. *I can't believe Dad would mess with the building like this!*

"Wow, this is some fast work, even for my dad!"

"The expedited redistribution of assets simply means I, not your father, am exceptionally skilled at what I do," David said. "Meaning the project is operational and..."

Staffers and varying crew members parted, granting Jaycee and David free passage. Each male and female worker could've been a top model anywhere in the world, but there they were, lugging equipment around.

David halted, swiveling his head.

"You ever notice the 'Stepford Wives' vibe of this place?" he asked aloud.

"I think I heard my mom talk about that once. It's an old person thing, right?"

"It has something to do with brainless bimbos," David said, grumbling. "I forgot; kids don't know anything."

She followed David around a corner and down the

length of half of a basketball court.

"I'll be sure to ask my dad about it when I see him."

Meeting up with Dad would be a whole lot easier if I didn't have to keep Mr. Boxworth from finding out I'm one of the superheroes he hates so much. I need to ditch him.

"Hey, if you're dunzo, what do you need him for?"

"I'm on my way to collect my absurdly large payment from Barry," David said, speed-walking.

"Ah, paycheck time, I gotcha."

Welp, scratch that ditch, Jaycee thought, frowning. *Not sure I could stop him from getting paid even if I wore my Powerhouse armor!*

They approached a set of sizable golden elevator doors. David pressed the "up" button, and the shiny entrance opened.

"Eric know yet?" Jaycee asked. "About the project's completion, I mean."

They fit with room to spare in the car designed for lugging huge pieces of equipment up and down the tower. Unlike the gaudy exterior, drab white walls dulled the lift's inside. Long blank metal plates lined the corners.

"What Eric needs to know is that I own the patent to the Mega—er, mega-top-secret invention."

"It's the MegaCore," Jaycee said, rolling her eyes. "I was there when Dad asked you to build it. Dude, I've been to your house. I've seen the proto—"

"Anyway," David said, curling his lip in frustration. "With the money I'm making from this top-secret project, I can get us as far away from Pantheon Solutions as possible."

David tapped the top button on the slick panel by the door.

"You can't go! What about Eric's flying?!"

David scoffed.

"I'll, eh, buy him a new drone to stick on his back, and he can fly around all he wants."

"You think it's just his anti-grav backpack that makes him fly?" Jaycee asked, blinking with rapid-fire speed. "Even after all those experiments we did?"

Afterimages of Eric anchored with weighted belts and strapped to a wheelchair flashed in her mind. She had aided David as much as she could to find a way for his son to live a normal life. Each trial and every method of holding the boy down proved futile.

Eric defied gravity, sure, but it fought back, Jaycee thought. *He still can't go without floating or flying for too long—simply standing on the ground for a prolonged time hurts Eric, and it's only getting worse.*

"I think you kids idolize teenage crime-fighters too much," David said. "Scientists are the real heroes."

The elevator's muffled buzzing cut off as they came to a soft stop. The doors opened, but Jaycee stalled. She saw a gargantuan structure's broad outer base and luminescent dome down a gray walkway.

"Whoa, this is so much bigger than the original MegaCore!" Jaycee blurted.

She followed David into the rooftop enclosure. The air smelled different, faintly acrid, with a lightness to it.

"Alright, that does it!" David said while marching forward. "I thought you were more than just the boss's daughter—just some spoiled rich girl."

David reached the end of the path, his back to the hull of the engine.

"You won't listen to me; that's fine. I'll let your dad tell you to leave."

Jaycee's jaw unhinged, gasping at David's

outburst.

"Huff and puff all you want," he said. "Every exhalation is sucked up by the filtration matrix of the MegaCore. But you apparently already knew that since you're so smart."

The massive black panels covering the surrounding walls shut out all light save for the industrial lamp banks positioned around the vast engine. With little room to spare, the big battery took up nearly the roof's entire surface. Dissimilar to the original device, sleek chrome panels encased this modified MegaCore's base. Walking along the enormous circular structure was itself a pilgrimage.

Stepping over thick tubes and other bundled power cords, Jaycee followed David to a tall edifice attached to what Jaycee arbitrarily considered the rear of the gigantic dome. The hum of the surging power coursing throughout the machine became louder as she realized that no other servicemen or any other workers were present. They were alone up there.

"Hey, Barry, where are you? It's payday!"

"Eric," Jaycee whispered, feeling more uneasy by the second. "If you're hiding up here, you can come out any time..."

The white vertical construct in front of them blinked with orange hazard lights. Two wide silver steel strips complemented the front of the structure, glinting in the limited light.

Mr. Boxworth may be kind of a jerk, but, man, he designed one big, cool machine!

She peered above the dome at the ceiling's darkened grid of reinforced ventilation panels. Jaycee took a step toward the smooth, featureless face of the bulkhead in front of her. A hatch slid upward, revealing the short passageway hidden within.

"Are you sure my dad is in there?"

"He ought to be," David said, walking inside. "If he wants me to show him how to use this thing, that is."

She entered behind him, feeling slightly claustrophobic, trapped between two corridor walls. Hexagonal patterns adorned every surface, some with open circuitry. The hum intensified.

The hatch shut behind her—there was nowhere for Jaycee to run. A triangular door waited on the other end, a handful of feet away. A silver bar ran diagonally across the front, over ridges of black-painted metal. David pulled the door open, revealing the immense open space on the other side.

"What does my dad want with your machine anyway, Mr. B?"

David darted his eyes as if searching for some confidential non-comment.

More secrets, huh? Jaycee thought, unamused. *Like I'm one to talk, but this is getting ridiculous!*

"Er, you'll find out when he uses it—very publicly," David said. "Everyone must see how brilliant I am."

He took a step.

"I've actually never been inside before," David revealed, panning his head to take in the scope of the interior's enormity.

Jaycee guessed that it spanned over fifty meters in diameter. The main frame's piping pattern decorated the interior curvature of the dome's underside. The pipes connected to the thick black metal ring encircling the base.

She closed the door behind her. Jaycee's eyes followed the flowing streams of energy pulsating through the translucent tubing wrapped around the foundation.

The looping bluish-red flashes accelerated,

warping faster around them. The dome crackled with purple light, reflecting on the grid-like floor. Jaycee's lungs fought to keep oxygen. The top of the MegaCore stole each breath—absorbing air via the rounded ceiling's microscopic particle collection network.

"Are there cameras in here?" Jaycee asked, eyeing the ceiling. "Maybe we can find Dad on a surveillance feed or something.

"No, you want to know why?"

"Warning! Unauthorized personnel prohibited," David's recorded voice boomed over the speakers lining the upper rim of the dome. "All recording devices are forbidden. Warning!"

"That's why," he said, a smug grin stretching across his face. "Couldn't have said it better myself."

"Primo dad joke, Mr. B," Jaycee said, rolling her eyes.

Jaycee's gaze landed on a group of six large dark gray stasis pods erected in a circle around a wide golden tube in the center of the core. The floor's geometric multicolored wires connected the featureless steel husks to the smooth glossy rod. The cylindrical centerpiece touched the thirty-foot ceiling, attached to a bulky clamp-like apparatus.

"What's with the space odyssey monolith tribute?"

"Oh, that movie you've seen," David remarked.

He stepped inside the inner circle.

"None of my plans called for any ritualistic assembly. This is all your dad."

Jaycee nearly tripped over a dull gray metal block with grooved panels riveted to its sides. A grid of circular ports protruded from the top.

"Hey, careful with that!" David warned.

"What is this thing?"

"It's a portable power generator," he explained.

"We used them during the construction."

A sullen frown replaced the aggravation on his face.

Eric told me that Dreadnaught killed his mom by blowing something up—something that would cause a huge explosion, like a generator, Jaycee remembered, shivering. *Too horrible to even think about.*

"When the MegaCore is mass-produced," David said, sneering, "no one will need those... things... ever again."

"I should think not," Baron said, emerging from the entrance hatch. "Things have been explosive enough lately, no?"

"Dad!"

Jaycee ran to hug her father with open arms. She hit the brakes when his hand raised.

"You can't be here, Jaycee."

"I tried to tell her, Barry," David said from behind her.

"But, Dad, I—"

"Your mother is waiting on you at school."

Baron brushed by, panning his head to take in the MegaCore's depth.

"Fully constructed far ahead of schedule, and even under budget," David said with his hands on his hips. "Not bad for a blackballed inventor, eh?"

"The truth will be in the test," Baron said. "Which will commence imminently."

"Isn't there the matter of a deposit? Or maybe write an old-fashioned check? You know, the kind with a lot of zeroes at the end?"

"As it states in the contract, David," Baron said. "After a successful demonstration, compensation will be delivered."

He turned to leave.

"Safety gear has been provided for you. I will return momentarily with a protective suit of my own."

"Dad, please, talk to me!" Jaycee begged, tugging at his sleeve.

"Jaycee," Baron said, lifting his arm. "Yesterday afternoon's perfunctory meeting was for your mother's sake. She's been sent all the paperwork she needs to finalize the..."

Her eyelids fluttered.

"Ahem, the matter of sole custody," he said, staring ahead at David.

Her father pursed his lips, wiggling his mustache like an angry caterpillar. Airing their family matters did not sit well with Baron. With an annoyed grunt, he straightened the jacket of his sophisticated dark gray suit. Jaycee chased Baron as he approached the hatch.

"You can't just leave!" she called out, her eyes watering.

A tear pelted onto the smiling cartoon elephant on her t-shirt.

"This is for your own good," Baron said, facing her. "What is about to take place is too dangerous for you—"

"But there's still so much we haven't—!"

"Go home, Jaycee!"

The menace in his eyes emanated a strange horror. Stunned, Jaycee watched him leave through the hatch.

Chapter Five: *TRANSCEND*

JAYCEE

"You Maddox's are a strange breed," David said, apparently incapable of caring any less about Jaycee's heartbreak.

Jaycee stared at the hatch, but it did not reopen. Baron had gone; his image replaced by welling tears distorting her vision.

David inspected a pod with a cocked eyebrow.

"All your products are too clean—what're you hiding? You shouldn't be afraid to show some diodes and circuit boards."

Jaycee palmed her eyelids, rubbing tears away. David scoffed.

"Everything has to be so smooth and pristine," he said, pecking at the outer shell.

Tap tap tap.

"Seriously—do these open or wh—?"

The pod's door popped open, startling David.

"See?" he said, poking his nose into the gray-padded interior. "How's anybody supposed to know what this even is?"

He stood inside, thumbing an array of small red dots on the inner side of the door.

"Would it kill Barry to add some labels? What does this even do—?"

Hissssss. Gas poured in from dispensers above David's head. The door slammed shut. The fumes behind the window clouded his terror-stricken face. Jolted, Jaycee hurried over only to see a metal sheet sealing itself, hiding the viewing panel.

"Step inside the control station, David." Baron's voice commanded, booming from the speakers.

"What the—!" Jaycee said in a sharp breath. "Mr. B's already in! Dad didn't see that?"

She patted down the pod.

"How do you get this thing to—?"

The pod behind her opened. Inside, a black mask sat on the pod's base. A wide visor wrapped around its otherwise featureless design.

Okay... she thought. *The dark nightmare hockey goalie mask is a new one.*

"Wear the face-covering to protect your vision," Baron blared over the sound system. "The transference will begin soon."

Jaycee's head shook like a bobblehead doll as she sifted through different strategies in her mind.

Don't think. Just move.

She lugged the weighty power generator box into the open chamber. She swiped the mask and slipped it onto her head. After pushing the cube onto the pod's floor, Jaycee hopped on top of it. Straight across from Jaycee, the massive central goldenrod warped her pod's reflection.

The door to her pod shutting caused Jaycee's head to snap back. She peered through the glass panel before her—assisted by the portable generator's height boost. A few shaky breaths later, Jaycee lowered the oversized mask. She tugged at the curved end extending over her chin.

With barely enough room to bend her arms, she waved her hands over the compact, backlit operations panel.

"Keyboard, screens, touchpads," Jaycee said, looking through the black-tinted visor. "Basic control stuff. Okay, Powerhouse, whatever's going on, you can do this."

"I must apologize for Jaycee's disobedience, David," Baron said through the speakers. "It will not happen again."

Jaycee scoffed, blowing a disgruntled puff from her curled lips. Despite knowing that her father would not hear her, Jaycee's words burst out loud.

"So, you'd rather talk to Eric's dad instead of your own daughter?" she said, flaring her nostrils as she fought off a sniffle.

No waterworks, hero! she commanded herself, stiffening her lip. *Focus on what needs to be done!*

"Warning! Unauthorized personnel prohibited. Warning!" David's recorded caution played.

Jaycee's eyebrows arched under her mask.

"You want to hear Mr. B, then that's what you'll get!"

Jaycee's fingers blurred over the keys. A navigation menu appeared on the monitors.

"Spending so much time watching Dad work in his computer lab may have killed my social life, but it's paying off now."

A few password entries bypassed a short series of firewalls.

"The mobile app stonewalled me but not this! Access to the secret Super Society network is cake— guess you didn't count on anyone on the team being stuffed in here, huh, Dad?"

Her fingertips slid over a touchpad, breaking down digital doors and into the Super Society communications page. Pictures of Supercut, Extra, Go-Go, and Eric Icarus appeared on the pad.

"Better go solo 'til I know more deets."

A flick of her wrist brushed the images away. Jaycee resumed diving deeper into the virtual catacombs.

"Datacombs!" That 'would've been perfect! No one's around to hear me say it, though. Oh well.

"The initiation sequence is quite simple, David," Baron said. "After inputting a basic command, your only requirement is to monitor your device's activity—as only one with your expertise could."

Half a foot in front of her face, the central monitor listed a catalog of audio files below the window.

"Well, Dad, like I've heard you say a thousand times, 'David Boxworth is an arrogant never-was that just likes to hear himself talk,'" Jaycee said before taking a deep breath. "Here's hoping Mr. B gave me plenty of material to work with."

She pressed a touchpad button with a microphone icon on it.

"So, lemme get this straight," Jaycee said, squirming within the cumbersome cockpit.

Pleeeease let my audio wizardry come throooough...

"I will supervise the experiment from this..." Jaycee said. "...upright desk fused with a medieval torture chamber?"

The sound of David's voice repeating her words through the sound system was music to her ears.

So flushing cool! It worked!

In the center of the pod assembly, small, imprinted squares cascaded across the golden shaft's circumference. The twinkling plates seemingly flipped into nonexistence, uncovering Baron standing inside dressed as Truther from the neck down. Steel restraints clamped over Baron's arms and legs.

How did he get in there? I thought I knew about all the secret passageways in the building.

The brace around Baron's bicep squeezed his ivory-colored cape, causing the top portion to puff up over his shoulders. Light streaked down in front of Baron, suggesting a transparent shield protected him.

He thinks I'm Eric's dad, so this is a total secret identity fail on Dad's part! Why no mask, Truther?

Wiggling her head, Jaycee regained her focus.

"Is this your secret man cave where you LARP as Truther?" she said under the guise of David's voice.

"The time has come to unveil the truth," Baron said with no delay from his lips to the speakers in Jaycee's pod. "You, and every person alive, shall witness my ascendancy. I am the sole inheritor worthy of the next step in humankind's history!"

"Is this about my son?" Jaycee asked as David. "We can study Eric together! Imagine the two of us working alongside one another again! Sciencing in a lab like the good ol' days!"

Silence.

"Any previous affiliation you had with me was, at best, insignificant," Baron eventually said with a flatness in his tone that weighed upon Jaycee's ears. "After years of hypothesis and trials, my unprecedented genomic research on exchanging superpowers is about to come to fruition. Something no one would ever be able to accomplish but me. Once the power transference is finished, I will show you just how little you truly are."

"Power transfer?" Jaycee said, careful to hold

down the microphone button. "What's really going on here, Da—er, Barry?"

Jaycee spotted motion from the pod a yard to her left, positioned farther along their pseudo-ceremonial circle. A metal sheet slid open, revealing a clear windowpane. Inside, a woman stood with her eyes closed, seemingly unconscious.

What the... Jaycee thought, mouth agape. *Hey, I've seen her before! That's...*

"It seems super weird to have Eric's mom, I mean, my wife here, um, and a little overkill, huh, Barry?" Jaycee said with a nervous laugh.

Especially considering she's dead!

"As callous as this reunion with your beloved is, it was necessary to relocate Eliza here. She is, after all, the source of my impending superiority."

Baron would've surely seen her bugged-out eyes and slack-jawed shock if Jaycee's face weren't concealed.

"Eric isn't in one of these other pods, is he?" Jaycee asked, afraid of what she might hear.

"The boy is in a safe location."

"If everybody is gonna see this big transcendence of yours..." Jaycee said, scrambling to think of what David would say.

What does Eric or his dad know—or don't know?

"Then, ah, why not just have Eric here to bear witness?"

"Eric knows that his family bloodline is the catalyst for the new age of man," Baron said. "That is all he needs to know for now."

The screen below Jaycee's fingers showed a figure representing the ring of pods surrounding the central pipe. Real-time data scrolled up the digital display. Instructions appeared, indicating tapping a key would begin the power shift.

Sweat dripped from Jaycee's forehead. She blinked a bead from her eyelash.

Can't risk taking the mask off! If he sees I'm not Mr. B, then I'm toast!

She released her finger from the microphone symbol on the touchscreen, free to speak in her voice.

"I gotta come clean," Jaycee said, her chest heaving. "Dad'll be mad, but at least he'll stop whatever crazy experiment this is!"

She looked over to the pod with the sleeping woman inside.

"But if there's even a chance that's actually Eric's mom, and something happened to her—or his dad— because I didn't do this..."

"However unlikely it may be, just in case money— among other things—isn't enough, David," Baron said. "The knowledge that the Boxworths play such a pivotal role in this should be enough to motivate you."

On a separate screen, Jaycee returned to the Super Society contact list. She lingered over the pictures of her teammates.

Maybe I should alert the guys after all.

"There's nothing more important than family," Baron said. "Soon, I will no longer be forced to lie to Jaycee about her destiny. It will be an honor to stand as father and daughter, overseers of a true super society."

Jaycee's heart raced. Her hands trembled.

"I've indulged you long enough, David!" Baron yelled. "My whole life has been building to this moment! Now! Press... the... button!"

Jaycee's finger pushed the enter key. Orange light flooded the area.

"Warning! Operation sequence commenced," David's recorded voice played. "Unauthorized personnel prohibited. Warning!"

"Your cooperation is much appreciated," Baron said.

The alert repeated itself. Baron let out a breathy chuckle.

"You always were an arrogant never-was that just likes to hear himself talk. Your crippled hubris is merely an added bonus, Boxworth."

Jaycee couldn't see far beyond her window frame, but the hyperactive flashing coming from above told her enough. The interconnected net of nanites swarming within the dome's dense material went into overdrive. It didn't take a genius to figure out that the particle converter had been centralized over Baron, so the redirected energy would zap straight into him.

"The humbling of this earth is long overdue," Baron said.

Even through the tinted lens of her visor, Jaycee saw Baron's curled, snarling lip under his mustache.

"And I am the vessel to squeeze humanity into subservience!"

His gold chamber was most likely used for its conductive properties. Jaycee knew, though, that her father sure liked to flex for a guy talking about humility.

"I've always known myself to be evolution's conduit!" Baron shouted.

Baron closed his eyes in what appeared to be a meditative state. The flickering lights stopped, blanketing the room in the ominous dark orange of hazard lights. It grew so quiet that Jaycee could all but hear the beating of her heart. Her frantic hands crushed any button she could reach, but the unresponsive controls denied her.

"Warning! Operation sequence commenced. Unauthorized personnel is prohibited. Warning!"

A sonic shockwave shot down like a vengeful thunderbolt, rattling the foundation. Dazzling neon-blue light surged from the ceiling, brightening the dome like an arena rock concert. Jaycee forced herself to look through her slit eyelids—a tornado of swirling electrical energy penetrated the big golden beam. Baron craned his neck to shriek at the heavens just before the radiance engulfed him.

The power absorption's force coursed through Jaycee's body. The dark visor's protection reached its limit—Jaycee shut her eyes, but the illumination battled through the blackness. She anticipated a light show from the conversion, but the blaring bombardment far surpassed her wildest expectations. The wave of intensity buckled her bones and clasped onto her stomach. A guttural grunt vibrated through her clenched teeth.

The monitors' info-crawl flashed in red numbers. Too much fuel overloaded the system—the MegaCore's ability to suck in molecules was performing too well. By Jaycee's reckoning, what Baron had built couldn't have been compatible with the original designs. Gauges and meters showed the danger level climbing to critical levels.

"Don't... stop... it!" Baron's voice boomed through the speakers.

As thick as her pod was, Jaycee felt it shake. Caution advisories flashed on various screens. The rapid scroll of numerals would be jumbled nonsense to a layman, but Jaycee deciphered that it warned of an imminent explosion of apocalyptic proportions. All that stored energy would have to go somewhere, threatening to go boom.

The touchpad under Jaycee's hand popped up an emergency protocol interface. Without hesitation, she tapped away. The shining bursts gradually faded.

Straining to see past the other pods, she confirmed that the panels on the dome's underside were retracting, one frame at a time. A dashboard screen showed a pixelated diagram of the roof's large square covering. The display showed the roof sliding and folding in real-time, doubly exposing the MegaCore to the elements. The speakers pumped in the gears' thunderous churning, moving the colossal exterior plating.

Baron howled in what had to have been pure agony. All at once, the hysteria ceased. Jaycee held her breath, afraid to look outside. There was silence, but, more precisely, it seemed more like soundlessness.

In a controlled breath, Jaycee released the air from her curved lips. Slowly, Baron reopened his eyes. From within his pod, Baron hung his head low, unmoving. Jaycee extended her neck as far as she could to see Eliza's pod. Her stoic living death had been untouched. Jaycee couldn't detect any scorch marks or other signs of damage to the equipment.

The whirring sounds of mechanical parts snapped Jaycee's attention back to Baron's pod. The clamps holding Baron unhinged. Jaycee tapped at the controls, but the lights dimmed, and the screens deactivated.

"Uh... I want out now..." she said, but the microphone wasn't working.

Any button or screen she pressed froze, locking her out of any control.

Uh oh, the Super Society network must be down, along with everything else!

Baron's gloved hand slapped the pane in front of him. With his head still down, Baron dragged his fingers down the glass.

The curved door slid open, and Baron took a feeble

step out of his golden chute. Wind pushed through Baron's dark hair as he shambled out of Jaycee's view.

"Dad? Dad!"

Jaycee's heart rate spiked, and her sweat grew cold. Slamming her fists onto the armrests, she fidgeted in a frustrated fit. Jaycee glanced at every area she could in the confined cell and found no discernible way to escape.

"The roof is open. Okay…" she told herself. "Someone will see this. They have to. And then they'll rescue me. Okay. Okay…"

"You haven't outlived your usefulness yet, Boxworth," Baron's faint, sickly voice spoke through the still-functioning speakers.

Click click click. Inner mechanisms shifted, and the door to Jaycee's pod opened. Extreme caution slowed her body. She leaned her head forward. The heavy pods stood assembled around her, silent and still. Winds swooshed in thanks to the retracted roofs of both the MegaCore and the roof of Pantheon Tower itself. The torrents wailed like restless ghosts.

Baron's hunched-over frame lurched in front of Jaycee, sending shudders up her spine. He looked her up and down. Anxious, she slid her sneakers over the portable generator. She raised the black mask, revealing her small smile.

"Hi, Dad," Jaycee whispered as the wild airstreams tousled her blonde hair.

Squinting, he shivered as he forced a thin smirk.

"That's my genius girl."

For a moment, she surrendered to a faint grin.

"Mr. Boxworth is out cold in one of the pods! He got sprayed with knockout gas!" Jaycee spouted. "Whatever's going on with Eric's mom, you can tell me—!"

Baron coughed and growled in what sounded like terrible pain.

"Are you okay?!"

"The regenerative process may have weakened me," Baron said, wiping spittle with his glove, "but, if my calculations are correct, I shall soon transform into the most powerful person alive."

He clawed at the "T"-shaped emblem on his shoulder, tearing his white cloak away.

"The question is..."

He let the cape drift in the wind.

"Are you willing to change along with me?"

Chapter Six: *ARRIVAL*

ERIC

GHOSTS WHISPERED THROUGH THE FOG in Eric's mind.

"Reserve your energy, young Mr. Icarus," the voice of Baron Maddox echoed.

Memories swirled like a discolored haze—afterimages of humanoid shadows blurred behind Eric's eyelids.

"You've caused quite the deviation from my plan," Baron said, sounding like he was speaking from another room. "While I realign my path, you should rest, Eric. You're going to need all of your strength for what's coming next."

The mere thought of Baron triggered flashbacks of a steel door slamming in front of Eric's face. Claustrophobic feelings caved in, shrouding his senses in darkness. The pod encased Eric like a metal coffin. Gas hissed from above his head.

"Good night, sweetie," Eliza said in a distorted wave as if Eric's ears were going in and out of tunnels.

"You're..." Eric slurred, mentally adrift. "You're not my..."

"It's time to get up, Eric," Eliza said, sounding

clearer, like she popped out of his happiest memory—she sounded real. "You have a big day today."

"Mom?" Eric said as his eyes flashed open.

Crystalline twinkles shimmered before him.

Wait, so did I just wake up or not? Eric thought.

He blinked away the disorientating sparkles.

"Chandelier?" Eric muttered, then his vision refocused. "Chandelier!"

The large, glistening light fixture hung a few centimeters from his nose. Brushing his drooping brown hair from his forehead, Eric realized his body buoyed, flat, and facedown—he was floating. Far beneath him, a white floor waited. The chandelier's golden chain suspended from high above—the vast ceiling sprawled like its own pale sky.

Recalling gravity activated its existence, and Eric fell. He screamed, flailing his limbs, fighting a losing battle against panic. A silver, circular object slid directly under him. The thing resembled an extra-large serving platter, shiny and ready to collect Eric's crumpled carcass.

Whatever it is, it looks hard!

Closing his eyes, Eric anticipated a crunch and a splat. Instead, his instincts—and superpower—kicked in, and his descent slowed. Through a cracked eyelid, Eric saw his scrunched face in the reflection of the chrome surface.

"My fault, my fault, my fault!" David babbled, stumbling nearer with uneven footsteps.

Eric shook his head and willed himself upright. The disc-like device *whirred* under Eric's hovering sneakers.

"Wh-what is that thing?" Eric sputtered, struggling to get his mental gears turning.

Grogginess sat heavily on his brain.

"Is it some kind of assassin drone sent to take me out?!"

"Huh?" David said, walking toward Eric. "No, that's just the robot vacuum cleaner."

David lifted his leg to kick the droid away but halted, no doubt not wanting to scuff his black loafers. The robot rotated its metal outer shell and scurried across the marble floor.

"Sorry for the free fall!" David said. "I was testing my latest invention!"

He held an angular hunk of dull metal in his hand. It resembled a clunky remote control.

"This device redirects brainwaves!" David explained, grinning from ear to ear. "It essentially 'tricks' the brain into thinking it's performing a separate task than what it's actually doing! I call it the 'Super Mind-Changer!'"

Still afloat, Eric rubbed his eyes. He hovered in what appeared to be a huge foyer of a lavish building. Wide, red stairwells sat on either side of him, connecting to the mysterious place's second floor.

There's one level right after another! Eric thought, astonished. *This place just keeps going!*

"I, uh, must've miscalculated a configuration," David admitted, tinkering with his device. "I accidentally made your brain think you were, er, skydiving, I suppose..."

"I must still be kinda loopy from the knockout gas," Eric said.

He eyed a giant mechanical arm perched over a set of tall metal cases. The stylish, layered crown molding lining the walls contrasted with the near-featureless steel canisters arranged a few feet from Eric.

"Am I still dreaming, or did someone spill a science lab inside a big fancy house?"

Machines of various sizes spread throughout the spacious room. Bladed tools and gun-shaped apparatuses adorned black carts near the foot of one of the staircases.

"Isn't it amazing?" David said, stepping closer to Eric. "I've only been here a couple of hours, and I've already built three new inventions! Two of them successful!"

Eric looked down to inspect himself. His plain, orange t-shirt and dark blue jeans were his typical unfashionable outfit, but not the clothes he remembered wearing before he fell unconscious.

What was I wearing if not this? Eric pondered, struggling to push out thoughts as if they each weighed a ton. *Why can't I remember everything?*

"I'm not sure how much earlier the drones dropped you off here—before I woke up here, that is," David said. "But I figured you needed the sleep, so—"

Eric's nerves jittered, snapping out of his funk.

"Wait a minute!" he blurted. "Knockout gas! I was put to sleep! I was locked inside a pod!"

Eric flew over to David.

"Baron Maddox keeps test subjects in pods! He makes fake people!" Eric rambled, eyes bulging. "He has Mom! She's alive, well, in a coma or something, but she has flying powers like me! Mr. Maddox is gonna steal them!"

"Deep breaths, Eric," David said. "One thing at a time."

"No, you don't understand!" Eric pleaded, grabbing his father's arms. "Baron Maddox is Truther! He's gonna end the Super Society! Mr. Maddox is totally evil! Like, 'take over the world' evil!"

"Son, I can expl—"

"We need to get out of here!"

Eric pushed himself upward, then soared across the long stretch of the floor toward a set of enormous burgundy doors. Eric grabbed the curved, silver handles, but the locked doors didn't budge. Pushing and pulling to no avail, Eric grew more frustrated.

"Do you have a key or something?!" Eric shouted, pounding on the thick wooden door.

He zipped over a few feet to the right of the doorway, floating in front of a row of tall, narrow windows. Dark green leaves pressed upon the glass, blocking any sort of view.

"Where are we?" Eric asked.

"In the heart of the woods outside New St. Cloud City," David said, taking a careful step toward Eric. "More specifically, the Gilroy Mansion."

"Wait," Eric said, gazing at the wide floor between the stairwells—and the seemingly endless hall of deep red doors behind it. "Like, Patrick Gilroy? Leader of the original Super Society—Judge Justice?!"

"The same home where Patrick used his wealthy family's old money to bankroll the first Super Society, yes," David explained. "Including fostering his kid sidekick, Sidebar. Who, of course, grew up to be Truther, who, as you've said, is—"

"Baron Maddox sent us to the house he grew up in?"

Eric floated above David, then hovered over the stairs.

"If you know what's happening, then you've told the police or somebody about Mr. Maddox, right?"

David walked up a few steps.

"I know a heck of a lot more than I did a week ago, that's for sure," David said. "Your flying power is, indeed, real; I realize that now! I never knew about your mom's... abilities, but... Look, I don't know every little detail about whatever Barry is up to."

"Wanna know the craziest, worst thing Mr. Maddox has done?" Eric said, flying up, noticing how identical each floor appeared. "He created a clone of mom! Well, a synthetic non-robot thing, but he replicated her! How absolutely sick is that?!"

"Well, look who's awake!"

The familiar voice caught Eric's ear, but his head did not turn.

"You've got to be kidding me," Eric whispered.

A shy glance confirmed his fear. Eliza stood next to David, whose creased brow begged for understanding. Eric decided he was fresh out. He speared his body downward, then swooped up to confront them.

"Dad, why is this thing here?!"

"Watch your tone, young man!" David barked.

"You knew about her, didn't you?" Eric said, fighting a soft tremble.

"Are you hungry, Eric?" Eliza said as her unblinking eyes fixated on nothing. "I'm making popcorn later for movie night!"

Eric bolted away, scoping out the expansive room. High above the front doors hung a huge portrait. The painting depicted a middle-aged, auburn-haired man with a sullen face Eric did not recognize. Next to the fancy-dressed guy stood a grinning boy—a teenager in dark dress clothes.

"That must be Gilroy and young Mr. Maddox," Eric said to himself. "I really need to get out of here!"

"Eric, please, you have to understand!" David yelled.

Prying his eyes from the creepy painting, Eric looked down, only to be further repulsed. Eliza wore her light hair in a ponytail while wearing a yellow, floral-patterned blouse and pink-striped bottoms.

Mom would never wear anything so bright and tacky, Eric thought, squinting one eye in disgust. *Mom was sophisticated and smart, and—ugh, I can't believe Dad!*

Gliding higher, Eric zipped across the pearl-white walls. He found nothing but concrete waiting for him at the end of the room. Dodging a few extended antennae of stationary droids below, Eric soared in the opposite direction. Another dead end greeted him.

"There's gotta be another way out of here, right?" Eric shouted in frustration.

"Eric, if you would just stop for one minute!" David said. "What I did find out about Baron—I didn't learn until pretty late in the game, okay?"

Eric pushed himself past a stairwell, where he found a cushy sitting area. Big, throne-like chairs surrounded a round glass table.

"So, Mr. Maddox promised you could housesit this swanky pad?"

A skinny robot with a spherical base rolled by Eric. Its flat face emitted spasmodic blips of orange light. It buzzed, then moved on.

"What is up with this crazy place?!" Eric said.

"I'm—I'm sorry about Dreadnaught," David yelled, his voice carrying a faint echo.

Eric flew beyond the back of the stairwell until he spotted a set of wide wooden doors.

"Baron wanted to set up some fake villain fight for you," David said. "He wanted it to be with Ultranaut—a public confidence booster, I guess. He said people needed to see you score a big win."

The silver handles did not move, and the doors would not budge.

"I wore the armor, yes, but I was going to rescue you—"

"But instead, your piece-of-crap suit reset back to its killer mode!" Eric said, unable to bring himself to say, "Dreadnaught."

Eric propelled himself, speeding toward the ceiling. His high view saw the automatons and bulky machines litter the extravagant interior. Locked doors and a lack of windows filled Eric with a growing dread.

"Are we trapped in this place?" Eric said. "Tell me we aren't trapped!"

"We're not prisoners," David said, sounding small from so far below. "Trust me, when I get paid for the new MegaCore, we can buy an even bigger mansion!"

"And you still haven't even gotten paid!"

"We're safer here!" David shouted. "We have everything we could possibly need!"

"You've been Baron-pilled!" Eric yelled.

Hunger and dehydration sent stinging reminders to Eric's guts and throat—he had no idea how long he was unconscious. Adrenaline carried him lower to the vertical window slats by the main doors. Eric knocked on the glass of each one in the row.

"Come on! There's gotta be a surveillance drone or something out there!"

"Eric, I realize this is a lot to take in—"

"I thought you hated Mr. Maddox, Dad," Eric said, pressing his face against the warm glass, trying to see anything through the shadowy leaves and branches outside. "You despised him right up until he gave you a twisted Mom-replacement-bot, is that it?!"

"Eric Nikola Boxworth!" David snapped. "Fly your butt down here this instant! You need to get your act together and apologize to Eliza and to me! I don't care how mad you are; I'm still your father! And even if I have to hold you down and pry your eyelids open, we will have movie night as a loving family!"

"Forget it!" Eric said before rocketing upward.

He hovered over the open area by the chandelier where he awoke.

I had to've sleep-floated from here, Eric surmised. *Maybe my costume or my phone is in a room—but which one?*

"Down. Now!" David bellowed, only to be ignored.

The urgency in Eric's bones softened at the sight of the rows of identical doors. Panic snuck into Eric's body, smuggling a nervous tremble with it.

"I wish super-speed ran in the family instead of flying," Eric muttered. "Someone has to stop Mr. Maddox, though. I'll check every door, every inch of this place until I bust my way out and—!"

The world wiggled—Eric's eyes twitched.

"What the—"

Plunging, Eric's hands outstretched. His fingers gripped an imaginary curve.

"Come on, come on!" he yelled, terrified as he fell.

His right leg kicked and kicked until his descent slowed. In a swooping motion, Eric floated upright in a sitting position. Hovering a foot from the floor, Eric looked ahead at the stairwell banister in front of him. Unable to move his head, he merely positioned his hands around an invisible wheel.

"Uhhh, Dad? Dad!"

Eric pushed down with his right foot, pressing on nothing.

"Your flying power kicked in instinctively—how fascinating," David said as he approached.

Eric's right hand reached for an immaterial knob. He maneuvered the make-believe lever, repositioning it.

"I can't stop," Eric said. "Why am I pretending to drive a car—and why is it not on purpose?!"

David stepped in front of Eric, holding the control device in his hand.

"I redirected your neural pathways using the Super Mind-Changer," David explained. "Cars stay on the ground, so now you do, too."

"I don't even know how to drive!"

"All the more confusing to your brain," David said. "Made it easier to, well, manipulate you."

Twitching in anger, Eric looked at where a rearview mirror would be.

"Sweet, it'll be real handy for when I get my learners permit," Eric said, seething with sarcasm.

"I know how insane all this is, alright?" David said with a heavy sigh.

"You mean, 'criminally' insane, Dad," Eric corrected. "Mr. Maddox is stealing Mom's powers, and he said he had big plans for me."

Eric fought to move his head to glance at David.

"I wasn't joking before; he literally said he wants to take over the world! Are we seriously just going to stay here and do nothing?"

"Let me explain something to you," David said as he walked around Eric. "Planned or not, nobody asks to be born. We exist whether or not the world has any room for us."

"Not following," Eric said, pantomiming fastening a seatbelt—with a curled lip to prove how much he hated doing it.

David stood by Eric, where the passenger seat would be in the imaginary vehicle.

"I've learned a lot about destiny recently," David said. "Fate has no say in my intellect or how despite it, I've been down and out. We just live, Eric."

"I'm hoping the eventual point you're getting to involves leaving here to go rescue Mom!"

"Hey, just lemme pass down some fatherly advice, okay? The smartest thing anybody can do is recognize opportunity and know what to do with it."

David stepped in front of Eric.

"Barry put us here, in this legit mansion, together," David said. "We are safe, purposely omitted from whatever scheme he's got going. Lately, we've seen a new impossibility every single day. The one thing I wasn't sure was ever going to happen again, though? Well, it's here. Now. Us together as a family—a normal family."

"That clone-bot-whatever is not Mom."

"No, but she's a way for us to press the reset button and take advantage of an impossible opportunity. That sounds pretty smart to me."

"Person detected at front gate," a monotone voice stated.

A small, black disc rolled up to Eric's sneaker.

"Person detected at front gate," it repeated.

"How many vacuum cleaners does this place have?" Eric said.

"No, that's not the—"

"David, dear," Eliza said. "It's for you!"

David hurried over to Eliza by the front doors.

"I have a visitor?!" David asked.

"Well, my memory can be a little wonky-doodle sometimes," Eliza said, "but it does seem like you've met this lady before."

Eliza tapped on a silver panel, and a monitor appeared as if materializing from nothing.

"Hello? Is anyone there?" a woman said from the screen's speakers.

With his neurons determined to drive, Eric fought to steal a glimpse.

"Hey, is that—?" Eric said.

"Eric's teacher?" David said, leaning to get a closer look at the monitor. "What's Barry's ex doing here?"

He gestured for Eliza to step out of view.

"Where's the microphone on this thing?"

David's tapping on the glass screen produced a *doot* sound.

"Um, can I help you?"

"David Boxworth? Oh, I, uh, I apologize for disturbing you," Valerie Cooper said through the intercom. "But I am at my wit's end—"

"Ms. Cooper, help, I'm trapped—!" Eric yelled before dropping onto his butt.

"Is someone else there?" Valerie said, exasperated with confusion. "I thought I heard—"

"Valerie Cooper, that is you!" David said, cutting her off with the fake-charm voice Eric had heard a thousand times before.

Curled in a fetal position, Eric felt the smooth marble floor on his cheek. His lips contorted, unable to produce the slightest syllable. Through squinted eyes, he saw David holding the Super Mind-Changer device behind his back.

Dad must've turned that gizmo up a notch, he thought. *I'm thinking we just skip Father's Day altogether this year.*

"Valerie, it's great to hear from you," David said. "It's been years, hasn't it? The last time we saw each other was right before the..."

David swallowed a grunt, sounding like a sick dog.

"The Dreadnaught demonstration."

"Erm, yes," Valerie said. "Well, our last interaction certainly wasn't at a PTA meeting."

"Ya know, I've been meaning to go to one of those."

"Your association with Baron was confidential at the time. I understand that, but still, I wish Jennifer and your son could've properly met earlier... Maybe things wouldn't have turned out the way they did."

I wish I could go back and change everything, Eric thought.

"Speaking of school," Valerie said. "Eric wasn't in class again today. Is everything—?"

"What're you doing all the way out here, Valerie?" David asked.

"I've looked everywhere else," Valerie said, sighing. "This is the last possible place I can think of... Jennifer, she... She didn't come home from school today."

Jaycee?! Eric thought, his heart quickening with stress.

"She went to a tutoring session and was supposed to come back to class," Valerie explained.

"Hoooold on," David said, sounding like he was trying to reel in a lost thought. "Jaycee ditched school today? She never did leave and go back to class, did she? Hm. Then that means we haven't been here for that long..."

"I'm sorry?" Valerie said. "Listen, I don't want to be a bother, but I searched the campus, her usual hangouts, checked with what friends I could actually contact... Coming to the old Gilroy Mansion, I know, is desperate—Jennifer has only been here once as a child, but I am running out of places to search."

"Did you happen to swing by Pantheon Solutions Tower?" David asked, his voice coming from the side of his mouth.

"I received the typical false courtesies whilst there—the 'model' employees get increasingly dense as time goes on. Anyway, with Baron 'predisposed at the current moment,' I got nowhere fast."

"I wish I could be of more service, but, uh," David said, stalling.

What else is Dad not telling me? Eric thought.

"I'm sure she'll turn up," David said. "She's probably at the tower. Look, this is Barry we're talking about. He could be... covering for her?"

Even he doesn't sound convinced, Eric silently observed while rummaging through his solidifying memories. *I last saw Jaycee at Pantheon Tower, right before Baron revealed his master plan to me... Jaycee was stressing about not being allowed back in the building. Maybe it's not too crazy to think she snuck over there after all.*

"It's doubtful Baron would disrupt his cooperation with our, ahem, legal proceedings," Valerie said, then took a long breath. "Between you, me, and the trees out here, Baron is agreeing to give me sole custody of Jennifer. It'd make life vastly less complicated if we were to resolve this matter before the authorities' attention became necessary."

"Ah, well, I'm sorry, that does sound messy," David said. "The 'no cops' thing sounds pretty good, though."

"I must say, David, you are probably the last person I'd expect to find here."

"I entered a new partnership with Barry, and, hey, working with him lands you in some crazy spots, right? I should really be g—"

"I wish it were under better circumstances, but it is good to visit with you."

Even under the mind-manipulator's influence, Eric managed to roll his eyes.

Are you for real?! Stop talking and get me out of here! First thing I'm gonna do once I'm released is—!

Stabbing pains rippled through Eric's body. His muscles seized, tensing as if he just had a violent sneeze.

I've been grounded too long! I don't know how

much worse the pain gets the longer I go without flying—and I don't want to find out!

"I never did get to thank you for watching Jennifer," Valerie said. "When she and Eric left school sick. I do apologize for them sneaking off to see my ex-husband like they did."

"Teens do dumb things; it was no prob—"

"Now that I see you, I wish I could thank you in person. The HD monitor out here is very flattering—I hope on your end I don't look like the mess I feel like."

"Oh, erm," David blurted, fumbling his words. "H-hey, the years have been a friend to you, too, Val—"

"Yoo-hoo, David, honey!" Eliza chimed in from somewhere—searing pain dulled Eric's senses. "I need you in here with me, darling!"

"My apologies, David!" Valerie said, flabbergasted. "I-I didn't know you had, um, that you were—"

"Yeah, that's my, hm, my, well, I—"

"I'm not thinking clearly," Valerie said, catching her breath. "I'm sorry to have disturbed you."

"I hope you find Jaycee!" David spouted as the intercom's audio cut off.

Every fiber in Eric's muscles tightened.

"Let me go already!" Eric grunted more than spoke as tears leaked from his shut eyes.

"Sorry, Eric," Eliza said.

Her footsteps grew closer.

"For the time being, leaving the property is only permitted under a special condition," she said, sounding much closer. "Only a member of the Super Society is allowed clearance to exit the mansion."

"Lucky me," Eric said through his teeth. "I'm a member."

"Oopsie," Eliza said. "I meant, only a member of the original team. And since there aren't any around, I guess we're stuck together!"

Agony's grip over Eric's body loosened. Relief enveloped him, and he blew out shaky breaths. David approached, holding the Super Mind-Changer. His thumb firmly pressed a button that seemed to relinquish control over Eric's brain.

"I really am sorry, buddy," he said. "I hope, in time, you'll see this is for the best."

Chapter Seven: *DRIFT*

ERIC

LIGHT DANCED IN THE DARKNESS in flickering spasms while screeching screams bounced off the walls. Thick, buttery popcorn filled the theater room with an overpowering aroma. David and Eliza snuggled on a cushy leather couch. The Super Mind-Changer rested by David's lap. Eric hovered above them; legs crossed in a sitting position. His floating foot fidgeted.

"I'm really trying to lay off the 'moody teen' routine," Eric said, "but really, this is the movie you decided to watch?"

"You ought to like it," David said. "It has zombies in it."

"This is your go-to for 'family movie night?'"

"Of course, it's a classic!"

"Classic just means black and white and boring," Eric said.

Despite the film's plodding monotony, it provided a much-needed alternative to seeing David and Eliza get cozy. The sight sickened Eric—thinking of what demented acts Baron could be doing worsened his nausea. The huge screen rivaled any real theater, but Eric directed his focus to more urgent matters.

I've wasted too much time already. There's got to be a way to sneak out of here!

His floating view of the five-row private cinema room saw only one exit.

"I've gotta pee," Eric announced.

"I told you to cool it on the soda," David joked. "Just because this place is stocked to outlast the apocalypse doesn't mean you have to consume it all at once."

Eric slipped through the lone door and floated into the spacious hall.

"Hey, Eric," David called from the couch.

Eric froze, buoying above the patterned carpet.

"If you get any ideas," David said. "I can change your mind."

Drifting farther down, Eric shuddered.

"Dad is straight up threatening me now," he whispered. "He's gone nuts, and I'm his prisoner..."

Each crimson door looked the same. The film's score played through the theater's closed door, murmuring like a faint memory. With a ghostly touch, Eric twisted the silver knob of the first door on his left. To his surprise, it opened, revealing a dimly lit room. Peering inside, but not too deep, he saw twin sinks and a maze of strings suspended from the low ceiling. Photo negatives floated in the sink's still water. Squinting in the dark, red overhead lamps' light, Eric saw what resembled a grainy group photo of the original Super Society team. Beside it floated a picture of what appeared to be founding member Aqua Queen and a blurry image of a man in civilian attire, not in a flashy costume. In the low light, Eric discerned only their sorrowful faces.

Shaking off the room's creepy vibes, Eric moved on. The next few doors remained locked, but Eric found luck in one close to the end of the lengthy hall. Careful to keep quiet, he cracked the door open. Inside, racks of white plastic storage bins stacked up to the ceiling, oddly higher than the previous photo dark room. Uneven stretches of duct tape labeled each tub. Eric mouthed the words as he read: "Gloves, masks, utility belts..."

It made him think of the sewing room in Pantheon Tower, where he first encountered the fake Eliza—an unwelcome flashback. At the edge of where Eric could see, a bin on a bottom shelf stuck out in the cramped area.

"'Ashes,'" Eric whispered, reading the label.

His imagination convulsed, dreaming up endless possibilities of where the remains of the deceased members of the first Super Society ended up. No urn, no shrine, just a little box hidden away in a small room is where the legendary heroes did all their eternal resting.

Or it could be anything, Eric thought, snapping himself out of his whirlwind trance. *I've been gone for too long; I better act fast if I'm gonna bust outta here.*

After trying the rest of the doors without success, Eric floated to the final one at the end of the corridor. Peeking over his shoulder, Eric swore the row of red doors had extended—he also decided ghouls or demons haunted this strange old place. Thinking of Baron's plan to steal his still-alive mother's secret superpowers sparked enough courage to turn the door handle.

Relief swelled within Eric when the door opened. The short-lived solace dissipated back to buzzing nerves as he flew inside. A bank of monitors lined up the wall—surveillance footage displayed on each screen. A lone gray chair occupied the glorified closet. It sat pushed to the edge of a metal desk, replete with a matching black mouse and keyboard. The middle monitor showed a corner-mounted view of David and Eliza snuggling on the couch.

Disgusting and live on camera, Eric thought. *No guard or anybody on duty, but I can't be sure if this feed doesn't go straight to Mr. Maddox.*

Each screen depicted a different room or hallway of the vast estate. The footage switched in sequential blips, cutting to different angles and areas. Slivers of light allowed shadows to dwell in the darkened views of the bedrooms.

"Could this place get any creepier?" Eric said in a quiet, careful tone.

Closing the door behind him, Eric pulled the seat back and sat, arming himself with the modest mouse and bland keyboard.

"Not the hi-tech equipment I expected, but it'll be enough to call for help."

Clicking and tapping like a madman, Eric successfully deactivated and reactivated screens, muted the volume, and flipped through several security camera feeds.

"Come on, alt-control-delete, don't fail me now."

Rebooting the system bounced Eric right back to the surveillance stream.

"Are you for real?!" Eric said in a frustrated huff. "Last resort time."

Sliding into a crouch under the desk, Eric sifted through the rat's nest of tangled wires until he found the power cord. He pulled it out of the surge protector strip. After waiting a few moments, he plugged it back in, and the computer hummed to life. Eric willed himself backward rather than pushed, then bumped his head on the underside of the desktop. In a clumsy ascent, Eric collided with the white-coated metal wall next to the desk. Grunting out an unintelligible curse, he lowered to the seat while rubbing the back of his head.

The sting lessened at the sight of the central monitor booting up a home screen. The default wallpaper of an unnaturally green field indicated that this operating system was a few generations old, but Eric's smiling face didn't care. Free from security camera footage limbo, Eric grabbed the mouse as if wielding Judge Justice's coveted weapon of choice, the Golden Gavel. A single folder icon named "Videos" drew Eric's attention, and curiosity lured him to click it.

It opened a lengthy list of files with dates going back years. Disappointment waved through Eric as he deduced that the dates referred to an archive of surveillance feeds.

"Do I really want to comb through hours of video just to see a drone fly in, carrying my unconscious body? Or Dad's, apparently?"

A subfolder caught his eye just as he scrolled the cursor to exit. Its cryptic name, "Sidebar - secret origin," practically begged to be unearthed. A window popped up, and Eric clicked on the file with a trembling finger.

"I'm violating my own personal rule of 'if you look for messed up stuff, you will find messed up stuff,' but here goes..."

A square screen appeared, playing shaky, close-up camera footage of the original Super Society team. In her neon-striped costume, Laser Lass and Avenging Eagle's patriotic getup made them stand out even in what looked to be an overpass's shadow.

"I recognize that area," Eric said under his breath. "What were they doing on the outskirts of New St. Cloud City?"

"How much did you see?!" Sureshot said, bursting into the frame in his bright red tunic.

Sureshot vanished and almost instantaneously rematerialized—his masked face scowled right up to the camera.

"Answer me, kid!"

Sureshot leaned in for an extreme close-up, shaking whoever the cameraperson was, wobbling the frame. A white-gloved hand eased Sureshot away.

"Everybody, take a breath!" Judge Justice commanded, entering with his black robe flowing behind him like a majestic cape.

The oversized Golden Gavel spun in his hands. His baby-blue mask turned to the camera.

"It's okay," Judge Justice assured. "What's your name?"

The camera wavered.

"Baron..." a young voice answered.

"Mr. Maddox!" Eric whispered; his eyes glued to the screen.

"Nice to meet you, Baron," the Judge said under the sound of the traffic on the bridge above them. "Are you okay? Are you injured?"

"What're we doing talking to him?" Sureshot chimed in from offscreen. "Just drop him off at the police station like any other civilian! It's his word against ours, who cares—?!"

"You really want the cops to know about this?" Avenging Eagle asked.

"He came out of nowhere!" Laser Lass said. "I didn't see him—he just got in the way and..."

The camera lowered, providing a view of what looked like a body, obscured by the shadow of street railings around a thick concrete pillar.

"I don't like this," Laser Lass said, shaking her

head, causing little streaks of pinkish light to flicker from her forehead.

"We defeated a supervillain," Judge Justice said, maintaining eye contact with the camera. "And in the chaos of battle, it is an unfortunate consequence that, yes, there will be... environmental damage. That's all this is."

"I wouldn't say 'defeated,'" Sureshot said, pacing in the background, in and out of frame. "Teknosaur is long gone by now!"

"So, we'll get him next time and finally strip that dino-armor off him," Judge Justice said.

"This isn't about some cyborg psycho," Avenging Eagle said. "This is about a guy dying in our crossfire with zero ID on him whatsoever! It's like he fell out of the sky!"

Sureshot rushed to him in a blur.

"Are you serious with the play-by-play, AE?!" Sureshot said. "We don't even really know what this kid saw!"

"He saw everything," Aqua Queen said from off-camera.

The POV shot panned to the aquamarine-colored costume of the hydro-heroine.

"Only question is," she said, spiking an eyebrow under her green-tinted goggles. "How much did your little camera record?"

The camera straightened, viewing the team in a steady motion.

"The truth?" Baron said. "I was pretty proud of these glasses I built—hidden camera between the lenses. But I guess the frames weren't fooling anybody, huh?"

The Super Society crowded around him.

"Wirelessly uploading the footage to my computer

back at—"

The glares from Sureshot and Laser Lass caught the camera's eye, seemingly making Baron reconsider his next words.

"—a computer in a location you don't need to know about," he continued. "I'm pretty proud of that, seeing how I have such little to work with."

"He's blackmailing us?!" Laser Lass exclaimed.

Eric lifted from his seat, floating but too excited to notice.

"He's lying," Avenging Eagle said. "But if he's not..."

He clenched his red-gloved fist, lighting up the crimson stripes on his uniform. The ruby-red light pulsated with energy.

"I have ways of getting the truth out of people."

"Just lemme teleport him 'im somewhere far," Sureshot said, his eyes bulging under his mask. "I can make this go away in the blink of an eye!"

"How about we ask him what he wants before teleporting to conclusions?" Aqua Queen suggested. "So, mister...?"

"Maddox," Baron said. "Baron Maddox."

"What are you after, young Mr. Baron Maddox?"

Baron's lens looked left then right.

"I want to be one of you—" he said.

"We don't have time for this!" Laser Lass said.

"Police and media will be here soon," Avenging Eagle warned. "If we are dealing with this, then we do it now—"

"—but better."

All eyes fell on Baron. Eric's jaw hung open, equally shook.

"What exactly do you mean," Aqua Queen asked slowly with a careful step back. "'One of us?'"

"A costume, name, mask, and, well, not powers," Baron said. "When I was younger, I fell for the illusions, but I know your abilities aren't real—it all comes from your tech."

"Younger?" Avenging Eagle blurted. "You can't be more than fifteen as it is! Listen, I don't know what you think is—"

"I can make your gear better," Baron said. "I can help you."

"You mean you can extort us!" Sureshot hissed, gritting his teeth and struggling to keep his voice down.

The camera lowered, peeking past the legs of Avenging Eagle and Laser Lass. The shadowed body appeared to be a casually dressed man in bright clothes, nothing out of the ordinary, but his obscured head ignited Eric's imagination.

This guy looks like he was dressed for a Sunday picnic, Eric thought. *What's he doing under a bridge? Was he spying or something?*

"Hey, look at me!" Sureshot ordered.

Baron's camera panned up, met by suspicious glares.

"You don't just threaten us and get away with it," Sureshot said.

"This shouldn't even be a discussion," Laser Lass added. "I mean, come on, he's just some kid, and we're the Super Society!"

"That's right; we are the Super Society!" Judge Justice said, stepping back in front of the team. "That means we help—no matter who, no matter how."

Eric held his breath. The audio quieted, leaving only the sounds of the bridge traffic.

"I'll train you, son," Judge Justice said, looking at the camera and raising his Golden Gavel to his chest. "And in exchange, you let us handle this. Quietly."

He glanced at the others. Their silence served as all the consent—or unwillingness to oppose—their leader needed. Judge Justice reached out his hand.

"What do you say, Mr. Maddox?" Judge Justice asked. "You want to join the Super Society?"

Static. Blackness.

Eric plopped to his chair, exhaling a huge breath.

"The original Super Society killed a guy and covered it up," he whispered as a shudder snaked up his spine. "And Mr. Maddox blackmailed his way onto the team!"

Eric clicked open a browser and typed his way into his email.

"This is big," he said. "This will break the Internet—this will break the planet!"

His foot pattered in the air as he waited for a text box to open.

"I wish I could tell Jaycee in person, but an email is better than—"

Error notifications popped up. Firewalls prevented him from opening his inbox. Eric grunted in frustration.

"No way to send a message!" he said while rummaging through a junk-filled drawer. "S'gotta be something around here..."

Eric's fumbling hands searched the desktop, flipping over a stapler, tilting a monitor, and brushing a pair of pens aside. His fingers found a small, rectangular object hiding behind a stack of unlabeled compact discs. His eyes widened at the sight of a light gray thumb drive.

"Everybody has to see this."

The wall of monitors flashed the same notification: motion detected from the theater room. A window appeared on the central screen in front of Eric.

Pixelated footage of David walking to the exit, Super Mind-Changer in hand.

"Gotta make this quick!" Eric said to himself.

Sliding off the chair, he crouched back under the desk. The computer tower sat nestled by the entanglement of cords. On his second try, Eric successfully inserted the thumb drive into the USB port. As he willed himself backward, something caught his eye. Pushing forward into the dim underside of the desk, Eric squinted to read the sticker slapped onto the top of the tower.

"'Property of New Horizons Orphanage,'" Eric whispered. "No way, this can't be the same computer..."

He popped up and got to work on saving the video.

"Soooo, I'm totally using the same computer Mr. Maddox used to extort the OG Super Society," he said with a shaky breath.

The file transfer box showed three minutes remaining.

"Not sure what's weirder, that Mr. Maddox uses his childhood computer—with a crazy secret blackmail video on it—as his security system, or that it's in this unlocked room... when he knew we'd be here, easily able to find it."

Two minutes left.

"If this is all part of Mr. Maddox's big evil plans, then that must mean he doesn't care if I find this," Eric said, his pupils fixated on the green progress bar. "Super-frightening as that idea is, I still have to get this to people!"

One minute.

"C'mon, c'mon, c'mon," Eric muttered, fidgeting.

A new motion detection alert appeared above the loading bar. The screens showed David entering the hallway.

Thirty seconds remained until the transfer was complete. David tried a few locked doors, then moved on.

Ten seconds. Eric tapped his fingers on the desk, eager to fly out of the small office. A thousand terrible lies coursed through his brain, each with no chance of getting out of trouble with his dad, but Eric didn't care.

Just as long as this thing finishes in time, he thought.

The progress bar halted at five seconds.

"Are you kidding me?!" Eric said, seething through his teeth.

The monitors displayed David approaching the door. The static green bar sat as if frozen in time.

Click. The handle jiggled.

The status bar completed, electrifying Eric's nerves. He tapped at the mouse to safely eject the thumb drive. The door opened, and Eric jolted, bumbling into the adjacent wall. His momentum pushed against the white-painted metal wall, causing it to shift. Eric gasped as the wall slid, opening a secret hatch.

"It's no use hiding, Eric," David's voice said, heard but unseen in a blur of motion.

Kicking the chair, Eric felt himself sinking through the metal chute. He disappeared into darkness.

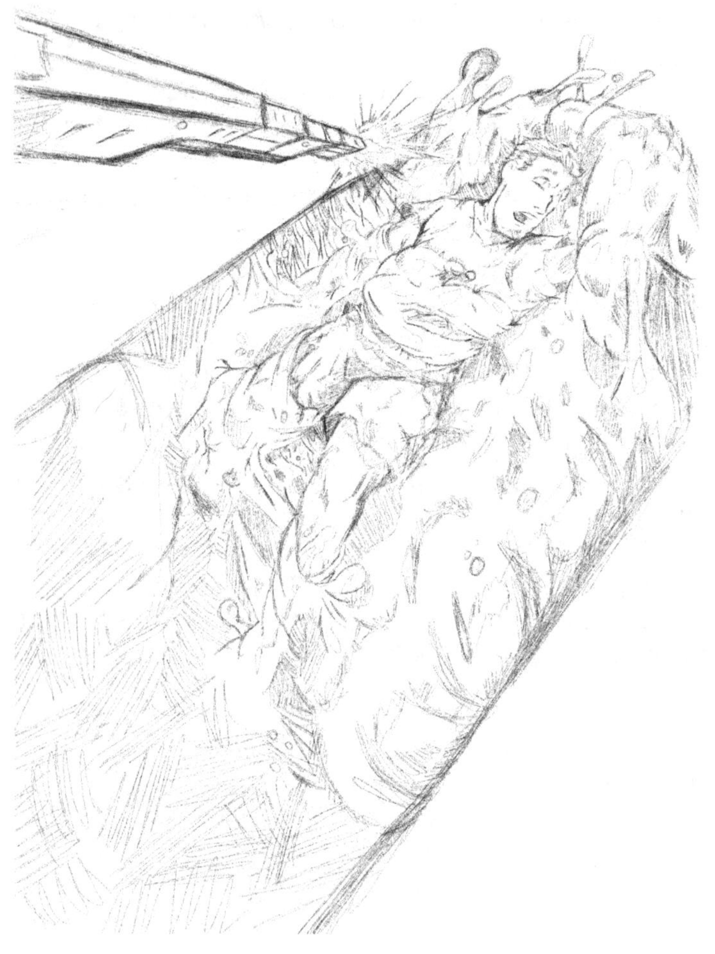

Chapter Eight: *TERMINAL*

ERIC

TUMBLING DOWN THE CRAMPED, STEEL chute, Eric thought to use his floating ability, but his body didn't get the message. He bounced like a pinball until jettisoning from a rectangular opening. Gravity warped around Eric, swirling his innards until his flying power kicked in. With his sneakers hovering above the gunmetal gray floor, Eric's jaw unhinged at seeing what appeared to be an industrial factory surrounding him.

"What the heck...?" he drawled out, slack-jawed while looking at the conveyor belts, valves, and various levers sprouting from the bulky machines.

A dull hum filled the air. The inactive devices smelled of faint, acrid cleaning chemicals. Eric let out a sharp sigh of relief as he felt the thumb drive in his hands. He pocketed it, then gave it a little tap outside of his shorts to reassure him he didn't just imagine securing it.

Aimlessly floating, Eric bumped into a workstation. Beside a keyboard and a boxy monitor, a metallic glove wobbled. Copper-colored coils spiraled where fingers would be, and the uncovered panel over the wrist exposed a tangled tapestry of multicolored wires—a flat, "T"-shaped sheet of metal lay next to the janky glove. Eric leaned in, inspecting it.

Is that a proto-Truther gauntlet?

The assembly line of mechanical arms, cylindrical power generators, oversized drills, and other tools lined the walls of the spacious room. Fluorescent lamps hung from the high ceiling. Eric ascended to the opening he fell out of, then peeked inside. Eric heard no sound from the top, only the soft hisses of his echoed breaths. The darkened tunnel curved upward.

If that wall resealed itself, I might not have a way out of here, Eric thought, forming a grim frown. *Since the chute was big enough for me to slide down— barely—I'm guessing it was designed to be a secret entryway.*

Twisting as he backed away, Eric spotted a mounted costume display on the floor to his right. A bright red tunic stood propped up next to an open tool cabinet.

How'd I miss this?!

A black wireframe filled out the arms, legs, and chest. A white mask covered a blank mannequin head atop the frame.

This is gotta be teenage Mr. Maddox's secret lab, Eric thought, gulping. *This is where he built all his gear when he was Sidebar... then eventually created his Truther suit.*

Willing himself closer, Eric floated, gazing upon the sidekick uniform.

"Mr. Maddox was pretty lanky when he was around my age," he said, sizing up the slim costume. "No wonder he could slide down that chute."

Eric's childhood fandom of the original Super Society pushed fond memories to the surface of his brain. He recalled the excitement of his miraculous flying ability landing him as a current roster member. Nostalgia clashed with dread. He raised a trepidatious hand, making a slow move to touch the tangible history before him.

"Alert! Alert!" a robotic voice blared from hidden speakers.

Rattled, Eric recoiled his hand. The recorded alarm replayed, sparking panic. Eric swiveled in a jerky motion, scanning for trouble.

Krrrrrr! The mechanical whirring startled Eric. His muscles tensed at seeing a long, thin cannon emerging from behind the neighboring tool cabinet. A black steel arm positioned the sleek rifle at Eric. A circular scope mounted on the automated weapon lit, emitting a fiery red glow.

"Whoa!" Eric spouted, backing away.

The floor beneath him separated into twin panels, then retracted into itself. A pair of robotized arms sprang from slots on the openings' edges. The black rectangular arms' skeletal fingers clamped onto Eric's ankles. He yelped as the metal digits yanked, pulling Eric into a strange pink substance.

"What is this stuff?!" Eric yelled, flaring his nostrils at the sour smell.

The robot arms tugged with incredible strength, sinking Eric farther into the thick goop. The square hole in the floor opened wide enough for a person to slip through. Eric didn't want to think about how long it'd been since anyone met the dense blob hidden below.

"Why am I not surprised Mr. Maddox has a trapdoor?!" Eric quipped, struggling to move.

Fighting and flailing fell him over, sending Eric onto his back. The weird clay-like matter softened his landing. The smooth glop welcomed Eric's body, eager to submerge him. It slithered over his stomach, legs, and arms.

The cannon snaked around the Sidebar costume, lowering at Eric's head for perfect aim.

"You are being deeeeee-tained for attempted theft," the cannon's tinny, robotic voice said between spats of crackling static. "Thievery is a supervillain-level offense. Appropriate action will beeeeee taken."

"Are you for real?!" Eric said, eyebrows spiking. "I didn't even touch the costume!"

The cannon's red scope light blinked. Fidgeting tightened the pink goo's grip on Eric's upper arms. The sentry gun blasted an eerily silent, thin bolt of crimson energy. Eric moved his head out of the way. Sparks flashed from the point of impact, a mere two inches from Eric's temple.

"You got it all wrong!" Eric shouted. "I wasn't going to steal anything!"

Steam plumed from the scorched area beside Eric. The laser's damage left a small trench, splitting a patch of the goop apart.

Whatever this stuff is, it can be cut, Eric thought. *If I can't get free, then I'll be sliced along with it!*

"My program activates based on supervillain activity," the cannon stated. "Threats will not be tolerrrrrrr-rated."

The scope blinked, followed by another pulse of scarlet energy. The laser missed Eric's thigh, leaving a little steaming, jagged wedge in the putty-like substance. Eric wiggled his legs, but his feet descended deeper. Muscle fibers and tendons tightened, spreading terror throughout Eric's body. Unable to pry himself from the mysterious sludge, Eric froze as a familiar tingling ignited his nerves.

"Oh no, oh no, oh no!" he said. "I've been grounded too long!"

The weakness simmered, pecking Eric's legs, and clawing up his spine. The black-coated steel fingers kept their hold on Eric's ankles. The dense slime covered the clamps up to their chrome knuckles.

"Hey, talking cannon!" Eric said, grunting in pain. "You respond to villain threats, right? Well, I'm gonna take down Baron Maddox!"

"Zeta-level threat registered," the glitchy gun stated. "Threats to creator are met with maximum force."

The scope blinked red and bolted out another round of laser fire. The blast hit the glop wrapped around Eric's left wrist. The blow jolted him, but Eric found relief when he realized it didn't hurt—the pink matter absorbed the heat. The shot carved into the stuff, freeing Eric's hand.

Only my other arm, chest, and legs are left to go... No pressure, Eric!

"You haven't been used in a long while, huh?" Eric said, both taunting the device as much as satisfying his curiosity.

"I am overdue for software updaaaaaaate," the cannon said. "I still operate at a functional level— enough to eliminate enemies of creator-or-or-orrrrr."

A spike of searing stinging attacked Eric's body.

Is gravity punishing me or what?! he thought. *I'm so over this weakness!*

"Are you a good enough shot," Eric coughed out, "to eliminate me before I destroy this entire lab?!"

"Sigma-level threat registered."

A bright flare of energy hit an empty spot of the pink mess, a few inches from Eric's ribs.

It bought the lie but can't shoot straight, Eric

thought. *I have to raise the supervillain stakes.*

"It's no use trying to stop me!" Eric shouted. "I'll steal every Super Society costume!"

"Repeated thievery attempts. Upsilon-level threat registered."

The cannon's rectangular barrel shot a brilliant burst, hitting Eric's midsection. The sudden impact rattled Eric, but the solidified ooze covering him took the heat. The blast severed the sludge, relinquishing Eric's upper body. His right hand remained encased, though, and the vises around his ankles maintained their hold.

"Once I'm free, I'll unleash my shrink-ray on everyone!" Eric declared in his most convincing bad guy voice. "I'll put New St. Cloud City in a bottle and sell it to aliens!"

"You are in Omega-level threat territory now," the cannon said. "You will beeeeeeee neutralized."

Another blast, another near miss, hitting a blank spot by Eric's shins.

"I'll use a mind-control device!" Eric said, sitting up as far as he could with his hand still stuck. "I'll force people to, um, think they're driving a car!"

"Seems unlikely, buuuuutttttt—" the cannon said before firing off a laser.

The bolt hit the pink matter by Eric's knee.

"How's this for an evil plan?" Eric yelled. "I'll make synthetic clones of people! I'll steal superpowers from a comatose mother!"

"Only serious threats are registered."

His weakness seizing his insides, Eric growled in frustration.

"I'll blow up an orphanage!"

"That's going too far," the cannon said. "Even for a supervillain."

"Really?!" Eric said, crinkling his brow in disbelief.

A surge of reddish energy hit the slop over Eric's right forearm. The pink goo split, releasing his hand.

"Well, you haven't seen anything yet!" Eric said, fully freed from the waist-up.

The scope blinked, warning of the next barrage of laser bolts, but Eric grabbed the cannon before it could discharge. The weapon's support crane offered no resistance as Eric forced it down. Eric held his breath as the cannon unloaded a short beam, aiming it at his left foot. The metallic claw loosened its snare, and the pink dough around Eric's ankle ripped apart. Wriggling his sneaker free, Eric struggled as the cannon wobbled, trying to reposition itself.

"Attempted theft of creator's property registered," its shrill, monotone voice reported. "Initiating defenses."

Wrestling the rifle felt like wrangling a short but wild ironing board—its flat frame buckled in Eric's grasp. Eric strained, training it on his other foot. A piercing blast hit the metal hand and the glop surrounding it. Rising, Eric heaved in oxygen, relieved of his weakness-induced anguish. The rush of manhandling the gun spiked his adrenaline, replacing the short-lived solace.

"This insurgence will be reported to creator," the cannon said as it wriggled under Eric's grip.

"I'll tell Mr. Maddox personally!" Eric said.

He pulled the narrow barrel, aiming it at the empty cabinet beside the Sidebar costume. A soundless energy surge hit the tall case—sparks erupted from its blue-painted steel frame. The impact knocked the cabinet onto its side, crashing with a loud *BLANG*—uncovering the cannon's base behind it. The weapon's onyx-colored arm connected to what appeared to be nothing more than a skinny black metal box.

"That's your power source, huh?" Eric said, guiding the cannon to face it.

"Affirmative. Threat to destroy creator property registered. Extreeeeeeme termination authorized."

The scope flashed red, then shot a bright beam. The energy bolt struck the black box base, exploding it into a flickering fit of light. Embers popped from vents on its sides, followed by billowing smoke. The scope faded, and the cannon dropped. The mechanical arm made a slow descent to the floor, lifeless.

"I can't believe I just won a fight with a talking raygun," Eric said, exhaling a deep breath.

He gazed upon the open floor panels and the exposed square of pink clay. The sludge lay pelted by multiple laser blasts, warped and scarred.

"Sticky pink goo under metal floorboards," Eric said, brushing his hair back while shaking his head. "Mr. Maddox must've been around my age when he built this crazy stuff—and I thought I was a strange kid."

Rummaging through his pocket eased a mini-heart attack—the thumb drive never slipped out. Untouched by the goop, the plastic and metal casing remained intact.

"Okay, seriously, time to leave now," Eric said while ascending to better view the lab.

Machines, tools, and devices lay cluttered, spreading to the walls.

"Don't tell me the chute is the only way out of here."

A twinkle caught his eye and then vanished. Moving his head back and forth, then up and down, Eric spotted the tiny sparkle. Against the back wall, behind a wide, bulky workstation, the top of a silver hinge stuck out. Eric advanced to the pearl-colored station, looking past its dust-covered monitor screens and segmented keyboard. Eric noticed a horizontal sliver next to the metal latch. Then over lamps' light streaked across the silver surface. The top shelf of the tall workstation covered it, but Eric deduced what he saw.

"There's a door behind here..."

Stretching to grip onto the sides of the upright station, Eric pulled, but the thing did not budge. The closed drawers at its base did not open. Eric didn't know what was in those compartments, but they were heavy. He tugged under the protruding keyboard shelf, but it merely wobbled a bit. Shaking the structure like a vending machine with a stuck chocolate bar also failed to move it.

Catching his breath, Eric backed away. The station was lodged between a large, olive-colored cylindrical power generator and a multilayered machine. Curling his lip, Eric dove back in. He pulled at the walls encasing the twin monitors, the only stable grip he found. Sheer determination produced a squeak of metal sliding across metal.

He released the station, exasperated and disappointed. The station moved roughly a centimeter. Eric made a careful effort to lie flat on the floor for a breather. Blinking sweat from his eyelashes, Eric saw wheels below the workstation. Small, black crescent shells covered the wheels. Little grip necks stuck out, lowered in a locked position.

"You gotta be kidding me."

He stretched to unlock the wheels, and to Eric's relief, the station rolled out with no problem. The door became visible after nudging the heavy frame far enough out of the way.

"Of course, no knob or handle or anything."

Eric took a long blink, collecting himself. Steadying his hand, Eric reached out to touch the stone-gray steel surface.

"If there are any more laser cannons, I'm not an evil bad guy trying to poison the city's water supply or whatever!"

He tapped at the blank, smooth door.

"Access denied," a deep, computerized voice announced.

Startled, Eric pushed himself backward.

"Super Society members only," the disembodied computer stated.

"Original members," Eric said, remembering what "Eliza" told him.

He sighed, craning his neck and placing his palms over his face. He turned, peeking through his fingers at the Sidebar costume.

"Stealing is an Upsilon-level threat, eh?" he said, lowering his hands. "Maybe I have some villain in me after all."

Chapter Nine: *G-FORCE*

ERIC

SILVER DOORS REFLECTED A BLURRY image of a figure in red.

"I can't believe that worked."

Eric tugged at his white gloves and straightened his bright red sleeves. The thin material stretched over his skin, threatening to tear if extended too far. The smooth tunic was thick, like some cross between spandex and leather.

Hopefully, this outfit is durable enough to last until I finally escape this freaky place, Eric thought.

The mask fit snugly over his head, covering his hair. The small openings at the sides pinched his exposed ears. Looking through the mask's white lenses disoriented Eric—though he saw clearly, a faint white tint twinged his view of the world. Circuit boards pressed into his scalp, indicating a tech-based aspect to the cowl.

I wish I knew how to turn on whatever Mr. Maddox programmed in the lenses.

He caressed the line where the mask ended, revealing his mouth and chin. It cut into his cheek, stretching to accommodate Eric's larger head.

"For a guy who grew up in a mansion, wanting for nothing," Eric said, "Mr. Maddox just didn't eat, apparently."

Ding! The elevator stopped with a jerky motion. Above the door frame, a dark, translucent red panel blinked. A thin vertical bar of light scrolled from left to right. The red beam wavered over Eric's masked face.

"You have reached the top floor," a deep, robotic voice said from corner-mounted speakers. "Happy hunting, Sidebar."

The doors slid open, unveiling a grated metal pathway between swaths of lush foliage. Eric floated, moving forward under half-lit lamps. The mounted dim lights stood upon thick, black poles sticking just barely over fifteen-foot-tall thickets of leaves.

Eric looked around at the shadowy shrubbery ahead—a dark path awaited him, promising danger and uncertainty. The costume absorbed the humidity, but the balmy warmth seeped through enough to make Eric sweat.

Great, he thought. *I have to find my way out of this secret nightmare garden, and I'll get pit stains on the costume.*

Rising, Eric peered above the high wall of droopy banana leaves and tropical greenery. The night sky hung over him, blocked by a thick glass ceiling. A pale moon stared back at Eric—an unattainable symbol of freedom. He pressed against the smooth pane, pushing himself down. Torpedoing back up, Eric pounded on the glass—he would fit through its wide frame if only it would crack. Impatient frustration expelled from every pore.

This can't be it! he thought, shaking. *There's no way out, is there?!*

His balled fists beat on the dense glass until he

finally eased downward.

"Don't freak out," Eric whispered to himself. "Focus on how absurd this whole place is."

The clear ceiling stretched far into the distant blackness. Eric reckoned this to be the top of the mansion. He also reasoned that he might be stuck unless he spotted another sensor of some kind—or anything resembling an exit.

"Nope, nope, nope," Eric told himself. "Don't think about being trapped. Concentrate, Eric! Mr. Maddox designed a big, stupid building."

He calmed his breathing.

"He probably blackmailed Judge Justice into putting this-this-this plant nursery whatever up here. A nursery!"

He forced a chuckle.

"Probably was just building a practice Plant Pipeline—"

His breath quickened.

"—just like in the Pantheon Solutions tower."

Eric focused on the full moon while descending farther.

"Mr. Maddox must've been planning his empire since he was a kid. And I'm wearing the uniform he did it in."

The thought of young Baron Maddox dreaming up wicked schemes while dressed in the same attire turned Eric's sweat cold. The fading lamp beneath him grew darker.

"I wish this mask has night vision—"

"Night vision mode activated," a computerized voice announced as if emanating from Eric's skull.

The path ahead illuminated a vivid, white silhouette of leafy plants and huge stems. Eric shut his eyes, taken aback by the intense light.

"Okay, voice command is apparently a thing with this mask."

Eric positioned himself a foot above the metal walkway. The walls of leaves on either side of him blended together, forming a white mass under the night vision lenses. Eric registered new shapes as the lenses digitally altered his sight, forming the world around him. The grid pattern of the glass ceiling seemed to have no end. The foliage continued in a bright, white eternity.

Creeping farther along the lone walkway, a mist of iridescent water sprayed in front of Eric. Another drizzle burst into a whitened cloud, like a ghost fading out of existence. Eric flinched, feeling the wet droplets spritz onto his tunic. The moisture wicked off his sleeve, yet the damp coolness unsettled him. The still silence jarred him even more.

"I could really do without any more surprises."

He guided his floating body forward a few more feet until the afterimage of a rectangle appeared—an outline of a door grew clearer as he neared. The closed door showed no sign of a handle or controls, but it still meant hope for escape. Eric's excited breaths blew into barely visible wisps in front of him. He flew to the entrance and reached for its surface when a blinding white hatch swung open beside him. Eric recoiled, willing himself backward.

The curved hatch lid hung motionless. The slender door appeared to be a featureless slab of light, but the shell's opening it connected to remained pitch black. The hatch stood adjacent to the main door.

It's getting harder to distract myself from the creepiness of this mansion, Eric thought, gulping.

He waited a moment before flying farther. Eric halted when a solid, white silhouette emerged from the hatch. Eric held his breath while moving backward. The person possessed a familiar frame.

"Get lost trying to find the bathroom Eric?" the fake Eliza asked as she stepped onto the steel path.

Petrified, Eric watched in silence.

"I told your father I needed to powder my nose," Eliza said, taking slow *clanking* steps closer to Eric. "I can just tell him we both got turned around in this silly place."

The shape of her head looked around but did not indicate she saw Eric.

I'm hovering right in front of her, but she can't see me, he thought. *It must be pitch black down here.*

"Eric, I know you're here," Eliza said, taking cautious steps. "We both followed you and saw you on the surveillance monitors. David couldn't fit through the skinny, little chute into the lab—so he said he's finding an alternate way to come here."

Eliza resembled a phantom possessed by pure light under the night vision lenses. Her image grew closer and brighter.

"David doesn't know this place as well as I do," she said.

Eric ascended, hovering over her, careful not to make a sound. A few strands of her hair wavered and made a sudden stop.

"Why don't you want to stay with us, Eric?"

He buoyed, still as a statue.

"Wanna know a secret?" Eliza asked, resuming her plodding stroll. "The pod I just came out of? I have to go in it once a day—sort of a pick-me-up. Recharge the batteries. Better than any cup of coffee!"

Eric lowered, slow and steady. He faced her back.

"It's just how Mr. Maddox wanted me to be," she continued. "All his people are like that. Isn't that funny?"

All of Mr. Maddox's "model employees" have to regenerate, Eric thought. *Guess that explains why Pantheon Tower has so many pods.*

Keeping his eyes on Eliza, Eric backed himself closer to the door at the end of the path. Eliza's pod door hung open but whatever interior lamp had turned off. Eric's special lenses saw the main exit standing like a lone monolith—light peeked through its edges.

"Not even your father knows what the pods really do," Eliza said. "There. Now we share a secret. We've bonded!"

Eric felt the imprint of the thumb drive in the side pocket on his leg.

How many other secrets does she know about?

Eric flattened himself an inch from the leafy wall. He moved horizontally toward the exit, careful not to make a sound. He advanced, edging closer. She turned, facing Eric.

"That door won't lead you out of here," she said.

Eric froze.

"It's super important for us to get along, Eric," Eliza said. "We're gonna be spending a lot of time here together. At least until Mr. Maddox calls you up for your part in his big show!"

She walked forward.

"I know I'm not your mother," she said. "But I just know that we'll be the best of besties after we get to know each other."

Eliza stepped even closer, a breath away from Eric. Panic took the wheel and lifted his body. The warm air flushed over the exposed part of Eric's lower face as he rose, yet he felt chilled to the bone. Weightless, he hovered, hiding in the open space between the plant walls. Eric's trembling breaths sputtered out in sharp, faint mists under the mask's lightened lenses. He prayed he flew high enough so that the darkness would conceal him once more. Below, the silhouette of Eliza looked up.

"Wearing the Sidebar costume is pretty clever," she said. "It could use some tailoring, though. Why don't you let me make some alterations? Don't worry; I'll make sure it's quick and painless."

Eliza sidestepped, disappearing into the white mass of leaves and flowers. Fear struck Eric's body, ripping the air from his lungs. Eric forced himself to fly to the door. The night vision showed no trace of any controls whatsoever. His open palm patted the metal surface, feeling for anything that would open it.

"Come on, open! Open!" he yelled, no longer caring about stealth.

The slick door slid upward, unleashing a flood of intense light. The bright wave sent Eric reeling, shutting his eyes as he twisted away. Then, rubbing the cowl's smooth material over his forehead, Eric allowed his boot to land on the walkway. His eyelids parted in slits, and he felt around while the lenses adjusted. The outlines of the pathway and the surrounding leafy walls lay before him. Eric's mind ached as he gathered his bearings.

"This place is creaky and old," Eliza said from somewhere. "I'm sure you've noticed by now how some of the tech is a little outdated, huh? Kinda faulty?"

"I've noticed that some of Mr. Maddox's newer inventions are glitchy, too," Eric said, his heart racing. "Especially the synthetic people inventions."

"I'm afraid I don't know what you're talking about," she responded from the shadows. "Hey, wouldn't it be the most fun ever if we remodeled this old shack? It can be something we do together as a family!"

Slowly backing, Eric darted his eyes, looking for any sign of movement from the jungle.

"After all," Eliza continued, "Mr. Maddox put us here to be happy. To be safe. This—this new life—it's Mr. Maddox's payment to your father for all of his hard work."

Eric peeked over his shoulder at the open doorway—the luminous light from the hallway inside stung Eric's eyes. He told himself to make a break for it.

Just fly through the door, Eric, he ordered himself. *You're already busted, so you should just leave! ...And end up lost in some maze and stuck all over again.*

"Why so quiet, Eric?"

"Oh, I'm, you know, trying to figure out just how freaked out I should be over a robo-clone of my mom hunting me like she's the Predator."

"Speaking of movies," Eliza said, unseen, "we still have to finish what we were watching! You don't need those three-dee glasses, though. Night vision mode off."

Eric's sight went dark. The sudden switch rattled his senses, and his nerves shook.

Voice command, Eric thought. *She's not as dumb as she lets on.*

The doorway's light behind Eric provided enough brightness to make out the immediate area around him.

"Don't spoil the ending if you've seen it before," Eliza said, sounding too close.

Light from behind Eric guided him—he swiveled, lifting from the ground to fly to the door. Eliza jumped in front of him, stopping Eric mid-flight.

"I need to see if the hero dies at the end!" she said, lunging at Eric.

Startled, Eric resisted, but her strength outmatched him. She pushed him down by his shoulders, shoving Eric to his knees.

"I'm not sure you realize how nice you have it here," Eliza said with an unnatural grin. "You could've still been locked up inside a pod, sleeping away in dreamland."

Eric yelped as her fingers dug into his collar.

"It'd mean so much to us if you put in a little more effort," Eliza said, shaking her head. "If you don't work on that attitude of yours, mister, then I'll be forced to punish you."

"I want you to know how sorry I am," David said.

With Eliza's claws still restraining him, Eric leaned as far as possible. His father stood, shrouded in the doorway's light.

"But you took it too far," David said.

"D-dad," Eric stammered through the anguish. "P-please!"

"This isn't how I imagined any of this to go," David said. "I really did want us to be a family again."

David stepped closer.

"But," David said, "this outburst has shown me that it's simply too much to ask for. You'll have to go back in your pod, and that's all there is to it."

"Dad!" Eric coughed, sinking lower as his legs crumpled under Eliza's surprising might. "No, Dad, you can't do this!"

David sighed.

"I really thought I could fix this."

"You'll see one day how this is all for the best, Eric," Eliza said with a maniacal smile.

Her grip released Eric, and he skittered away. Eric heaved in oxygen as he levitated. Mouth agape in confusion, Eric watched Eliza stand straight. She started doing the robot. Eliza made a stiff rotation with her hands pointed. She bent over, tilting her head. David stood a few feet behind her, Super Mind-Changer in hand.

David approached her as she let her forearm dangle. Eric's eyes adjusted well enough to see the strap slung over David's shoulder. The bag carried something large, poking out from behind David's back.

"I need to reprogram this thing," David said, fiddling with the Super Mind-Changer. "It was supposed to make her do the chicken dance."

He paced around Eliza's robotic dancing.

"Barry told me about her, ya know," David said, shaking his head as he stared at her. "He said he originally created her to replicate your mother's abilities—which obviously didn't pan out. But I was all too happy to take the hand-me-down clone-wife."

He tapped a button on the device. Eliza stood upright, motionless. Her unblinking eyes stared at nothing.

"I truly believed I could handle knowing," David said in a hushed tone. "I thought this was what I deserved."

His sunken eyes glanced at Eric.

"What we deserved."

Like how prey stiffens until it's safe to move, Eric waited in silence. His eyes followed David as he guided Eliza down the path. She turned, taking rigid steps toward the exit.

"For a second, I even thought this was better than actually getting paid money," David said, directing Eliza to the pod by the door.

Eliza stepped inside the cylindrical chamber. The light from the hallway revealed only gray padding inside. Eric wondered how she'd eat or go to the bathroom—or if she needed to.

Just how organic are those... things?

David took a lingering look at Eliza's face. Shadows blanketed her frozen smile. The dark reflection of his mother's memory sent shivers up Eric's spine.

"Barry may've lied about how exactly he'd compensate me for my work," David said. "But it wouldn't have made a difference. I would've taken this anyway."

He closed the hatch until it made a *click*.

"I would've screwed this all up all the same."

David took a deep breath and then looked at Eric.

"Son, I know we have a ton to talk about," he said. "But first, lemme just say I'm not loving the costume change."

"What's that behind your back?" Eric said, fighting to steady his nerves.

David spiked a brow as if he'd forgotten the object slung over his shoulder.

"Oh! Yeah, there's a bunch of goodies just lying around here. Can you believe this awesome laser rifle was back in that lab?"

Swinging it around his waist, David revealed the laser cannon.

"I managed to unhook it from its robot arm," David said. "Its battery hub was damaged, though."

"Just be glad it doesn't have any power!"

"Sure, it does."

David tapped at a panel on the flat back of the rectangular gun.

"There's a backup battery."

The scope woke up, fading in its ominous red light. Eric raised his arm, shielding himself. Looking past his trembling limb, Eric watched David lower the weapon. Letting the cannon hang at his side, David raised his hands.

"Hey, wait, whoa, I don't even know how to fire this thing!"

David took a step, but Eric swooped himself upward. Eric looked down, but his body tilted, prepared to fly away. They shared a moment of tense silence.

"What's going to happen to her?" Eric finally said.

"She—they—go into some kind of stasis hibernation. I don't know the details, but, I mean, she'll be okay if that's what you're asking."

"Dad, I'm going to find a way out of here, and when I do, I'm taking down Mr. Maddox."

Eric shifted his eyes to the starless night sky above the glass ceiling.

"After that," Eric said. "I don't know what's going to happen. But everybody will know everything. Like, the news and police—everybody."

David let out a confused, breathy chuckle. His creased brow and half-smile dissipated into a knowing frown—his eyes relaxed, downcast at the steel path under his loafers.

"I'm getting used to being locked up," David said, nodding. "I don't know if there's a category for the unbelievably rotten things I've done, but..."

Eric considered soaring off. In his gut, he knew there was no time to waste, yet he remained.

"My big new life lasted less than a day," David said, scoffing. "I'm complicit in a mad scientist's evil scheme. I betrayed my only son in the most outlandish way possible—just another failure for David Boxworth! So, whatever reason they find to take me away, I deserve it."

Eric found himself sinking despite his instincts demanding that he flee. Planting his white boots onto the path, Eric took careful steps. David looked down—after spending so much time airborne, Eric nearly forgot how tall people are, especially adults.

"You don't have to risk not flying and getting your weakness to act up," David said.

"If there's any chance to save Mom, you know I have to do whatever it takes."

"Raise up a bit," David said.

He motioned for Eric to go up.

"If you're gonna take one last look at me, then look me straight in the face. Eye-level."

Eric levitated to David's height.

"I spent my entire life building things," David said. "Fixing and experimenting on machines. Inventing new technology. But, Eric, you—you are something that defies science."

Eric fought to quell his lips from quivering. He willed back tears from welling up.

"You—and your mother," David said. "You can fly. By no way that makes any kind of logical sense—you can fly."

David lifted a hand, reaching for Eric's shoulder, but stopped himself from making contact.

"Out of all the things I've had a hand in doing, you're the best thing I've ever made."

Eric winced.

"Oh, don't be gross," David said. "What I'm trying to say is, I have a magic flying superhero for a son. And that's the best thing that could've ever happened to me."

David looked up, gazing at the moon. He let out a soft breath, twisting his lips in a tight smirk. Eric knew this look well—the face David made when he knew he was beaten.

"I wish I was brave enough to go with you."

"The laser cannon is activated by supervillain threats," Eric said.

David's head dropped, facing Eric with squinted eyes and pursed lips.

"It does what now?"

"Say you're going to do something a bad guy would do, and it'll shoot."

David held the rifle in front of him, sizing it up. He took a firing stance, pointing the gun at the windows above them.

"Bad guy stuff, eh?" he said, steadying his aim. "Okay, how about this? I'll put on killer robot armor and fight my son. I'll then kidnap my son and use a machine to control his brain. Then, I'll force him to live in a creepy mansion with a psycho clone of his mother!"

The rifle pulsated, then unloaded a crackling surge of red energy. Eric looked away from the bright burst. The laser struck the ceiling, shattering a windowpane. Eric and David crouched, covering their heads from raining shards.

The last of the glass bits fell around them, bouncing off leaves. David swung the cannon behind his back. Eric's saucer-like eyes glared at him in disbelief.

"What're you waiting for, a permission slip?" David said. "I don't expect to win father of the year anytime soon, so letting a minor go off into danger alone isn't that new for me."

Clunk! Clunk! Clunk! Eric and David looked around but couldn't see where the metallic noise came from.

"Dad, I—"

"Go get your super team together and settle this! Trust me; I'm not going anywhere."

The thuds of metal hitting metal grew nearer.

Bronze-colored steel plates extended across the ceiling, covering one windowpane at a time. Darkness spread thicker and faster with each sheet as they blocked out the moon.

"Must be a security shield!" Eric said. "Neither of us is leaving unless we drop everything!"

"What do you mean?"

"I mean, you're heavy enough as it is!"

"Huh?"

"Lose the cannon!" Eric said as his eyes trailed the expanding metal plates.

David side-eyed Eric as he lowered the weapon to his feet. Eric wrapped his arms around David.

"Er, okay, we're hugging!" David blurted. "I'm gonna miss you, too. I'm glad we could have this mome—!"

"The Super-Mind Changer," Eric said. "I'm flying us out of here, but that thing stays."

"It weighs less than a pound—"

"If I'm ditching my regular clothes, you can lose the thing you controlled my brain with."

David stared into Eric's eyes. Eric's face trembled with adrenaline and panic, but his eyes locked onto his father's. David let the device slip from his fingers, bouncing on the metal grating below. After a deep breath, Eric hoisted them up, rocketing toward the broken window.

Metal sheets closed in, covering the area surrounding their escape. *Clunk. Clunk. Clunk.* Eric grunted as he carried his father's weight. The plates linked, encompassing the ceiling like a steel cloud.

Eric grimaced as the G-force pulled his flesh. Their combined mass would barely squeeze through the opening—a miscalculation in Eric's aim would splat them across the metal.

"Eriiiiiic!" David yelled.

They shot out of the open windowpane, hurtling into the night air, and headed straight for the moon.

Chapter Ten: *SOAR*

L IKE A STALKING BIRD OF prey, Valerie watched Jaycee's every move.

"I can have cameras installed here by tomorrow," Valerie said. "And I already have new locks on my shopping list."

"For the thirty-seven-thousandth time, I'm sorry, Mom," Jaycee said as she leaned back in her chair. "I'm not going anywhere. I have nowhere to go."

"With the way today has gone," Valerie said, "I don't want any more surprises."

Valerie scanned Jaycee's room before making her way to the door. From her cluttered desk, Jaycee eyed her unmade bed.

"Today has been stressful," Valerie said. "So, I'll overlook this sty. Only today, though."

Jaycee curled her lip as she watched her mother close the pink curtains on her window, covering the night sky.

"Get some sleep," Valerie said as she exited. "You have school in the morning—school you will not be ditching."

Jaycee waited until Valerie's footsteps took her

far enough down the hall to flip open her laptop. The screen displayed a grid of Melvin, Tiffany, and Yvette.

"Does your mom really think she can keep you locked up at school all day tomorrow?" Melvin asked from his little video box.

Jaycee shushed him as she got up to shut her door. She cursed herself for not muting the online call.

"I'm lucky she's even letting me ride the bus tomorrow," Jaycee said, sitting. "She has to be at school extra early, so I'll take whatever freedom I can get."

"You'd think we'd get personal drivers by now," Tiffany said. "I mean, what else do the privileged foster kids of Baron Maddox have to do to get a chauffeur?"

"Will we even see you tomorrow, Jaycee?" Yvette said.

"I doubt my mom will let me out of her sight."

"She and all the other teachers have to be in some early meeting tomorrow morning, right?" Melvin said. "They're decidin' how tomorrow will go and all that— who says Ms. Cooper, er, yer mom will even be around to notice if you've left?"

"Melvin brings up a good point," Tiffany said.

"Of course, I do!"

"The whole city will be out tomorrow," Tiffany continued. "Let's say you volunteer to stay behind and, I don't know, nerd out at the library."

"This isn't exactly a regular field trip," Yvette said. "Any counselor would be cool with you not going."

"So, I can be tethered to my mom or be the only kid who doesn't ditch school," Jaycee said, blowing a blonde strand of hair from her forehead with a sigh.

"Jaycee Maddox would be cooped up in class," Melvin said. "But Powerhouse can make an appearance."

"Awesome idea," Jaycee said. "And I can't believe I

didn't think of it myself, but—"

Their faces on the monitor leaned closer, anxious for Jaycee's reply.

"—I'm in enough trouble as it is and—"

Groans erupted from the laptop speakers.

"Come on," Jaycee said. "If I get caught, I'm looking at being my mom's assistant for summer school! Or whatever cruel and unusual punishment she can think of!"

"I'll just say it," Melvin said. "It's a joke that we're supposed to be in costume tomorrow anyway!"

"Melvin, please—" Yvette said.

"I'm serious. Any function or event we show up to as the Super Society is a total lie! We aren't a team anymore!"

"Super classy, Supercut," Tiffany remarked.

"This wasn't exactly a planned thing," Yvette said. "Look at it this way; we get one last go as our super-selves."

"A farewell to all my adoring fans," Tiffany said.

"Now who's classy?" Melvin said, scoffing.

"I'm really sorry, guys," Jaycee said, frowning. "Just say that Powerhouse is on a secret mission with Truther."

"Wait," Tiffany said. "Truther isn't going to be there either?"

"What a shock," Melvin said. "Truther is M.I.A.; what else is new?"

Jaycee gulped.

Uh oh, she thought. *Why'd you open that can of worms, dummy?! Okay, Jaycee, damage control!*

"Hey, guys, I gotta log off," Jaycee said. "Best of luck tomorrow!"

"Boo!" Melvin said as their respective video boxes blipped into blackness.

Jaycee caressed her mouse's smooth surface. She hesitated, then moved the cursor to a Super Society double-S symbol icon on her desktop. Clicking it open popped up a different video call window. The frame showed the back of a black chair in a dimly lit room. The scarce details of the background hid in shadows, but Jaycee recognized Truther's lab.

"The time for deceit will soon come to an end," Baron said, his voice sounding like sandpaper scraped across gravel. "Take comfort that these necessary lies protect your friends—your siblings."

Jaycee sat uneasy, peeking over her shoulder. She mentally willed her mother to stay in her room.

"Even Eric?" Jaycee said, careful to keep her voice low.

"Eric Icarus has his place in this," Baron said from behind the chair. "When I am strong enough, he will understand, as everyone will."

Jaycee lingered on the screen, staring at the back of the leather chair. She winced at her father's labored breathing.

"It'll be weird with just three members up there tomorrow," she said, unsure of every word. "I know it's best just to sit tight, but, uh, I was thinking maybe—I dunno—I show up, just to, like, show my face, ya know?"

Baron's breaths cut between raspy coughs. Jaycee gritted her teeth and squinted. She imagined him regretting including her and how she'd end up disowned.

"When I inherited the team, I wanted this new iteration of the Society to be young, as I was," Baron said. "As much as I planned for everything, the other children—they ended up being a stroke of luck. They entered the Pantheon foster youth program with perfect timing. But you, Jaycee... I initially did not wish this life upon you."

Jaycee sent her head back, eyes closed.

You just had to say something, didn't you?

"Your eagerness—your bravery," Baron said. "The willingness to face danger head-on was evident even at a very young age. I soon realized that you were born for this, so it'd behoove me not to deny you."

Jaycee's finger recoiled from the mouse. She didn't know if she should even breathe.

"Do you have your uniform, hero?"

Jaycee blew out a sigh of relief. She looked at her bookbag on the floor by her bed.

"Got it!" she answered with an eager grin. "I remembered to grab it from the mid-level hangar at the tower and—"

"You'll need it for tomorrow."

"Thank you, thank you!" Jaycee whispered, barely able to contain her glee. "What about you, Dad? Will you be there?"

"My recovery from the power transference is proving to be a lengthy endeavor," he said. "The transformation of my body is an unpredictable process. I would not endanger you or myself if I felt my presence was compromising."

So, in other words, you have no idea, Jaycee thought.

"When I achieve my true potential," Baron said, "you and I shall stand as father and daughter, reigning as paragons of power."

"We'll take crime-fighting to the next level!"

Baron replied with silence. Jaycee's excited smile withered.

"When can we tell the others?" she said.

"In due time. The dissolution of the Super Society

as we know it is all part of the greater mission," Baron said. "Their ignorance absolves them of involvement if the plan goes asunder. They are playing their roles. But Jaycee…"

The chair swiveled. Jaycee peered from the corner of her eye at the screen. Baron remained mostly concealed. His chair rotated a bit more. The golden "T" of his Truther mask protruded at an angle—it stuck out from behind the back of the leather chair.

"…Once I prove that the superpower can be safely replicated in myself, I can move on to others—to you, as part of the worthy elite. I cannot guarantee the same ascendance for the others."

"So, the team is done? For real done?"

Baron wheezed in what sounded like an attempt at laughing.

"Just like I learned when you were much younger," he said. "Keeping secrets from you never lasts long."

He hacked. Jaycee scowled at the gross wet sound.

"Go-Go, Supercut, and Extra served me with honor," Baron said. "But it is not their destiny to join us on our path."

Jaycee tapped her fingers, failing to keep still and quiet.

"And Eric?" Jaycee asked. "His mom is the source of your, um, powers. She's in a pod at the tower. Is Eric… Him and his dad—are they, like, cool with this? Wherever they are?"

"The radical nature of Eric's familial inclusion is not ideal, but unavoidable."

"What will happen to Eric? Is he also elite or just another power source?"

"Do you recall when I first assigned you to gather intelligence on Eric?" Baron said, turning slightly closer to his camera. "It is up to Eric to decide how easy things are for him. He can be more than simply a power reserve if he goes along willingly. If he sees our vision, he can help mold the future of this city—this world. This may take some time, though."

"And if he doesn't?"

Baron turned completely, fully revealing himself. Jaycee's pupils focused on the monitor though her head pulled away. She forced herself to see her father's frayed face, sunken and etched with unnaturally aged wrinkles. Jaycee spotted the dark veins on Baron's cheeks even in the lab's low light. She wondered what else the Truther mask covered.

"If Eric Icarus cannot control his emotions," Baron said, "I'm afraid I would be forced to see that his journey comes to an end."

Her eyes drifted from the screen.

"Don't be disheartened," Baron said. "This is a thrilling time—you are on the cusp of becoming a true superhuman!"

"I am excited," she said. "After all..."

Jaycee peeked at her bookbag—the zipper opened enough to see her Powerhouse uniform inside. She looked back at the monitor, thinking of her mission as a superhero. She nodded, then stiffened her upper lip.

"...I was born for this."

DAVID

David's armpits burned with pain. Eric's grunts didn't sound like a picnic either. His son's noodle-like arms wavered, and David felt Eric's small hands losing their grip on his underarms, slipping from his black shirt.

"Do you need to take yet another break?" David asked, casting his sleep-deprived eyes on the Horton River far below his dangling legs. "It's not like we're in a rush. What's another coupla hours?"

"We could've called a cab," Eric said, tightening his arms around David's chest. "But you left your phone and wallet at the mansion. Something you maybe could've mentioned before."

Sunlight twinkled across the lazy waters as the morning blossomed. The city skyline awaited them— glistening windows sparkled on each skyscraper, and shimmering daylight streaked across the upper deck of Metro Memorial Stadium. The familiar beauty of New St. Cloud City always struck David, but an oddity stood out.

"For a kid in a bright red costume carrying a grown man while flying through the air, we aren't drawing much attention."

"Hopefully, it stays that way," Eric said.

"There're usually a ton of drones buzzing around," David observed. "And the highway traffic looks like it's all headed in the same direction."

"Maybe we just got lucky for once."

The wind attacked David's face as Eric pushed them faster. David closed his eyes, trying to dissociate from the arduous flight. Unfortunately, his brain's habit of racing prevented any escape. Boxworth Dreamineering's abysmal future intruded at the forefront of his thoughts. The collapse of any hope of a normal family weighed upon his spirit. Despite being unsure of what kind of incarceration surely awaited him, David secretly looked forward to it.

All that time locked up will give me plenty of opportunities to write a memoir, he thought. "*Nuking the Opportunity of a Lifetime – The Pathetic Story of David Boxworth.*"

David opened his eyes to see the upward-pointing lightning bolt emblem of Pantheon Solutions. A giant black square border hid the rooftop. They were too low to tell if the MegaCore still sat atop the tower. David felt it was a safe guess that it remained barricaded by the metal walls.

The bottom half of the Pantheon Solutions Tower remained static, covered in glass. The building was made of reflective metal and solid concrete from the midsection up. Eric veered toward the middle of the tower, zeroing in on the level above the floors of windows encasing the Plant Pipeline visible within. The clear panes shined in the sun, making it difficult to see the workstation rings surrounding the mammoth tube running down the center of the building. David knew that Baron's "model employees" lurked inside, most likely with orders to confine him.

Back to my gilded cage, I suppose.

"So, you think we should just sign in at the front desk?" David said. "Maybe it's not a good idea to go charging in the main entrance."

"I don't think we'll have to," Eric said. "I think they knew we were coming."

A massive stretch of metal curving the center of the tower opened. The huge panel slowly lifted, partially retracting into itself. David heard the booming grinding gears from several feet away.

"Looks like we attracted some attention after all," David said.

A wide-open space waited inside the horizontal hatch. Industrial lights lined the ceiling.

"Why is there a big garage in the middle of the Pantheon Solutions Tower?" David said.

"I'm pretty sure that's a hangar," Eric answered.

Eric landed them on the gray concrete floor. Flickering orange lights guided them from the deck while hazard lamps blinked from the sides of the entrance. David took quick but cautious steps across the wide interior until he found a stairwell. He grabbed the railing, steadying himself while the winds whipped him. The stairs led to an unmarked door, which David considered bursting through to get inside to safety. The sprawling view of the cityscape held him in place.

Eric landed near the edge, also taking in the city. David's gaze shifted to the back of the hangar. A set of wide, riveted silver doors closed off the room. Nothing else occupied the space, which David found peculiar.

"There's enough room to hold a decent-sized aircraft in here," he said, unheard over the ruffling noise of the flowing wind.

Crates and bolted-down computer stations lined the walls, yet no crew operated them.

"Where the heck is everybody?" David said, scratching his temple.

Rapid chopping sounds faded into his eardrums. Eric raised his arms, preparing for anything. He looked at David, and they both shared a fearful expression.

"The chickens have come home to roost," David said.

The silver Super Society helicopter descended outside the hangar's entrance frame. The sleek, aerodynamic vehicle positioned itself close to the edge where Eric stood. The *Pegasus'* blades sliced the sky, pushing air into the confined area. Eric budged, moving backward while afloat. David gripped onto the guardrail for dear life.

A door on the 'copter's side slid open, revealing Melvin, Yvette, and Tiffany inside—they wore their colorful uniforms as Go-Go, Supercut, and Extra. The teenage trio held onto the edges of the hatch, hunched over to peer into the hangar. The craft's overbearing engine pummeled David's ears, adding to the disorientation of the oppressive airstreams coming from the whirling blades. David saw what looked like a handheld device in Supercut's hand.

"Eric Icarus?" Supercut yelled, his voice amplified by the loudspeaker held to his mouth. "What are you wearing? A Sidebar costume? Is this some kind of sick joke?!"

"What?" Eric shouted back, covering his brow.

Go-Go grabbed the device from Supercut.

"Eric! We received word that you were here but didn't believe it!" she yelled. "You're lucky we circled back! You're just in time!"

The redheaded Extra yanked the loudspeaker.

"You're extra lucky we were given your costume," she shouted. "Your real costume!"

She raised Eric's familiar blue tunic, complete with his decoy backpack.

"My costume!" Eric shouted, smiling.

The grin dropped.

"Wait," Eric said. "What am I just in time for?"

"You really don't know?" Supercut said, barely picked up by the loudspeaker's microphone.

Go-Go took back the device from Extra.

"Judge Justice's funeral."

Eric's jaw dropped, and David followed suit.

"Come on!" Go-Go shouted. "You can change in the *Pegasus* on the way!"

Eric's determined vengeance-filled face vanished. In its place, the scared boy returned.

"Go!" David screamed, hoping Eric heard him.

Eric ran to the edge, mere feet from the reaching

hands of his teammates. He glanced back with an unsure expression.

"But I need to be here!" Eric shouted to David. "And the world needs to find out what we know!"

"Yes, but if we do it the wrong way, it'll be a bigger mess!"

Eric's antsy fidgeting indicated he didn't get the message.

"Baron gets locked up; that's great!" David said. "Your power gets discovered, and then—boom! Every military and tech agency swarms this place! They test and experiment on you! They'll never leave you alone! It's what you wanted to avoid this whole time!"

"I don't care what happens to me as long as—!"

"Your mom will be dissected, Eric!" David said. "If I didn't know you or her, I'd be first in line to split you open and see how you work!"

Eric's lip curled and quivered. David knew this was the face he made seconds before erupting in tears.

"It'll be easier if you just go along with things for now!" David yelled. "I'll do what I can from here!"

"But—!" Eric said.

"You not being at this funeral would only draw more attention—attention we don't need!" David said. "We go in half-cocked, and it's over before it started!"

Eric walked forward, stepping onto a short bridge extended from below the helicopter's hatch. Both ducking, Go-Go pulled him in. Eric stared at David from within the 'copter's cabin with tensed eyes.

"Trust me!" David screamed.

The silver door began to slide shut and the mini walkway retracted.

"Eric!" David shouted. "You're braver than I could ever be! Your mom would be so proud of you!"

The door fully closed. David doubted that Eric had

heard him. The helicopter turned and then flew away. The air stilled around David. He watched as the silver craft disappeared on the horizon. Behind him, the metal doors rose with a heavy churning sound. A larger elevator platform and two figures waited on the other side.

"Welcome back, Mr. Boxworth!" Chelsea said with a beaming smile.

Dahlia joined her as they walked into the hangar.

Craaaaank. Craaaaank. Thick mechanical levers and gears lowered the hangar door, sealing them inside. David released the railing and approached his handlers.

"So, I suppose Barry knows I, eh, declined his offer after all?"

"Mr. Maddox knows all about the hubbub at the Gilroy Mansion," Dahlia said. "And don't you worry, we sent some handy-dandy drones to watch over your wife!"

"You mean the fake one?"

Chelsea and Dahlia smiled at David with empty eyes, clearly not understanding.

"I don't suppose I could see my real wife now, huh?" David asked, cocking an eyebrow.

"Oh, Eliza's pod is off-limits," Chelsea said.

She and Dahlia took David by his arms and led him to the back.

"Lemme guess," he said. "Back to genius jail?"

They giggled.

"I know it's hard to tell," David said as they entered the lift, "but my son and I are going to do this big rescue mission thing. We're going to figure out a way to free the real Eliza. Stop your boss, Mr. Maddox."

The twins paid no mind. Dahlia pressed a button, and David felt the elevator go up. He sighed.

"I should've kept the Super Mind-Changer."

Chapter Eleven: *DEPARTED*

ERIC

ERIC STRETCHED THE COLLAR OF his costume over his face.

"He died yesterday?!" he said, muffled under leather and spandex.

"What?" Supercut said. "Someone get Icarus a comm; I can't hear anything!"

The *Pegasus'* roaring engine nearly drowned out what his teammate said, but Eric made out enough.

"Judge Justice died yesterday!" Eric repeated louder this time.

"No, Judge Justice died yesterday!" Supercut said. "Seriously, someone get him a communicator!"

Eric shimmied his dark blue top on, then strapped on his metal backpack. The hollow weight of the pack felt familiar. Even its mass pushing Eric forward in his seat soothed him—it meant at least something had returned to his new normal.

The metal door that closed off the cockpit weakened Eric's ease.

"Hey, who's flying the helicopter?"

Despite the cramped quarters of the 'copter's interior, Supercut leaned in closer, practically cheek-to-cheek with Eric.

"Autopilot, dude."

"How did it happen?" Eric shouted, strapping on his blue gloves. "Judge Justice, I mean."

"He was, like, really old, so..."

"And there's already a funeral?" Eric asked.

"This wasn't exactly a planned thing," Extra said, looking bored in the seat across from Eric. "But the city's most beloved hero gets the rush treatment. And now we're late because we went back to get you. Seriously, where have you been?"

"There's so much I have to tell you!" Eric yelled. "About my mom! And the original Super Society! And about Mr. Maddox!"

"Here's what we know so far," Go-Go said, apparently not hearing him. "After the service, the casket containing the Judge's body will be taken onto a special Pantheon jet."

She stuck her chrome visor in Eric's face. He looked at his perplexed reflection on the shiny surface.

"There will be a separate jet acting as a decoy," Go-Go continued. "Truther intercepted reports of a planned attempt to steal the body! So, it's our job to escort the jets to safety!"

"Wait, who's gonna steal what?" Eric said, scrunching his lips in confusion. "Oh, and about Truther, you really ought to know that—!"

"It'll look better if you're flying alongside us," Extra interrupted.

"It's for, you know, optics!" Supercut said.

"Melvin is actually right—" Extra said.

"Of course, I am!"

"—because we are supposed to look like a team," Extra went on. "And I need the content. I can't live stream as Extra—which is so lame—but I can use the footage for my personal brand accounts!"

"Is Jaycee going to be there?" Eric yelled.

"Sorry, can't hear you!" Go-Go said, pointing to her earpiece. "You're supposed to guide us to the landing site!"

The door slid open, blowing in blustering winds. Go-Go took Eric by the shoulders and positioned him at the edge of the open hatch.

"Remember to wave to the people!" Supercut said. "But it's a funeral, so look sad!"

"See you down there!" Go-Go said before shoving Eric out into the air.

Spiraling high above the earth, Eric fought to control his gravity—the only way he understood how was to simply do it. The silver helicopter sped ahead, descending upon a sea of people. The massive crowd packed the large parking lot of the New St. Cloud City convention center. The electronic marquee above the building's entrance displayed a memorial image of Judge Justice in his prime.

"Everyone in the city must be down there!" Eric said.

He willed a burst of speed and dove after the *Pegasus*. A stage sat at the foot of the main entrance, surrounded by wreaths, mounted portraits of the fallen Judge, and security personnel in black suits. Eric couldn't distinguish who stood at the podium—the golden casket by the stage gleamed in the daylight, making it difficult to see much else.

"Back at the convention center," Eric said. "Last time his Golden Gavel was on display at the comic-con, now it's Judge Justice himself."

He pressed on a pocket on his utility belt. He breathed a sigh of relief—the thumb drive didn't get lost in the shuffle.

"How can I tell the team anything if they won't even listen to me?" he said. "I've got to get this over with as soon as possible!"

Police held onlookers at bay from a circular landing pad near the stage. The helicopter lowered for a soft touchdown. The officers held onto their hats as the blades pushed the air. Supercut, Go-Go, and Extra exited, and the crowd greeted them with thunderous applause. Eric dropped to join his team and floated alongside them as they walked. Fans huddled to the metal guard railing, reaching out toward Eric and the others as they passed. Cheers and tears poured from the clustered people.

The 'copter's engine powered down and the mourners' murmuring could be heard more clearly. Eric followed his comrades down a path guided by dark-suited security guys. The curved walkway outside the main building led to the stage.

"Guys, please," Eric whispered as they moved. "I was in a pod, then my dad and I were trapped in—!"

Extra shushed him as a security guy gestured for them to get on the stage. The audience clapped loudly despite their solemn faces. Eric got shuffled to the last in the row of his fellow heroes. A reverend and a few local politicians Eric never bothered to learn the name of stood near the back of the stage. They wore stuffy-looking suits and applauded at the Society's arrival. A man with gray horseshoe hair around his bald head shook Go-Go's hand.

Pretty sure that's the mayor, he thought. *And even the governor is here? Oh man, this is too much. I don't care what Dad says, this is just wasting time. Maybe I can fake like I'm crying hysterically and be excused.*

"To help us honor the memory of Judge Justice and the original team, please welcome the Super

Society!" the mayor said.

News crew cameras pointed at the stage from scattered areas in the crowd. The media presence made Eric even more nervous. Kev and a handful of Eric's classmates stood in the mass of people. The audience braved the sweltering midday sun to be in attendance. Seeing the bodies pressed together made Eric even more grateful for his suit's special temperature-control insulation. Nervous sweat, however, dripped down his forehead.

"It is bittersweet that we all gather here at the convention center," the mayor said. "A week ago, this was where we celebrated the extraordinary career of Judge Justice and his amazing compatriots. Today, we celebrate his life."

Eric spotted Valerie Cooper, his science teacher—and Jaycee's mom—in the crowd with a few other instructors.

I wish I could tell Ms. Cooper what really happened at the Gilroy mansion! Eric thought as his heart raced. *If she's here, then maybe Jaycee's here, too... Somewhere.*

"And now to say a few words..." the mayor said into the microphone.

His voice echoed from the row of speakers on the stage.

"I hope we don't have to say anything!" Eric whispered, gulping.

Supercut scoffed beside him. Down the line next to Supercut, Extra leaned backward to face Eric.

"You still have stage fright, Icarus?" Extra whispered, rolling her eyes.

"...is a man who knew the great Patrick Gilroy more than most," the mayor said. "A man who was guided into adulthood by Judge Justice. A man who dedicated his life to preserving the legacy of the Super Society—that's right, please welcome to the stage, CEO of Pantheon Solutions, Baron Maddox!"

Alarms blared inside Eric's brain. His body tensed, stiffening so much that Supercut nudged him with an elbow.

"Eric," he whispered. "Don't freak out; it's not like we were clued in on the schedule either. Now try not to look like such a robot!"

A cluster of people parted at the side of the stage, giving way for an entourage of security. They walked in formation, hiding a hobbling figure. The politicians bowed and nodded as the security detail ushered the unseen Baron to the podium. A pair of muscly bouncer-looking guys helped Baron to the microphone. The crowd gasped and broke out into a low chatter.

The men in black suits finally moved out of the way, and Eric saw him. Eric's jaw dropped. His teammates did a better job at concealing their shock.

"Thank you all for being here today," Baron said in a raspy voice.

Hunched over, Baron appeared to be as feeble as Judge Justice had been when Eric last saw him at the retirement home. Lines cut into Baron's sunken face, and dark bags tugged at his eyes. His bristly mustache drooped over his lips. His black suit and tie hung loose on him as if he'd shriveled.

"What happened to his face?" Supercut said under his breath.

"He can't have any powers looking s-so frail!" Eric whispered with an uneasy shakiness.

"What?" Supercut whispered back.

"Do I have to separate you two?" Go-Go hissed at them.

"The loss of my mentor has taken a toll on me,"

Baron said, spittle spraying onto the mic. "I feel the city's pain deep in my heart. Judge Justice was the last of the original members of the first incarnation of the Super Society. It is truly the end of an era."

The crowd hugged, shook their heads, and prayed.

They have no idea what Mr. Maddox has done, Eric thought. *But what has he done to himself? Are people actually buying this grief-stricken stuff?*

"Truther regrets not being able to attend today," Baron said. "As his former sidekick, Sidebar, Truther decided the best way to honor the Judge was to remain on patrol."

Baron trembled, and a security guy rushed to his side. Baron waved him off.

"Though today is a tragic one," he said, "we must choose to remember all the good Patrick Gilroy did for our world. We must focus on the shining example he set as a defender of the innocent. As Judge Justice, he ushered an unprecedented reign of heroism that has grown into the gold standard for heroes everywhere. I have strived to live my life in service of humanity, an extension of the hope Mr. Gilroy represented."

Eric's chest heaved as his anxiety turned into anger.

I can't listen to much more of this, he thought, seething.

"Eric, dude," Supercut whispered from the side of his mouth. "You need to seriously chill out!"

"People need to know the truth," Eric muttered.

Audience members held their phones to record Baron's speech. Little round drones with black lenses on their "faces" floated near the media cameras, all filming the farce.

"Please forgive me," Baron said. "This devastating loss has tortured my soul, and I must rest. I will now open the floor to a valued member of the Super Society."

"I think I just got over my stage fright," Eric said.

The security guys huddled around Baron as they escorted him off the stage. Feeling lighter, Eric willed his body up. His boots raised a handful of inches before stopping cold. Jaycee approached the podium in her Powerhouse costume, met with excited applause.

"Well, look who decided to show up after all!" Supercut muttered.

"Jayc—Powerhouse!" Eric said, careful to keep his voice down.

Powerhouse nodded to Eric, Go-Go, Supercut, and Extra.

"She tells us she won't make it because she's too afraid of her mommy," Extra whispered through a fake smile. "Then she upstages us. I'm almost jealous I didn't think of it."

"I, uh, didn't expect to be here today," Powerhouse said, gazing at the large crowd. "But I don't think any of us could anticipate the Judge's passing."

Eric gawked at her; his jaw unhinged. He wondered if she was still angry with him.

The last time I saw her, I bailed on her mid-apology, he thought. *And it was a sloppy apology at that. All just to chase down who I thought was Mom and...*

Eric shook his head, snapping himself back to reality.

"The Super Society has endured many changes," Powerhouse said. "I don't know what the future has in store for us, but I can assure you, this city will always be under the protection of heroes."

The crowd clapped and cheered. Camera flashes bounced off Powerhouse's yellow-tinted domes that covered her eyes.

"Sureshot, Laser Lass, Aqua Queen, and Avenging Eagle," she said. "We would not be here without them. Today is about Mr. Gilroy, but the other founding members never got their proper sendoff. They retired into obscurity and led quiet lives into their twilight years. We respect their privacy, yet we'd be remiss if we did not acknowledge their contributions to the city."

Their ashes are in boxes in a small closet in the Gilroy mansion, not what I'd call respect, Eric thought. *I don't think anybody except for Mr. Maddox knows what really happened to them.*

"They paved the way for the next generation," Powerhouse said. "Go-Go, Extra, and Supercut have been at my side each time we went into battle while protecting the fine citizens of New St. Cloud City. When the threat of evil casts its shadow, we answer the call. We do this with the obligation and duty to honor those who came before us."

Sunlight glistened across the steel encasing her arms. She brushed the golden hair back that protruded from the top of her mask. Eric resisted the urge to rush over to her and tell her everything.

"I'm saying all this to, ah, well, say," Powerhouse continued, pausing as if she needed to remember what line came next. "Er, that, like our predecessors, our incarnation of the Super Society... will be taking a step away from the spotlight."

Confused murmuring emanated from the crowd. Go-G, Extra, and Supercut looked at each, equally unsure.

"We're too young to 'retire,'" Powerhouse said with a nervous laugh. "This is more of a hiatus as we enter new phases of our lives. Judge Justice used his Golden Gavel as a symbol of hope. His passing may also mark the temporary disbanding of the Super Society, but we don't want to think you've been abandoned."

All eyes focused on the costumed teenagers standing at the side of the podium. They stood awkward and silent. Eric hovered in place, unable to mask the shock on his face.

"Truther wishes he could be here to tell you in person," Powerhouse said. "He is out on his final patrol for the time being. He told me that he wishes to express his gratitude to everyone in the city for allowing him to be your protector for all these years. We are hanging up our masks until further notice, but in our place, you'll be defended by our newest hero—"

Eric held his breath.

"—the maskless marvel with the unsecret identity," Powerhouse said. "The soaring superhero who will serve as torchbearer until we can rejoin him... Eric Icarus!"

Eric's teammates turned their wide-eyed heads in unison to look at him. The audience cheered Eric on as Powerhouse gestured for him to approach the podium. He floated to Powerhouse, who greeted him with her big smile.

"I just want to say, Eric," she said close enough to be picked up by the mic, "in your short time with us, you've proven yourself worthy as a fellow hero, a trusted teammate, and a good friend."

Puzzled, Eric's lips contorted, and one eye squinted. With his face still scrunched, Powerhouse went in for a hug.

"We are leaving the city in good hands," she said.

She stood, pointing to Eric as the crowd roared. Go-Go, Extra, and Supercut followed with weak, uneven claps.

"Jay—Powerhouse," Eric whispered, backing away

from the mic. "What is this?!"

"The people want to hear you pay your respects," she said, grinning.

She stepped aside, leaving Eric alone at the podium. The mayor and the other suits gave him a thumbs up. The swaths of people stared back at him, expecting words of greatness. Palpable anticipation filled the air. The audience quieted so that Eric could hear only ambient sounds of the city and low-humming drones. In the distance, the Pantheon Solutions tower stood—its upside-down lightning bolt logo twinkling in the sun's rays. Eric wondered what sage advice his father would give him.

"Uh," Eric drawled out. "I don't know what to say."

Powerhouse stood, feet shoulder-width apart, with her armored hands clasped behind her back. The other three Society members wore eager faces as if they expected Eric to shine some light on this confusion—as if he had a clue.

"I'll be honest," Eric said, too close to the mic.

Feedback squealed, and he winced.

"I thought I was going to step up here and say— well, I had planned a, um, different speech."

Recording devices, phones, drones, and cameras seemed to move closer.

"Now, I just want to say that..."

A twinkling on the horizon took his attention.

"I just wanted to say that... I see... jets?"

Thunderous engine sounds crept from the distance. A pair of twin aircraft sped toward the convention center. Everyone cast their gazes upward, gasping at the sight of the ivory-colored jets torpedoing closer. The large cargo vessels slowed and then descended over the parking lot. The iconic Pantheon lightning bolt emblem gleamed on their tail fins. The corporate slogan, "Think Infinitely," stretched across the sides.

Eric joined everyone in craning his neck to witness the winged machines hovering above. The jets cast a shadow over the masses, blocking the mid-morning sun. Their designs weren't unlike military vehicles Eric had seen pictures of, but each jet bore unique attachments on its sides.

"Infini-Jets," Eric whispered, recalling a vague memory. "Dad used to talk about these. Never thought I'd see one up close."

The jets' circular turbines rotated upward, pushing pummeling winds around them. The engines emitted a blue glow—a souped-up version of drone propulsion technology. Both vessels' hulls displayed their names—the *Aether* and the *North-Wind*.

"Dad and his Greek mythology," Powerhouse said, barely heard over the engines as she approached Eric.

"I think I'm starting to get why Mr. Maddox named me after a Greek tragedy," Eric said to her, but Powerhouse's confused face indicated the jets drowned out his voice.

City denizens dismissed common automatons, but they all looked in astonishment at these advanced airships.

The new MegaCore has taken over Pantheon tower's roof, Eric thought. *And that midlevel hangar would barely fit the Pegasus—where is Mr. Maddox keeping these things?*

Neon-blue light flashed from underneath the golden casket. People on the stage and in the audience clamored as the shiny coffin levitated. Disc-like thrusters on its base propelled it, flying it to a jet. The *Aether's* rear hatch opened, and the automated casket guided itself inside.

A tugging at Eric's arm jolted him back to earth.

"Follow us alongside the *Pegasus*!" Go-Go yelled, barely heard over the booming turbines. "We're escorting the jets—you ready for our final mission, 'torchbearer?'"

Chapter Twelve: *VELOCITY*

ERIC

*B**RZZT!*
Static exploded in Eric's inner ear. Pinching his gloved fingers, Eric adjusted the tiny communicator.

"You sure this thing won't fall out?" Eric shouted, tugging at his earlobe. "You can hear me, right?"

"Loud and clear," Go-Go said.

The little earpiece's speaker proved its worth—her voice sounded clear, even over the blaring jet engines a few hundred feet in front of Eric. His protective costume regulated his temperature, but the forceful airstreams struck Eric's exposed head. He bobbed up and down, then side to side, fighting to maintain a steady trajectory.

To his right, Eric saw Go-Go in the helicopter's side window, giving him a thumbs up. Powerhouse sat next to her.

"It won't be a long flight," Powerhouse said over the radio. "We're just going to DeSalvo county. But keep your eyes peeled, Eric! Based on the intel Truther gave us, whoever threatened to steal Judge Justice's body could come from anywhere!"

All the voices talking into his ear reminded Eric of an overcrowded podcast, making it difficult to get a word in.

"Jayce—Powerhouse!" Eric said. "If I could just explain—!"

"Focus on the mission, Icarus!" Go-Go interjected.

Despite being a flyer, Eric did not possess expert aviation knowledge. However, he knew enough that the Infini-Jets weren't at full speed, stalling to keep pace with the slower 'copter.

Good thing, too, he thought. *I still don't know how fast I can go. So far, my top speed is "try not to die."*

They zipped over the skyscrapers far below but still close enough to discern details on the rooftops. Eric assumed the lower altitude meant better visuals for cameras.

Why else have me flying solo out here? I may be the "torchbearer," but I still feel like the team mascot.

Buildings grew shorter and smaller as they soared, and it wasn't long until they passed over a tapestry of roads and fields.

"We'll be approaching the landing site in less than ten minutes," Go-Go said.

"It's a private strip," Extra added. "Local police are cracking down on paparazzi but watch out for media drones."

"Hopefully, we'll see some!" Eric said. "The world needs to know what Mr. Maddox is—!"

"This is your captain speaking," a deep voice bellowed into Eric's earpiece. "Well, I should say, new captain—the original pilot is taking a nap back on the tarmac."

"*Aether*, this is *North-Wind*," a voice chimed in, thick with a southern drawl. "Please identify yourself. Over."

Trouble in pilot paradise? Eric thought with a grim frown. *They've been listening to our chatter this whole time—I better be more careful about not using secret identity names.*

"You wouldn't recognize me now," the deep voice said. "Perhaps you knew me as 'New St. Cloud City's most wanted—African American male, late forties; embittered former employee of Slate Enterprises.' Ring any bells?"

"Whoever you are," Supercut said, growling, "you try anything funny, and we'll cut you right outta the sky!"

"You children are too young to remember," the baritone voice said smugly. "I was quite the thorn in the side of the first Super Society. Surely your elders told you of the leader of the so-called criminal organization, the Guerrillas?"

"*Aether*, you're gonna land your aircraft as soon as—" the *North-Wind* pilot started.

"You may address me as Extendo."

Eric held his ear, focusing on the audio exchange. The *Aether* flew directly in front of him, and Eric waited on a cue to take action—not that he had any idea what to do.

"The authorities have already been notified," Go-Go warned. "Have you injured any other crew?"

"It's just me," Extendo said with a mocking laugh. "Don't worry; your overpaid Pantheon bootlicker flight crew is back at the hangar. But trust me, they'll remember who Extendo is for the rest of their worthless lives."

"Call yourself whatever lame-o codename you want," Extra said. "You're just a footnote in the archives. We've beaten you Guerrilla-goons before, and we can drop you just the same."

"*Aether*, or Ex-Innuendo—" the other pilot said.

"It's 'Extendo!' Test me, and you'll see why I chose that name!"

"Sure," the unseen *North-Wind* pilot said. "As long as you stay in formation and land your craft safely, we can discuss whatever's got you all cattywampus."

"My demands are simple," Extendo said. "I want the corpse of your false idol. Robbing the city of its grief—stealing closure—that's the ultimate payback for a society that overlooked us for far too—!"

"Okay, so who else is bored?" Extra quipped.

Eric flew over to the *Pegasus*. Powerhouse looked back at him through the window. Eric nodded to the jet ahead of him. Powerhouse shook her head, silently telling him to hold off.

"You think you are so clever," Extendo said. "I know the body isn't in the gaudy gold casket—or any other decoys onboard."

Unsure if the communicator came with a mute button, Eric moved closer alongside the helicopter. Facing the window, Eric mouthed, "What is he talking about?" Powerhouse and Go-Go responded by exchanging worried glances.

Loud, mechanical clanking sounds emitted from the *Aether*, stuttering in a chunky sequence. Its aft hatch lowered, revealing a stack of golden coffins in its cargo bay. Gray netting held the stack in place—three-by-three, the shiny cases resembled a set of oversized gold bars. A hulk in jade-colored armor stood beside them in the large cabin.

"Extendo!" the *North-Wind* pilot said. "Close that hatch, now!"

"If you won't give me the oldest Super Society member," Extendo said, "I'll take the newest one!"

A thick, puke-green-coated metal tube shot

from Extendo's right arm. Large, flat metal claws sprang from the cylindrical rod's tip. The rectangular digits wrapped around Eric's torso—he yelped and squirmed under the heavy clamps. Unable to move his arms under the claw's pressure, Eric quivered as the cybernetic limb held him in the air. He felt like a rag doll tied to a kite string.

"I can't get out!" Eric yelled.

Powerhouse's face pressed against the glass of the 'copter's side window.

"Extendo!" she shouted. "Let him go!"

The pipe's curved outer plating pulsated, shaking the spinning little gizmos working inside the details of the transparent casing. Extendo's angular shoulder shell held his elongated arm—it remained firmly attached to his bulky frame.

"What kinda tech is that?!" Supercut said. "Is this guy a cyborg, or what?"

"Let's just say your boss Baron Maddox isn't the only genius in town!"

Extendo's mocking laughter stung Eric's ear as it boomed into the communicator.

"Hold on, Eric!" Go-Go said.

The *Pegasus* veered, getting dangerously close to Eric. The engine roared, overbearing Eric's senses. The blades whirred above his head like a giant buzzsaw.

"Hey-hey-hey! Wh-what're you doing?!" Eric sputtered. "One move from this guy, and I'll be a lot shorter!"

"That's not a bad idea!" Extendo said. "Give me the Judge's corpse, or your young friend will lose his head!"

The 'copter's side door slid open. Go-Go stood on the edge of the cabin, holding onto the doorframe. Sunlight streaked across her silver visor as she looked up and down, sizing up the situation. The wild wind torrents pushed against Go-Go's big, curly hair while she nodded at Eric. Behind her, Supercut leaned over, peeking outside. The crushing airflow fluttered the pointed tips of his mask.

"I'm waiting!" Extendo said.

Jolted, Eric felt a sudden force yank him forward. The arm retracted, pulling him a foot closer to Extendo.

"Eric Icarus boards my vessel—the hard way—or it's a beheading. Your choice, but the clock is ticking!"

Little dots on Go-Go's metal gear lit up into vivid purples and blues.

"Superspeed armor fully charged!" she said. "Supercut, you're with me!"

"Huh?" Supercut said. "Why me?!"

"'Cause I can only carry one person at a time!"

She dragged Supercut's rotund body from his seat.

"Go-Go!" Powerhouse said over the communicator. "Please tell me you aren't gonna do what I think you're about to!"

"How about don't say anything?!" Extra added. "Bad guy listening in, remember?"

"All you need to know, "Go-Go said, "is that I'm doing whatever it takes to protect my friends!"

"Cool, but why do I gotta be invol—?!"

Before Supercut could finish, Go-Go grabbed him. Then, moving like fast phantoms, they leaped. Their bright costumes swirled into a reddish-yellow blur, landing on the outstretched tentacle. Eric felt the impact of their combined weight, but only for a moment. Go-Go's superspeed leg braces carried her and Supercut. Go-Go's incredible inertia kept them from falling off the high-wire.

In a flash, Go-Go and Supercut appeared inside the *Aether's* cargo hold.

"End of the line, Extend—!" Go-Go started.

Extendo's free arm whacked her, then struck Supercut. Their bodies hit the interior jet walls next to the caskets.

"You talk too much. Just like your predecessors."

"No!" Extra screamed.

"We don't have time for this!" Powerhouse said. "Everybody, hold on!"

The helicopter advanced, then dipped, facing downward.

"What the—?!" the *North-Wind* pilot said. "Is your autopilot malfunctioning?!"

"Nope!" Powerhouse answered. "It's offline!"

The 'copter moved to its left.

"I'm in control," she said.

"Powerhouse!" Eric shouted. "Whatever this is, it's too dangerous!"

The helicopter's spinning blades moved near the extended arm. The *Pegasus* leaned down farther, almost completely vertical.

"You children are mad!" Extendo said. "What do you think you're—?!"

The whirring blades cut into the middle of Extendo's arm. *Chonk-chonk-chonk-chonk!* Each chop of metal-on-metal reverberated, sending shockwaves through Eric. He shook as sparks burst from where the steel arm had been carved. The helicopter blades sliced the remaining attachments, severing the mechanical limb.

"Gahhhhhhrrrgghhh!" Extendo grumbled through blips of static.

The sudden release catapulted Eric backward, with the severed limb still clamped around him. The thick, flat claws loosened as he spiraled through the sky. Finally, the vise relented, and the snake-like arm fell.

As Eric steadied himself, he saw the *Pegasus*

curving in the air, repositioning itself. He joined it in resuming their pursuit of the twin jets.

"Sitrep!" the *North-Wind* pilot demanded. "Somebody tell me what's going on!"

"Thanks to Powerhouse's rollercoaster piloting, I totally barfed just now," Extra said. "Thankfully, it was on the parachutes and not my costume."

"You guys might wanna strap on those parachutes!" Eric said.

Bright bolts of electricity flickered from the *Aether's* interior. With his good arm, Extendo pulled on the netting holding the caskets in place. His stout armored body stood with sparks flaring from his severed arm, which had not fully retracted—the remaining, vine-like arm drooped onto the cabin floor.

The 'copter sped ahead, closing in on Extendo. The *Aether* slowed to a halt, letting its turbines turn upright. The engines steadied the craft, holding it in place in the sky and still carrying Extendo, Go-Go, and Supercut. The *Pegasus* decelerated, placing itself behind the jet. The *North-Wind* sped ahead, soaring out of sight.

Eric trailed the *Pegasus*, getting a clearer view of Extendo. Eric scowled at the design choice of this strange cyborg colossus. Salmon-pink-painted metal rings coiled up Extendo's torso, making his appearance even more unsightly. Under his bright yellow helmet, Extendo grimaced, contorting his lips in a misshapen snarl. Extendo's body stood wide yet stunted.

For someone who calls himself Extendo, Eric thought, *he's maybe only as tall as Dad!*

Worried, Eric wobbled his head, searching every angle for Supercut and Go-Go. He did not see them but assured himself they must be hiding behind the casket stack.

"You've forced my hand!" Extendo yelled. "You won't give me what I want? Then I'll give you death from above!"

A quick snap of the straps connected to the net resulted in the coffins shaking loose. With a shove, Extendo forced the golden caskets to slide out in a barrage, torpedoing them at the *Pegasus*. An oversized gold bar crashed into the blades while another hit the cockpit. Eric darted over but quickly pivoted, narrowly dodging a shooting casket.

The *Pegasus* swiveled, hurling shards of glass and broken bits of metal. The bent blades struggled and then stalled. The 'copter fell in a swooping motion, flipping its tail rotor up as the cockpit faced the earth. Extra and Powerhouse's terrified screams garbled into buzzing feedback in Eric's comm.

Eric launched after them, only to roll out of the way again—Extendo's other arm stretched by him, speeding past like a bullet train. The pale green metal limb popped its slat-like claws. The multi-pronged clamps opened wide as they reached the plunging helicopter. The 'copter's winglike, horizontal stabilizer rudders screeched as they crumpled under the claw's grip. Extendo's protracted appendage held the damaged rotorcraft by its thick tail—the silver vessel swayed high above the ground.

The *North-Wind* emerged from the clouds. It curved, flying away, then finally headed back toward the dangling 'copter.

"*Pegasus*, I'm gonna position myself under you!" the *North-Wind* pilot said. "Icarus, you catch 'em if they plop out!"

No pressure! Eric thought, gulping.

Eric flew to the nose of the *Pegasus*, reaching through the jagged edges of the cockpit's shattered windows. Extra and Powerhouse sat strapped in the front seats. They appeared to be frazzled but unharmed.

"Truther is missing out on all the fun, eh?" Extra said with a nervous chuckle.

"I'm gonna fly you out of there!" Eric said.

They nodded and began to unbuckle their restraints carefully.

"Get them aboard, Icarus!" the *North-Wind* pilot ordered.

The *North-Wind* hovered below them, bobbing as it kept up with Extendo's wavering arm. The helicopter's tip buckled, threatening to drop like a giant lawn dart.

"I'm no fool!" Extendo said. "The body is on the second jet—the *North-Wind*! Use your flying boy to bring it to my vessel, and this ends!"

Extendo's steel arm whined, straining to hold on.

"My patience is running thin, and you're running out of options!" he warned.

Extra climbed to the 'copter's open side hatch. Extendo's arm released a new link, lengthening it further—the abrupt shift rattled the chopper. Extra wiggled, clinging to the doorframe.

"The body!" Extendo shouted. "Now!"

"We don't have it, alright?!" the *North-Wind* pilot said. "It's just a big show for the press! It's been a decoy, all of it!"

"Are you kidding me?!" Extra exclaimed, looking at Powerhouse. "Did you know?"

Powerhouse shook her head from the cockpit while holding onto a chair with her armored glove. Her eyes bugged out under the domes covering her mask.

"I swear, I had no idea!"

Extendo muttered, which grew into a loud

guttural grumble, then a squealing electronic audio distortion. Eric reached for Extra, but static hissed in his ears, causing him to flinch. Extra also winced at the earsplitting sound in her earpiece.

"The Judge is a deceiver 'til the end," Extendo said in a huff. "Since there isn't a body, I'll dump the rest of my cargo."

Using shards at the tip of his severed arm, Extendo cut the remaining netting. He kicked the last two golden caskets, pushing them down the cabin floor.

"By the way, your friends Go-Go and Supercut are inside."

"What?!" Eric yelled.

The cases slid off the jet.

"Looks like these caskets got some use after all!" Extendo said, snickering.

Chapter Thirteen: *FALL*

ERIC

"**N**o-no-no!" Eric said, darting his head back and forth at the falling caskets and Extra holding onto the helicopter's hatch. "I-I-I can't get you and—!"

"Eric!" Extra shouted, clinging to the 'copter's side doorframe. "We'll hang on; go save them!"

The shiny coffins tilted, spreading the gap between them and Eric as they plummeted. Eric bolted after the nearest one while keeping the other in the corner of his eye. He pressed his hands against the casket's slick surface, desperate to unlock it. But unfortunately, the lid did not budge, and Eric's feeble strength failed to lift the weighty case.

"C'mon, c'mon, open!"

He pounded the casket's lid, then noticed a flicker of blue light from its underside. Eric flew beneath it, and his eyes lit up at seeing a series of flat, circular thrusters. Ecstatic, he patted the casket's side, but nothing happened.

"Stupid thrusters; work!"

He slammed his fist against the bottom paneling,

and the disc-like emitters sparked into a brilliant blue. The casket slowed its descent, allowing Eric to push it upward. Tugging at the lid's edges, he guided it toward the other casket.

Eric let the powered casket hover as he nosedived after its rapidly falling counterpart. He swooped beneath, then pushed against its underside. Punching the metal panels, Eric silently cursed it for not activating. Despite blow after blow, the thrusters remained dormant. Eric glanced up at the hovering casket—its blinking thrusters weren't strong enough to keep it afloat. It fidgeted as it made a slow drop.

Frantic, Eric repeatedly beat the inactive casket, controlling his flight to fall along with it. The last strike triggered power, and the thruster rings burst into a neon blue haze.

"Yes!"

Eric rammed the back of the casket, aiming at its twin. The golden chests collided with a *blang*! He shoved the two caskets through the air, targeting the *Aether*—Extendo's husky frame waited inside. The jet's turbines held it afloat; the vehicle stayed stationary, helping Eric's aim. The caskets' bottom thrusters helped to steady their course and prevent them from straying. They held as if linked together, with momentum propelling them faster.

Eric hoped to hit his target, unable to see beyond the caskets' reflective outer shells. The *Aether's* open aft hatch filled his periphery as he neared. Grunting, Eric mustered enough strength for a final boost. The caskets fired like a duo of missiles, speeding into the jet's interior.

Bam!

"Argghhhahhhh!" Extendo bellowed in what sounded like terrible pain.

Flying to a safe distance, Eric blew a breath of relief—not only did he make a miraculous shot, but the caskets stayed inside. The excitement did not last, though.

That was a rough landing! he thought. *Please-please-please let Melvin and Yvette be okay!*

Buoying in the wind currents, Eric covered his brow, scanning the inside of the cabin. Extendo lay in a heap with his severed arm swaying like a lifeless eel. The other longer limb kept its grip on the helicopter below—until it snapped. The clamps released themselves, dropping the *Pegasus*.

"No!" Eric screamed as tears flung from his squinted eyes.

The *Pegasus* slipped into a crash course with the *North-Wind* hovering below it. Eric's exhausted muscles begged to stop, but he pressed on, though the 'copter fell too far.

As the *Pegasus* dropped, a cluster of Extras popped from nowhere, forming a chain of doubles. The link of redheads replicated one by one, ascending to the *Aether*. The top of the Extra chain grabbed hold of the stationary jet's lowered aft door. Extendo's lifeless tentacle swayed beside her. Each replicant held onto the other's ankles and wrists. Eric couldn't believe his eyes nor discern the real Extra. The copies wavered in the wind like a loose wire.

The *North-Wind* veered but not in time—the helicopter crashed into the vessel's curved roof. The jet rocked while pulling away, letting the *Pegasus* shoot to the ground like a silver bullet. A serrated chunk of shrapnel rocketed from the 'copter's fiery rotor.

Eric twirled, dodging the sharp remnant of the helicopter's engine. But unfortunately, Eric's corkscrewing maneuver hurled him off course—he gathered his bearings in time to see Powerhouse jump from the falling helicopter. His heart skipped a beat.

Powerhouse grabbed an Extra by her boots at the foot of the long ladder of duplicates. Powerhouse kept her head up as the Super Society's famous vehicle fell to the plains far below until it became a silvery speck.

The *North-Wind* increased its speed and raised its altitude as it swerved away into a bath of clouds.

"Mayday—" the *North-Wind* pilot said under spouts of harsh static. "—assessing the damage— emergency land—"

The crackling static ceased, leaving eerie silence. Eric lost sight of the jet, then swung himself toward Powerhouse.

"I'm coming to get you, Powerhouse!" Eric said.

"Hurry!" Extra said. "My duplicates won't last long!"

Eric spotted Extra—the real Extra—scaling to the top of the body chain. She made it into the *Aether's* cabin.

"They're holographic projections," Extra explained via the comms. "Nanites give them some tangibility, but they aren't designed for this kind of thing!"

"I know how your 'hard light' works, Extra," Powerhouse said through shaky breaths. "But thanks for telling me how I'm gonna fall to my death at any second! 'Preciate it!"

Powerhouse climbed a quavering replicant, but intangible patches stunted her ascent. Her fingers phased through a thigh, and her frightened gasp blared into Eric's earpiece. Only "solidified" objects on the humanoid hologram provided any grip for Powerhouse—she found a bulky orange utility belt pocket to hold onto.

As he neared, Eric rooted for the clump of

microscopic nanites to assume the shape of the pocket. He didn't fully understand how the tech worked, but Powerhouse didn't fall, which is all that mattered.

Extendo's limp arm swung by Powerhouse, flailing in the open air like a wilted stem.

"Hold on!" Eric said.

Adrenaline fueled Eric's dive, zeroing in on Powerhouse, though he couldn't help noticing the *North-Wind's* lengthy absence. But then, other worries intruded, storming as images and quick clips:

When's the last time you ate something? You need sleep! You can hardly breathe; how are you supposed to—?!

The roaring winds shifted Eric's concentration, and he shook the anxiety off. Powerhouse hung mere feet from his outstretched arms.

"Guhhhaugh!" Eric belted out in sudden anguish.

Large steel clamps constricted around his ribcage. Extendo's arm claimed Eric, yanking him from Powerhouse. The recharged arm swung Eric from side to side, jumbling his organs. Powerhouse reached out but missed him with each swipe.

The top of the Extra duplicate-chain dissipated, phasing into nothingness. Each double dispersed in descending order, tearing the tether to Powerhouse. Extendo's arm turned, swaying Eric upward like a pendulum swing. On the way down, Eric saw Powerhouse hanging from the last in the line of Extra copies. Powerhouse grabbed the otherwise motionless "Extra" dupe around its waist. With the other copies gone, she began to slip into the air.

The green dots on Powerhouse's steel-clad knuckles indicated a super-strength surge. She pushed herself from the dematerializing duplicate girl using whatever force she could. Powerhouse grabbed

Extendo's cylindrical arm, slipping until her powered gloves sunk into the limb's metal husk.

Powerhouse clung to the tube-like arm and wrapped her legs around it, sending Eric flashbacks of rope-climbing in gym class. She looked down at Eric, caught in the clamps at the robotic arm's tip. They exchanged freaked-out, mouth-agape expressions.

"Hey!" Extra said into the comm. "What's going on?!"

"We're good," Powerhouse answered. "Just having the strangest day of my life, but we're alright!"

Blips of white and red lights popped into view— bright twinkles scattered around them. Little black dots emerged, then neared enough to reveal their smooth, dome-like appearances.

"That's just flushing great!" Powerhouse barked. "Media drones have caught up with us!"

The lenses on the drones' smooth "faces" sparked with flash photography.

"Perfect timing," Extra said, groaning. "Now the whole world can see us get our butts kicked!"

"Just make sure Go-Go and Supercut are okay," Powerhouse said. "I'll get Eric out of this thing!"

A dozen round robots swarmed around them, bobbing in an unorganized cluster. Each soccer ball-sized drone shoved itself in Powerhouse and Eric's faces. Different network and production company logos stretched across their rounded surfaces. Eric's shocked face reflected in each one brushing by.

Powerhouse batted a drone away as she shimmied down the arm. She leaned, reaching for Eric. Her steel-clad hand pried a claw from Eric's midsection.

"There's a control panel back here for the door!" Extra buzzed in through their earpieces.

"I'll fly us up as soon as I'm outta this thing!" Eric

said.

"Hurry!" Extra said. "Closing this hatch is one of those 'good ideas' our team has from time to time!"

"Hold off!" Powerhouse ordered. "Shutting that door may cut our lifeline in half!"

"I don't know how long this Extend-dork will stay knocked out!" Extra said.

"Extendo's robot parts seem to be working just fine without him!" Eric yelled.

"Gimme a few seconds!" Powerhouse said.

She pulled a wide slat from around Eric's chest.

"Lift it a little, and I should be able to squeeze through!" Eric said, squirming with his arms stuck at his sides.

"The Super Society is going out with a bang, huh, hover-boy?" Powerhouse said with a smirk and crinkled brow.

The lights on her knuckles blinked, indicating her strength-enhancers going into overdrive. Eric wondered how much battery power her armor had left.

"This entire incident kinda suggests we should stick around!" he yelled. "Jay—Powerhouse, you gotta listen to me! Your dad—!"

"Got it!" Powerhouse said.

The steel clamp loosened, and Eric's torso stung in a bittersweet mix of soothing relief and residual pain from the pressure. He snaked his way to Powerhouse, cautious not to drift. She wrapped an arm around his shoulders—her thick armor weighed upon his neck but mostly rested on his metal backpack. Her free hand held onto the Extendo's arm's outer shell.

"Extra," Eric said. "Keep that hatch open; we're on our way!"

"Change of plans!" Powerhouse said. "Our ride's here!"

Confused, Eric glanced over his shoulder. The *North-Wind* lowered itself across from them. Its turbines stood upright by its wings, blasting energy, and keeping the craft afloat. Dents and scratches decorated the jet's white hull, but the canopy appeared free of marks or cracks.

"Finally, some good luck!" Eric shouted through the winds whipping at his cheeks.

"Eric Icarus," the *North-Wind* pilot said through the comm. "You have permission to come aboard."

A door slid open on the jet's side, revealing the spacious interior of the cargo hold. Inside, a withered-looking man sat strapped to a seat.

"No way," Eric said. "That can't be—"

"Dad!" Powerhouse yelled.

Baron clutched onto the black restraints while furious currents ruffled his ill-fitting suit. Drones scurried about, nearly bumping into each other in a mad rush to capture footage of Baron. A black ball-shaped drone floated by Eric's dumbfounded face.

"Mr. Maddox?!" he said. "He was in the other jet the whole time? Is he—?"

The drone loomed closer, and Eric reconsidered his nervous rambling. Cocking an eyebrow, he got a new idea.

"Hey!" Eric yelled at the spherical robot. "Weird question, but—do you have a USB port? 'Cause, I got something I think everyone needs to see!"

He reached for his pants pocket, feeling for the thumb drive.

Truther's unsecret origin is about to go viral!

"Eric, what're you talking about?!" Powerhouse shouted.

The drone zipped away, joining a group of other automatons huddling around the *North-Wind*. Eric puffed his cheeks, frustrated at himself. Risking another second with Powerhouse hanging from the dangling arm made him feel rightfully stupid. He swallowed his rage and wrapped his arms around her waist.

As they approached, he flew them through forceful gales of wind, locking eyes with Baron. The buzzing bots cleared, and Eric placed Powerhouse into the jet's cabin. She crouched by her father, smiling at the sight of him. Eric wore a thin frown. Baron welcomed a gentle hug from Powerhouse, but his sunken eyes remained on Eric.

Concentrating, Eric stilled himself enough to float outside the open door. The chaos of Extendo's attack and the craziness building up to it left him with a thousand things to say—and even more to scream. Instead, Eric hovered in the air, with words bottlenecking on their way to his tongue. Powerhouse gave Eric a flummoxed look, partially opening her mouth. Baron's unnaturally aged face crinkled, bending the strange lines etched in his cheeks and forehead.

He knows I know, Eric thought as his brow stiffened. *I will save Mom! Everyone will know your messed-up plans! Say it, Eric, just say everything already!*

"Guys, I don't know if you've been keeping up with the news," Extra piped in from the comms, "but I have an open hatch with some precious cargo in these caskets—which I haven't been able to figure out how to tie down!"

"The hatch will cut the arm!" Powerhouse said. "It's still dangling!"

"I know it's not very superhero-y of me," Extra said, "but I don't mind if Extendo falls out."

"Severing the limb could be disastrous,"

Powerhouse said. "We don't know if the shock will short-circuit Extendo's brain!"

"Where was this concern when you used the helicopter as a buzzsaw?!"

"That was different! Eric was trapped!"

"Look, even if I wasn't holding onto a seatbelt as if my life depended on it—which it does!" Extra said, "that metal arm is too heavy! I can't exactly roll it up!"

"Can you make some extra Extras to help?" Eric asked, keeping his gaze on Baron.

"My armor's battery is fried!" she said. "I'm singled out up here!"

"*Aether,*" the *North-Wind* pilot squawked over the radio. "Your autopilot should take you back on course. Both aircraft should be secured if all crew and personnel are safely on board—with the doors closed. Eric Icarus, this means 'you-know-what' or get off the pot!"

"Mr. Maddox!" Eric said, pointing an accusing finger at Baron.

Extendo's limp arm sprang to life, writhing like an angry viper.

"Does Jaycee kno—?!"

It clamped its wide claws on Eric's backpack, yanking him away from the open hatch. His backpack straps dug into his armpits as he resisted.

"Eric!" Powerhouse shrieked.

The iron claw pulled hard, and Eric swiveled—his arm slipped through a strap loop. The other strap loosened until it slid down Eric's arm. Extendo's clamps tugged, but Eric grabbed the strap before it flew away. He wrenched the blue-coated chrome backpack with both hands by its strap, but the claw's relentless strength lured him closer.

"We got a problem up here!" Extra said, panic

quivering in her voice. "Stretchy Robo-Freak is—well, his body is up!"

The claw's slat-like digits bit down on the other backpack strap—Eric played tug-of-war on the opposite end, and his strength faded by the second.

"Extra!" Powerhouse said over the comm. "Find something heavy and put Extendo to sleep!"

"Uh, his ugly-as-sin cyber shell is awake, but the head looks out of it and—Eeearrgh!"

Extra screeched into the earpiece.

"Extra?!" Powerhouse cried but received no answer.

Glances provided no sign of what happened to Extra, but Eric had a few guesses. Extendo's arm dragged the backpack, towing Eric with it. His heart racing, Eric felt the strap slipping in his palms. News drones bobbled over one after another. Each electric eye pointed at him.

If I lose the backpack, everyone will know it's just a decoy! I'll have no cover, and my secret, real power won't be so secret anymore!

Extendo's arm yanked the backpack with even more force, taking Eric with it. Powerhouse stood in the jet's open door frame—her image grew smaller the farther away Extendo pulled.

"Eric!" she yelled. "We're gonna move and get you!"

Zap! Zap!

Bright yellow laser blasts struck the hull around the open cabin. Powerhouse ducked as more beams hit the jet.

Another tentacle dropped from the *Aether*, and at its steel tip, the head of Extendo buckled. Eric's eyes bulged, shocked at the sight of Extendo's unconscious face encased in his lemon-colored helmet. His chain-link neck swished his head, narrowly missing Eric's nose with each flyby.

Extendo's drooping jaw opened wide, and his mouth lit up a blazing orange inside. The dangling head belched out a flurry of energy blasts.

The *North-Wind* made a lateral push, moving toward Eric. The onslaught of lasers halted its motion.

"We can't get close!" Powerhouse said.

A few news drones exploded into bits as more bolting beams attacked. The arm retracted a notch, pulling Eric even farther from Powerhouse. Above, the *Aether* hung, suspended, and unattainable.

Eric willed every ounce of grit, trying to put his arm through the backpack's strap loop. Extendo's clamps jerked it back, jolting Eric. The longer Eric held onto the strap, the farther both jets became.

He imagined the *Pegasus* as a broken heap in a cornfield far below. Media drones circled like vultures, keeping their distance.

"The backpack doesn't matter," Eric said to himself. "I can't keep this up; I need to fly!"

"Eric?" Powerhouse chirped in his earpiece.

"I am so over this dumb claw!"

"We can't get to you," Powerhouse said. "We've taken too much damage!"

The elongated neck wiggled like a charmed snake. Extendo's head threw up another round of yellow energy surges.

"We're gonna go up to the other jet!" Powerhouse said. "I'll jump over to it if I have to, but Eric—I have to close that hatch!"

"Extra will love saying, 'I told you so!'"

"Eric, you're too far out! There's nothing else we can—" Powerhouse said before a crackling wave of feedback cut into the comm. "—lasers won't stop!"

"Powerhouse, you know I can help!" Eric said.

The drones amassed around him. Each camera recorded him holding onto the metal backpack—as far as the world knew, if Eric released his hold, he'd be a goner.

"If you let go of the backpack," Powerhouse said, "then everyone with a phone, computer, and a TV will see!"

Even during the disarray, Eric observed that she protected his secret.

"It won't make a difference! Not after I...!"

Tell her, Eric! he commanded himself. *Why can't you just say you know Mr. Maddox's plan? What he's done?! Open your mouth and talk! Right now!*

His father's words echoed in his mind. He shook his head.

Even if I tell Jaycee and all these drones everything, it won't help Mom. She'll be taken to some lab before I touch the ground. It's one thing if my secret gets out, but she can't protect herself.

"Ahhh, my head!" Extra grumbled over the comm. "That's it! I'm closing this hatch!"

"We can't just sit here and take damage!" the *North-Wind* pilot said.

"Shut the hatch, Extra," Powerhouse ordered.

The stress seared into Eric's tendons. The struggle to keep his grip on the strap burned his muscles, and agony boiled within his veins. The leather strap tore into his gloved palm. Extendo's automated claw closed, swallowing the backpack. Eric clung onto the flapping strap poking out from a thin crease. The claw squeezed, fully enveloping the backpack, constricting tighter until—*crunch!*

"No!" Eric yelled. "I think he just crushed my—!"

"Eric, you have to fall," Powerhouse said.

He shook his head.

"Let go," she said. "You'll be okay; you're just going to have to trust me."

Pretend to fall?! Eric thought. *Control my descent until—splat?!*

Extendo's upside-down head unloaded more laser fire, blasting the jet. The drones' cameras caught it all.

"Eric, do you remember what I told you when we rescued that guy on the bridge?"

Eric squinted, focusing on Powerhouse in the growing distance. She clung to the frame of the hatch.

"We do get scared," Powerhouse said. "But we don't look down."

Eric released the strap. He looked at her for as long as he could while controlling his flight. He simulated falling, resisting his survival instincts.

"Closing the hatch!" Extra said.

Extendo's snakelike arm and neck dropped. The laser blasts ceased. The metal tendrils flailed as they fell. Like chrome noodles, the arm and neck wiggled and spread, falling alongside Eric.

The physical stress of carrying David earlier in the day, on top of maneuvering caskets and fighting mechanical tentacles, weighed upon Eric. The mental duress made his head throb. Eric willed himself down, faster and faster, until he passed out.

Chapter Fourteen: *PAYLOAD*

JAYCEE

THE *NORTH-WIND* HUNG HIGH ABOVE the bridge, its turbines keeping the craft upright and still. A gray dirigible vessel hovered over the jet, extending a white tube. A small opening on the *North-Wind's* wide, angular nose accepted the hose. Even from the street, Jaycee saw the scorch marks and skids left behind from Extendo's laser assault.

"The refueling process doesn't take long," Baron said, practically croaking as he found a rust-colored bench to sit on.

Jaycee leaned on a concrete pillar, peeking past the bridge's underside. This far outside the city proper never saw the likes of the suspended jet and blimp-like ship. However, their presence did not appear to stop traffic as the crushing sounds of speeding automobiles rumbled uninterrupted.

Her father sat as if waiting for a bus while he pulled a large leather sack over his lap. His black funeral attire hung loose on him, and his sunken cheeks and wrinkled eyes marred his usual appearance. Baron's mustache maintained its dark color, but the rest of him looked s different—no one would suspect him of being the multi-billionaire CEO of the country's leading tech company.

The security guys in sunglasses from the funeral stood as guards, surrounding the perimeter. One monitored the sidewalk a few yards beside Baron. Another patrolled the other end of the cavernous under-bridge area Jaycee occupied. Their jet-black SUV sat parked across from Jaycee, sticking out as the fanciest thing in the alleyway.

It looks like a cave troll's dream under here, she thought, frowning at the graffiti-tagged concrete walls.

Fortunately, the mild odors of trash did little to bother her. She looked at the curved street in front of Baron.

What is so special about an intersection?

"Are your Men In Black friends getting a ride back with us?" Jaycee asked.

"My ears are not themselves," Baron said, gesturing around his head.

Jaycee stepped from under the bridge, feeling unnerved. She wore her civilian outfit, making her feel vulnerable in the open. Her lime-green top contrasted with the industrial, cement-gray surroundings.

"You made your security guys drive out here," she said, approaching the bench. "I know you don't normally need to hire bodyguards, but there's room on the jet."

The passing cars thundered across the bridge, blaring an ambient hum of engines and bustling wind. The afternoon light died down as the early evening rush hour took its toll.

"Their services will not be required when we're in the air," Baron said. "I have my own personal superhero."

A shaky smile cracked under his hairy lip. Jaycee

matched with a faint grin.

"Extendo would not have been stopped if it weren't for you," Baron said. "He—what is left of him—is detained, safely locked away at the tower. All thanks to your incredible teamwork."

"Yvette and Melvin are okay, right?" Jaycee said. "Tiffany said they were fine, but can we call them?"

"They were transported to the tower where they are resting. You'll see them at school tomorrow."

"Are you sure we can't video-call Eric or something? I never got to explain the torchbearer announcement thing."

"His recuperation will go more smoothly if he is undisturbed."

"Okay, but a drone swooped him up before he landed. The impact of hitting the inside would still hurt, wouldn't it? Is he awake? Can we—?"

"He is unharmed and resting at the tower," Baron said before coughing.

"Shouldn't you be resting, too?"

"We're in uncharted waters," he said, closing his eyes. "I set contingencies in place and prepared for as many variables as I could think of—but the power transference's effects have been quite the x-factor. My body's physical adjustment is frustrating and unexpected, but certain matters must be attended to."

An empty parking lot sprawled out across the street before them. A short, rundown office building stood alone at the end of the lot. Shaggy patches of grass and overgrown weeds spread beyond the lonely-looking building, stretching into desolation. Jaycee wondered if this area once thrived.

That building has probably always been the last bit of the city before entering the backwoods, she thought, glowering. *"Now exiting civilization. Next stop: the middle of flushing nowhere.*"

Baron motioned for her to sit by him. She eyed the bag on his lap as she took a seat.

"Are we stretching our legs before hitting up the mausoleum? Where is the superhero cemetery, anyway?"

"This is Judge Justice's final resting place," Baron said, opening his eyes. "This is where it began for us, and this is where it shall end."

Jaycee looked at the condemned building across the street. The windows stood out as either broken or boarded.

"Mr. Gilroy used to work in that building?"

"Erm, no," Baron said. "Technically, our partnership began over there."

He pointed a wobbly thumb at the under-bridge area behind them.

"Here?" she said. "Are we even in New St. Cloud City?"

"This is considered a part of DeSalvo county. Outskirts, yes, but still within our fine city's borders."

"Glad we cleared that up," Jaycee said with a cynical smirk.

The smirk dropped, and her eyebrow raised.

"You didn't start out in his big forest mansion?" Jaycee said, looking over her shoulder at the stone-gray pillars holding up the bridge.

Baron reached into the big leather satchel.

"The life of a costumed crusader brings many surprises, does it not?" he said, pulling out a featureless white box.

He handed Jaycee the plain-looking container with a trembling hand. The smooth plastic felt lighter than she expected, not that Jaycee knew what to make of any of this.

"The Judge is in good hands," Baron said.

Jaycee's eyes popped. Unable to look away from the small package, her mind raced.

"You're kidding me, right?"

"I was 'kidding' the media with the show they anticipated," Baron said. "The dummy caskets are, admittedly, not something I would try again. Not that it matters much now, but Extendo was fooled. At least some purpose was served."

He coughed, then gurgled. Jaycee thought she might regurgitate something herself.

"No body," she said, frowning. "Decoy caskets. Big showy funeral for the cameras—"

"Keeping up appearances. Preserving the legacy. Tricking a supervillain."

"Right," Jaycee said, forgetting to blink. "All that. Which means I'm holding..."

"You have been bestowed the honor of spreading Judge Justice's ashes under the bridge."

Though her legs felt hollow, Jaycee stood. She cradled the container like she'd carry a baby bunny. She dared not drop it, as if the contents could feel anything at all.

"This is littering," she said, walking across the pavement.

"I won't tell if you won't," Baron said without looking back.

She stood at the foot of the area beneath the bridge. Jaycee placed her fingers on the lid's crease, but a slight breeze stopped her. She worried that an unwanted gust would blow the ashes into her face or at the security guys. The men in black looked away, either unaware of her or pretending not to notice her.

"Patrick Gilroy has joined his compatriots in their final form," Baron said from the bench.

"Are they, um, 'around' here, too?" Jaycee asked, looking at the pavement.

"Super Society members are cremated upon their passing. It's become somewhat of a tradition now," Baron said. "The others were also present for our first interaction. However, they are in a different final resting place."

"Uh-huhhhhhh," Jaycee said, confused as she looked around. "I thought the story was Mr. Gilroy adopted you from an orphanage."

"The New Horizons building was my, ahem, residence at the time," Baron said, grunting as if the words tasted foul. "But where you stand now is where I first encountered your predecessors."

Do the security guys have earplugs in? Jaycee thought. *Dad must be in worse shape than I thought if he's blabbing about secret superhero stuff!*

She removed the lid, peeking at the mound of gray ash with a squinted eye. A car honked, spooking her. Jaycee gripped the box with a death clutch. The horn's trailing sound wailed into the distance like a sad ghost. She shook her head, relieved that at least no one seemed to see her or care enough to stop and stare.

"It brings me great joy that you embrace the role of herald," Baron said, raising his raspy voice to combat the traffic noise. "You always were the only one I knew I could really trust."

Jaycee gave the box a gentle shake, tipping the ash the same way she'd sprinkle Parmesan cheese over spaghetti. She grimaced—it felt too simple; Jaycee thought something so sacred shouldn't be so matter of fact.

"Soon," Baron said before hacking, "we will pierce the veil and show what true human potential is. We are embarking on something that has never occurred on this planet. Who better than a Maddox to lead the way?"

Jaycee figured she ought to spread the dust around, so she rattled the container as she waved it back and forth. The ash fell, sporadically landing by bits of gravel and tiny chunks of concrete.

"Once we have the gift of flight," Baron said, "we will no longer need to hide behind comfortable lies and superficial half-truths. We will finally be able to take off our masks."

Jaycee patted the bottom of the box, knocking the last specks out.

"Did Mr. Gilroy die alone?"

Jaycee's question silenced Baron only for a moment. He leaned over, looking at her from the bench.

"He had been asleep a long time," Baron said. "Perhaps in his dreams, he remembered a time when his peers and partners surrounded him."

"Like you?"

He looked at her through slits, showing no sign of emotion.

"Curating the public's perception is tiresome. I do not enjoy withholding truths from you, Jaycee."

She flipped the box back upright. In the sky, the dirigible retracted its tube and flew away. She envied it.

I miss the Pegasus *already.*

"I will show you the entirety of my genesis as a sidekick," Baron said. "I want you to know everything and still come to me of your own free will."

Jaycee twisted her lips, uncertain what to think of the little piles of ash on the street.

"Once people see our second phase of life," Baron said, "they will flock to us. Willingly. The masses must welcome the new age with no resistance. Come here; I want to show you something."

She walked over as Baron retrieved a dark, blue-coated chrome case from the leather sack. It lay flat with mini airplane wings on its sides.

"You got Eric's backpack?!" Jaycee blurted with a dropped jaw.

She hurried over and sat beside him.

"A drone brought it as we were dropped off. You were doffing your uniform at the time."

"Can we not say 'doffing' ever again?" Jaycee said, gawking at the backpack. "And how did you find this? I thought it was crushed, or it'd be lost in a field forever!"

"Evildoers are often not as strong as they claim to be," Baron remarked. "And Pantheon Solutions makes sturdy equipment."

Her eyes fluttered as she swiped the backpack. She marveled at it, her eyes following her warped reflection on its shiny surface. Her funhouse mirror smile melted—the pack's straps hung loose, stretched, and ripped at the seams. To her surprise, the steel edges bore only minor dents.

"The farce has gone on too long," Baron said. "But before this can end, you must see the beginning."

Jaycee raised the hollow pack, and a rattling came from inside. She caressed the rounded cover, feeling for a latch. She flipped up the sky-blue middle panel. Jaycee sent a curious side-eye to her father while sticking her hand into the compartment. Her fingertips traced a small rectangular object.

"A... thumb drive?" Jaycee said, holding the slim gray device to her eye. "Did Eric store all his homework on here?"

"It contains something that was never meant to be seen."

"Oh! No, no, uh, look, if this is Eric's, erm, 'private'

collection, I don't want to see—!"

"What?" Baron said, wiping spittle from his mouth. "On it, you will see my first encounter with the original Super Society."

"It was recorded?! Cool!"

"View its contents away from my presence," Baron said, looking her dead in the eye. "My influence must not play a factor. For us to start an era of super-powered crime-fighting—an age of utopian order—there must be no secrets between us."

The thumb drive disappeared in Jaycee's closed hand.

"I would not give anyone else but you this choice," he said.

"The choice to do what?"

"To see heroes in their darkest hour. To know me at my worst and still go along with my vision."

Jaycee sensed a flurry of fearful thoughts scratching behind her eyes.

"Dad," Jaycee said, lowering her voice to a hushed tone. "What if the power transference isn't what you think? What if you're like this...?"

The remaining words failed to come. Baron sat unmoving, like a blinking statue. Nervous energy bubbled up within Jaycee, but she rebelled against her instincts. Steeling herself, Jaycee cleared her throat.

"What if it doesn't work?"

Baron leaned back and away.

"I know growing up," he said, "you thought having a superhero for a dad was the greatest thing. And you kept my secret, earning my trust."

Even in the fading daylight, the warmth of early summer beat down. Jaycee wiped the sweat from her forehead, then noticed Baron's dry, pale skin.

"Watching my body mutate cannot be easy," Baron

said. "But, on your tenth birthday, when we began your training, what did we do?"

"We swore to uphold and carry out the mission no matter what."

"The mission to continue the Super Society's fight for justice and the pursuit of truth," he stated.

Jaycee squeezed the slick tip of the thumb drive through her tightly cupped hand.

"Has Eric watched this?"

Baron looked away, staring off into the bleakness before them.

"You will have to ask him."

He shifted the leather sack from his lap. He vibrated as he summoned the strength to stand. Jaycee put the steel backpack aside and helped him up.

"Knowledge is power, Jaycee," Baron said. "What you do with the information is a heavy burden."

The security guys closed in, forming a circle around them. The *North-Wind* rotated above and then lowered. Its engines' booming collided with the bombardment of highway traffic. Beeps and shouts from passing cars rained down—the jet's maneuvering finally got the motorists' attention. The jet positioned itself over them, casting an expansive shadow.

Jaycee stared at the underside of the aircraft, squinting at the bright blasts from the turbines. The thumb drive felt heavy in her hand.

Chapter Fifteen: *STALL*

JAYCEE

"I CAN'T BELIEVE I'M SAYING THIS," Valerie said, sighing. "Due to the unforeseen robot attack during the Spring Formal dance last Friday—and after Judge Justice's funeral yesterday—the final exam has been pushed to, well, tomorrow. Personally, I think Principal Garza is being soft on you…"

Jaycee ignored her mother's droning with practiced ease. This time, however, her focus drifted to something especially distracting. The thumb drive sat in her bookbag, nestled behind a spiral notebook. The bag leaned against her shin, so she'd feel it if it somehow grew legs or was snatched up. Jaycee scanned the classroom. Her classmates directed their bored eyes at her mother.

With no one looking, Jaycee spread the bag's zipper open and reached inside. Her fingertips brushed against the smooth plastic of the little device.

"Jennifer," Valerie said, jolting Jaycee.

Jaycee's hand recoiled as if the bookbag's zipper teeth would bite her.

"Just because you spent yesterday at the library

doesn't mean you get to goof off today."

"Huh?" Jaycee asked, her mouth stretching into a confused grimace.

"Eventful as yesterday's funeral was, you were better off here on campus," Valerie said, straightening the collar of her cornflower blue blouse. "I trust you used your time wisely and read as much of the school's catalog as possible. Despite this, I will ask you to at least pretend to pay attention."

"Oh, yeah, right, sure," Jaycee said, melting in her chair. "I was at school all day yesterday and didn't go to the, um, thing. Yep."

Tiffany glanced at Jaycee from a few desks in front of her. Tiffany's perfectly plucked eyebrows raised in disbelief. Embarrassed, Jaycee twisted her lips in an awkward response.

Valerie began the morning's lecture, something about a course review to prepare for the test. The telltale thumb drive in Jaycee's bookbag called to her brain.

"Should've just used a hologram," Jaycee muttered softly. "Oh well, at least Mom bought that I wasn't at the funeral."

"Ya think they'll let us keep the Super Society holo-projectors? They'd be awesome for game nights," Melvin whispered from the neighboring desk. "And, yeah, your story worked. We sure were fooled."

Jaycee gave him a quick grin and a shrug, then they both sent their eyes to the front. They sighed in relief, seeing Valerie read aloud from a textbook, oblivious to their secret chatter. Melvin resumed doodling a dragon that resembled the one on his t-shirt. A final exam study guide poked out from beneath his stack of roleplaying game character sheets.

The girls at the desks around Tiffany giggled

at something while Valerie wrote on the board. A neighboring brunette snuck a note to Tiffany and pointed to a gawky girl in thick glasses sitting in their row of desks. Whatever was written sent the ladies into a snickering fit. A stern look from Valerie suppressed the girls' tittering.

Jaycee sunk her elbow onto her desk and planted her chin in her palm.

Melvin has his game guys, and Tiffany has her mean girl crew. I guess Dad was right not to involve them in the big superpower upgrade. They still have a chance at being normal.

Knowing the others bounced back from the Extendo incident comforted Jaycee but worries still weighed her down. She peeked at Melvin's desk—the seat normally belonged to Eric.

Eric's been absent all week, Jaycee thought. *Tomorrow's the last day of school—if he doesn't show up today, will they even let him take the exam? Ugh, since when am I the strait-laced student, and he's the rebel?*

"I know most of you were expecting to attend the last day of school as a formality," Valerie said. "Tomorrow is Friday, our final day and right before the break—I get it. But I implore you not to rush through the exam so you can get to making summer plans. It is not a blowoff day."

Jaycee pressed against her cheek, staring at her mother through squinted eyes.

"Depending on how well you perform on the test will determine whether or not some of you see me again next year," Valerie said. "Your parents will be able to see your grades online as soon as Monday. They'll be very interested to know if the ninth-grade year was so nice you have to do it twice."

Valerie looked at Jaycee as she spoke. Jaycee willed every ounce of strength to keep her eyes from rolling.

"All I ask of you," Valerie said, "is that you don't avoid this. Even if it's daunting, if you don't go through the hard parts, you won't advance."

Jaycee crinkled her brow as her nostrils flared.

I hate it when she's right.

• • •

Her sneaker tapped the red-and-yellow-patterned carpet, but not hard enough to make a sound. Jaycee's other foot rested, letting her bookbag's weight lean against it. A wall of periodicals stood before the desk Jaycee sat at. Behind her, picked-over shelves of audiobook cases lined the back wall. Jaycee leaned over, peering past her wide computer monitor—the skinny librarian reclined, lazily moving her mouse, engrossed in a thrilling game of solitaire.

The other tables in Jaycee's row remained unoccupied, which soothed her, but it wasn't enough. Nervous, she tugged the cuff of her yellow capris, trying to cover her legs.

Is it always this freezing in the library?

The librarian's coffee fumes sent flavorful wisps into Jaycee's nose. She fidgeted enough; the thought of a caffeine boost hurt Jaycee's head.

"Just watch it already," she whispered.

Her hasty reconnaissance of the area determined this spot to be the best for privacy. Still, even hidden in an ignored part of the vast room, Jaycee looked over her shoulder.

"You scanned for viruses," Jaycee told herself. "You were careful not to make copies or leave any trace.

The hardware and software are compatible—which is kind of remarkable since it's an ancient, pre-wi-fi device."

Jaycee shook her head, wiggling her ponytail.

"Mom isn't going to barge in," she whispered, nodding as she psyched herself up. "So, just finally watch this thing!"

She swiped the thumb drive from the desk and inserted it into a port on the back of the monitor. In seconds she located the folder named "Sidebar - secret origin." A mouse click popped up a video window. The play button waited, but Jaycee failed to launch.

"Gotta sync up the wireless earbuds!" she said, navigating the computer settings.

She found her device's name listed and waited for it to connect. Her little black earbuds rested by the keyboard, waiting for action. The black video box floated on the desktop, beckoning Jaycee to watch. The cursor made figure eight trails as she stared at her reflection in the black mirror.

"Jaycee?" Yvette said, approaching the table.

"Hey!" Jaycee said, gleefully welcoming the distraction.

"I thought you had Social Studies this period," Yvette said, shuffling the short stack of books in her hands.

"I probably do."

Jaycee recounted the week: on Monday, Valerie pulled her from class to meet at Pantheon Solutions Tower; Tuesday, the baseball game mishap that led to Baron's power transference; the funeral the next day, and now this.

"It's, eh, been a busy week," Jaycee said. "Who can keep track of things like class schedules, right?" Yvette said. "It's good to see you made time to study."

"I need everyone to keep thinking that I was here all day yesterday," Jaycee said, rattling the earbuds in her palm. "I figured it's a good idea to actually spend some time in the library."

"To be honest, I haven't processed everything. No time. After yesterday... I could use some chill."

Yvette placed the books on the table. She rubbed her arms, and Jaycee did the same to herself.

"You're in the right place, then," Jaycee said.

The air conditioning vent above them blew at full blast. Yvette's track outfit didn't look the warmest.

"Doing laps around the school is a great way to warm up," Yvette said.

"I'll pass. Extendo gave me enough exercise for a while."

Yvette leaned on the corner of the table.

"We've had dangerous missions before," Yvette said. "Something about this last one, though—I dunno, makes me think... I don't wanna sound too much like a nerd, but—"

"Too late."

"Cute," Yvette said. "Anyway, I'm looking forward to my biggest stress coming from worrying about getting good grades."

"That wasn't nerdy," Jaycee said, forming a devilish grin. "It was geeky. Dorky. No, we have to go old-school for this—that was downright dweeby!"

"And you've gone from cute to straight up precious," Yvette said, crossing her arms and smirking. "Judgey Jaycee is saying this as she apparently cut class to study in the library?"

"Shhh!" the librarian hissed from her desk.

Jaycee and Yvette puffed their cheeks, holding in laughter.

"People can say whatever they want," Yvette

whispered. "But I'm the recipient of the Pantheon scholarship this year—sponsored by Mr. Maddox himself. So, I guess I feel like I represent your—our—dad. Is that weird?"

"I think for someone who was basically the real leader of our superhero team, it's not weird at all."

Jaycee caught what she said.

Go-Go dedicated her existence to Pantheon, Jaycee thought. *Am I Dad's "chosen one" only because I'm his bio-daughter?*

"Hey, Yvette, make sure you come up for air once in a while, huh? Crash a party once in a while."

Yvette leaned in.

"Is that sage life advice from my little Super Society sister?" she said, cocking an eyebrow. "You know you guys are my squad. Well, Truther is more like a guy who works for your dad. But the rest of you are my friends."

"Eric, too, when he's here, right?"

"I didn't see him at the tower this morning, but I'm sure he's fine by now."

"Shhh!" the librarian spat, face full of scorn behind her coffee mug.

"I better get out of here before we get suspended," Yvette said, standing straight.

"Garza wouldn't dare this close to the end of the year."

"For you, he might."

"Shouldn't you have Senioritis?" Jaycee said, randomly moving her mouse, pretending to work.

"I don't have a class this period. I usually spend my free time here."

"You're hopeless," Jaycee said, rolling her eyes.

Yvette gave a friendly wave and left. Jaycee felt deserted on her abandoned island in the lonely library.

The air seemed to quiet, and the hum of computers also fell silent. Jaycee put in the earbuds, took a deep breath, and pressed play.

. . .

Jaycee nudged the remaining chicken tender on her plastic tray. She sat by herself, immersed in surrounding lunchtime conversations. Melvin squawked, deep in a tirade about mystical attributes from a table across from her. At a few tables farther, Tiffany pecked at her phone at rapid speeds while her glam girls crowded her. Jaycee looked at her phone—Baron's contact info displayed, yet she couldn't bring herself to start a text message. The thought of calling him made her cringe.

The chicken finger cooled by the second, on par to be as cold as her water bottle. A lanky jock in a loose-fitting Majors baseball jersey chuckled with his bros at a neighboring table. At another, a bearded teacher discussed what sounded like home improvement projects with fellow adult staffers. Everyone acted like the previous day didn't happen.

Jaycee stared at the ocean of people yet looked at nothing.

"Daughter of celebrity rich guy," she muttered. "Don't everybody come to my table at once."

Jaycee's phone's static screen waited.

"I can't unsee that video."

She struggled to even glance at her phone for more than half a second.

"He was my age—just a kid," Jaycee said, too low for anyone else to hear. "I mean, I do dumb stuff. So, he bullied his way onto the Super Society and helped cover up a rando they killed. No big dad deal."

Jaycee's head slunk into her arms, pressing her nose against the tabletop's dark brown laminate surface. The chicken strip's aroma vanished along with her appetite. Her bookbag sat upright by her shin. She moved her leg, feeling the bag's smooth material bulge against her skin. Inside, her folded and tucked armored Powerhouse uniform weighed the bookbag down, yet Jaycee refused to release it from her touch. With some effort, she slid it a few centimeters.

"Good thing this will be over soon," Jaycee mumbled. "Getting tired of lugging this thing around."

A vibration rattled her. Her head snapped up to see a new text notification from Eric. The message bubble showed a smiling ghost emoji. She snatched her phone, inspecting it as if she had hallucinated the alert. Her ponytail whipped behind her as she scanned the cafeteria. Another text from Eric rumbled in: "Meet me by the stairs. I need to talk to you about your dad. Tired of the lies. Make sure ur not followed."

Jaycee's eyes became moons, and her mouth shrunk to a dot.

"No flushing way," she whispered. "Please tell me you aren't gonna do something dangerous, Eric!"

She studied every letter, every punctuation mark, ensuring she understood what he wrote.

"That looks like an intense selfie," Yvette said, walking to her table.

The phone slipped through Jaycee's fingers, but she caught it before it landed on the table. She shuffled her arms, crossed, then uncrossed her legs as she tried—and failed—to look casual.

"Yvette! What are you, um, doing here?"

Yvette held her backpack straps with two thumbs.

"I decided to take your advice and come up for air. We won't get to hang out this summer, but we can go get an espresso."

"Now?" Jaycee said, bouncing her knee as if she'd already drowned in coffee.

"I got some Senioritis after all. Whattaya say?"

A text from Eric buzzed Jaycee's phone: "Hurry, don't have much time."

"That sounds awesome, but…" Jaycee said, slow to look up from her screen. "Something big just came up."

"Anything I can help with?"

Yvette waited; her beaming face began to fade.

"I'm sorry, I—no," Jaycee said, barely able to look at the older girl.

"Well, if there's something you need, you know you can—"

Buzz! Jaycee's phone's jittering snapped her patience.

"I said I was good!"

"Oh," Yvette said as her hands lowered to her sides. "Yeah, that's cool."

Dejected, Yvette stepped away.

"I'll see you later," Yvette said without looking back.

"Definitely!" Jaycee said, but Yvette kept walking.

Jaycee's lungs deflated, and she gently pounded the phone onto the table. She hung her head, pressing the phone's smooth pink plastic case against her temple. Jaycee slid it down, reading Eric's text: "Come alone."

The mass of kids and teachers ate at their packed tables, oblivious to Jaycee's existence.

"That won't be a problem, Eric," she said.

Chapter Sixteen: *HIGH*

JAYCEE

JAYCEE DASHED INTO THE HALLWAY, brushing past a pair of students taking down posters and flyers from a cork board. Hurrying like the villain Demono had returned to set the school ablaze, Jaycee turned a corner, nearly knocking Principal Garza out of his sandals.

"No running in the halls!" he said to her back. "Unless it's a true emergency, then we can discuss—I understand that some matters are more urgent than others..."

He trailed off as Jaycee raced past a couple of classrooms until she reached the base of the stairs. Stepping around a brick pillar, Jaycee searched, but no sign of a flying boy. No one occupied the normally busy spot by the adjacent wall. Jaycee frowned, disappointed to see the empty high-top chairs and round tables. Muffled breathing grabbed her ear. She looked up to see Eric hovering just below the shadowy underside of the stairwell.

"Why aren't you at lunch?" Jaycee asked.

Eric dipped more into the light. He wore his anti-grav backpack strapped around his shoulders, but his orange t-shirt and olive shorts resembled anything but a superhero's costume.

"I woke up in my room at the tower," he said, almost whispering. "I was starving, so I asked a drone for two extra-large pepperoni pizzas. I'm so stuffed, I dunno how I'm able to float."

He cupped a hand on the corner of one of the gray steps jutting downward. He poked his head out from under the railing. Eric's pupils bounced like tennis balls.

"You hiding from the paparazzi?" Jaycee said. "You got your backpack, which is amazing. Why don't you come down here?"

"Since the fall yesterday, I'm having trouble staying grounded," Eric said, positing himself to be upside down and flat under the stairway.

He lay his legs on the long, thin peaks of the zig-zagging under-stairs. He clutched his phone to his chest.

"I'll catch it if you drop it," Jaycee assured.

"I lost it recently, but when I saw it by my bed this morning, I think..."

"Think what?"

"I think that me having my phone is a message."

"Well," Jaycee said with a faint smile. "Of the communication devices I know about, the phone is up there."

"I could post anything I want. I could call anybody. And, like, everybody knows it."

"I know landing in that pod had to be intense—are you feeling okay?"

Eric pocketed the phone, leaning his head back, staring at the floor.

"I've spent most of my time in pods lately."

Jaycee set her bookbag down on a round table. Shedding the weight of her books and uniform relieved her, but only partially.

"About the fall, Eric—"

"You were protecting my secret," Eric said, eyes closed. "Just doing what your dad told you to do."

"Have you seen him?"

"No," Eric said, then raised his head to look at her. "What your dad's doing is wrong."

The statement hit Jaycee like a laser blast.

"Wh-what do you mean?"

"Mr. Maddox looked weird yesterday," he said. "He looked sick—too sick."

Eric deserves to know, Jaycee thought. *But telling him anything now is asking for trouble.*

"I don't know," she lied. "He hasn't told me anything."

Eric sighed and closed his hand into a loose, shaky fist. She could tell he was fishing for answers, but Jaycee refused to take the bait—despite how it killed her inside.

"I've barely seen my dad lately," Jaycee lied, feeling her stomach knot. "And you're right; yesterday... I was just following orders."

While technically true, Jaycee still felt queasy. She swallowed hard, hoping she wouldn't puke up the chicken tenders she had eaten. They both fidgeted, unsure of what to do next. A mountain of unspoken questions and concerns begged to be cracked open, yet awkward silence filled the air.

"I was worried," Jaycee said, breaking the tension. "We all were."

"I shouldn't have bailed on you," he said. "When you and Ms. Cooper—your mom—were at the tower on Monday... I was gonna say I'm sorry about how the dance turned out. I'm sorry about a lot of things now."

"Your disappearing act had me freaked out. But I figured you just fought your dad wearing the suit that, um, ya know... The armor that was involved with your mom's accident."

Eric snapped his head away, sniffing loudly. He blinked away the welling tears sparkling in the overhead lamp's light.

"You needed space," Jaycee said. "But I could've reached out, too."

Tilting her head, Jaycee gazed at the black TV monitors on the wall. Her mind went as blank as the screens, trying to come up with something to say.

How can I tell him that Dad used a big machine—a machine Eric's dad built—to steal powers from his mom? Good luck not sounding nuts saying that out loud.

"At the funeral, I was going to tell everybody about my power," Eric said. "I was going to tell everyone everything."

Jaycee fluttered her eyes.

"Whoa, really?!"

He lowered, assuming a standing position in the air. His shoelaces dangled a few feet above Jaycee's head.

"I thought the no mask thing would make everything easier," Eric said. "All it did was complicate my life—and everyone else's."

"Letting the world think your flying ability comes from a backpack—that can't be fun. Costumes in general can be sucky sometimes."

He unstrapped the backpack. Her eyes grew large, not liking where this was heading.

"It was never forever, right?" Jaycee said. "Is this the real reason you wanted to see me? To let me know you're going public—er, more public about your flying?"

Eric let the backpack strap hang on his palm.

"It hurts to come down," Eric said. "Even if I didn't care about people going crazy about me flying—for real flying, like something an alien would do—there's still my dad. Your dad and the others. And also—"

"We're disbanded. No one knows our alter egos. And as far as our secret identities go, just because people know that the 'Pantheon Pals' live, or lived in the same place at one time, or whatever—it wouldn't matter."

"Yvette, Melvin, and Tiffany don't know about my power," Eric said. "You do. I have to act like everything's normal. Otherwise, I put the people closest to me in danger."

"Just be straight with me, Eric. Tell me what's going on."

Eric gripped the backpack's short, flat wings.

"What would you do," he said, "if you could tell the whole world all your secrets—to be free of every burden—but it meant risking hurting the person you love the most?"

Jaycee stuck her hands in her pockets, letting the words sink in.

"As fed up with secrets as I am," Jaycee said, "holding off on the big superpower reveal is a good idea. At least for now."

"That's just it. We can both be cool about keeping the secret, but it's like you said—the decoy backpack was never supposed to be permanent. 'Eventually' is gonna come, and when it does, I don't know what will happen."

He strapped the pack back on.

"I don't know what to do now," he said. "Sometimes it feels like the whole world is in on a big inside joke, and I don't even know what the premise is. But I feel like the punchline."

Baron's grand plan swam through Jaycee's mind. The video of her father's first encounter with the original Super Society replayed in her mind's eye.

"Eric, did my dad ever tell you how he met the original Super Society?"

Eric breathed a long grunt as he willed himself to be eye-level with Jaycee.

"I saw who Judge Justice really was," Eric said.

A twinge of fear pulsated through Jaycee. She stiffened.

"What did you see?"

Eric's lips split, but he hesitated.

"A sad old man," he said after a quiet moment. "A lot of money went into his sendoff yesterday. He didn't get nearly that much fanfare when he was still around, though. Not toward the very end."

"I met him once when I was little," Jaycee offered, steering the subject to something less volatile. "I wish I... understood him more."

Seeing the video would devastate Eric, she thought. *He's so lost, but I don't want to confuse him even more.*

"I was going to do so much," Eric said. "But when I got the chance, I choked. Heroes save people. I'm famous for doing nothing."

"Come on, Eric," Jaycee said, creasing her brow as she formed an uneasy grin. "I wish I could tell you more, but you gotta believe me, things are gonna work out."

"I was dropped off here at school. I'm talking to you. I could see anybody. And your dad... Well, I mean, it's not a secret I'm here."

"Says the guy hiding under the stairs."

Eric flew around to the other side of the stairwell. "I think I know what the joke is. I'm... powerless."

"What are you talking about?"

Eric floated into the empty hallway, and Jaycee followed.

"In a few minutes, a pod is gonna come get me," Eric said. "A flying drone, like the one that got you when Time Thief 'froze' you."

"Thanks for that pleasant flashback."

"The pod will knock me out, and I don't know when or where I'll wake up. Wherever it is, I'll be trapped."

Jaycee trailed Eric down the hall. Kids stared at Jaycee and Eric through classroom door windows as they passed.

"I have the choice of doing whatever I want, but I'm afraid to," Eric said.

Eric levitated as they approached an exit. Excited clamoring emerged from the nearby cafeteria. Students flooded the hallway while Jaycee watched Eric push open the door.

"Eric, I don't understand," Jaycee said loudly, competing with the noise of the growing crowd.

I understand everything, Jaycee thought. *Eric is safe. He's frustrated and scared, and I hate that, but he's safe.*

Eric backed away, flying higher outside as a horde of hollering kids gathered under him. Jaycee hurried ahead, trailing the bottom of Eric's shoes. Staff and students covered the grass surrounding the flagpole by the main campus entrance. Teachers yelled for everyone to calm down, but kids with outstretched phones ignored them.

Jaycee held her ground, front and center, with blood pumping in her ears. The adrenaline rush and her thumping heart drowned out the herd around her. A familiar face caught Jaycee's eye—Melvin pushed his way to the front on one side. At the other end of the wall of kids, Tiffany had her minions part the sea of students for her to cut through. Melvin and Tiffany's jaws hung, stunned at the sight of Eric.

"There's something majorly messed up going on with your dad," Eric said to Jaycee, half-squinting his earnest eyes. "If you really don't know anything, it's best to keep it that way."

The midday sun enveloped Eric in light, making it difficult for Jaycee to keep a lock on him. A white orb appeared, descending behind Eric. The kids clapped and shouted at the spherical drone, and they blew up when it unspooled its metallic arms.

"Eric!" Jaycee shouted. "I'll cut class and follow you; I don't care! I'll figure something out! I promise!"

The silver tendrils coiled around Eric's legs and chest. The crowd roared, jumped, and barked into their phones.

"Hey, Jaycee," Eric yelled from above. "I don't want to sound corny, but, really, you should stay in school!"

Chuckling spattered throughout the crowd. Eric bobbed slightly, blocking the sunbeams enough for Jaycee to see his thin smile.

"Eric Boxwoth is making a joke?" she said, with a half-smile of her own.

The steel coils covered Eric's face, then mummified his body. The kids and adults in the crowd all gasped as the orb towed Eric away. Jaycee stood motionless save for her quickened breaths while the kids encompassing her gushed over Eric Icarus' sudden vanishing.

ERIC

Cool steel pressed against Eric's flesh, and his innards galloped. Being hauled like luggage through the air proved to be a rocky ride.

"This is overkill," Eric said, practically kissing the chrome coil centimeters from his face. "Where else would I go? What else could I do?"

His drone chauffeur accelerated, and Eric felt the cybernetic tendrils tighten their grip on his body.

"If I say something, anything could happen to my Mom. So, you won, Mr. Maddox. You already did; I just didn't want to admit it."

The tentacles' vise allowed no light to seep through, but Eric closed his eyes anyway.

"At least this way, the others won't get hurt. Jaycee will be safe."

Hisssss. Plumes of gas sprayed through thin, curved slits between tentacle links. The mist spread throughout the tight area around Eric's head.

"What a shock, knockout gas. Is that what you make all day, Mr. Maddox?"

"The embittered are usually jaded," Baron said as if standing next to Eric.

Eric flinched, expecting to be attacked by a mechanical spider or whatever weird invention Baron would devise. Instead, he felt and saw nothing.

"Only failures are that cynical, young Mr. Icarus. But I do appreciate you keeping a sense of humor."

"Where are you?!" Eric yelled.

"Am I speaking to you from a communication device I installed in the coils ensnaring you?" Baron said, his voice oozing into Eric's ears. "Or is this another dream?"

"I'll stay quiet!" Eric said, pleading with the steel ring pressing against his cheek. "My mom stays alive, and no one will even see me! I'll quit school, whatever you want!"

"Such sacrifices. So noble. Very wise to stick with the devil you know, eh? Can you imagine what the world would do to your poor mother if they found out she could fly? The vile things these madmen could dream up, playing with her extraordinary bloodline—truly reprehensible!"

"They can have me, then! Leave her alone!"

Eric blinked away stinging tears, letting them run down his hot cheeks. Baron's face faded in like a vengeful ghost. Eric shuddered, grunting out a wet-sounding shriek.

"How are—?!"

"An augmented reality holo-emitter perhaps," the disembodied head of Baron said. "Or has this barely conscious dream escalated to a full-on hallucination?"

Baron's head did not fill Eric's vision entirely; it reminded Eric of watching a movie on his phone close to his face. Strangest of all, Baron looked clean of any sickness, free of wrinkles and dark veins.

"You did well, Eric. Pandering, making jokes, smiling. Showing your teeth. Lying through them as well."

"I couldn't tell Jaycee what's really happening," Eric said. "About you. She can live with her mom, far from Pantheon Tower. I can save her, at least."

"Afraid, afraid," Baron mocked. "Your mother's fate. My daughter's well-being. And the burdensome secret of your flying ability. More anxiety arrows in your quiver of fear."

"I want to see my mom."

"You aren't interested in how your father is doing?" Baron said in an over-the-top, fake sounding concerned tone.

"He'll help me stop you!"

"David Boxworth? I made him an offer, and he betrayed you before I could finish my sentence."

The cyber-vines slid lower across Eric's body down to his sneakers, completing his mummification. The force of the drone leading him tugged hard. The cables' tenacity endured the breakneck speed yet shook as they climbed upward—the bumpy flight made Eric's organs somersault. Unable to see anything but Baron's smug face lurched Eric's stomach even worse. He took in as much oxygen as he could through the metal arms' cracks, settling his insides.

"The devil I don't know is the lesser of two evils."

"How very edgy ninth grader of you, Eric," Baron said with an unimpressed smirk and raised eyebrows.

"Anything is better than being your prisoner! What if I told the others, huh?" Eric said, wiggling his nose against a metal casing. "Yvette, Melvin, and Tiffany—I think they'd wanna know the truth about Truther!"

"Ah, the 'Civilian Pals' and all their non-superhero equipment. Didn't you tell them you weren't their friend the last time you saw them?"

Regret ate through Eric's chest as he flashed back to accosting them after the dance, the precursor to his duel with Dreadnaught.

"I don't want to," Eric said, "but I'll tell Jaycee everything. The video of you and the original Society— how you held my comatose mother captive for years. Your plan to rule the world!"

"Can you trust her?" Baron said, flattening his lips. "She's lied to you before."

Desperation crawled along Eric's frantic thoughts. He found it hard to breathe and began to wonder how long he could last under wraps.

"You're a smart kid, Eric," Baron said. "But I need you to be smarter. In fact, I need you to be a genius, almost on my level of intellect. Think it through."

The coils' steel surface grew warmer, and Eric's muscles turned to sand.

"Play it out in your mind," Baron said, sounding farther away. "Visualize how this ends if you stray. Imagine your parents suffering in silence. Your former teammates, even Jaycee—one hair-trigger impulse from me, and they're imprisoned in pods."

Baron's words circled Eric's head.

"Think of your 'friends' rotting in cells; meanwhile, every law enforcement agency in the country forgets they even exist. Think of who will be in charge. Then circle back and let me hear you say it again."

Even Eric's hair felt heavier as it became a fight to keep his eyes open.

"Say it, Eric. Two words and I go away."

Eric let the robotic limbs cradle his limp body. Sleep's release summoned him, and he offered no surrender.

"You won," Eric said in a daze.

Slumber slipped over Eric like a fond memory. He closed his eyes, welcoming darkness.

"That's my genius boy," he heard Baron say from some faraway planet.

Chapter Seventeen: *SUSPENDED*

DAVID

H E SQUEEZED GRAY PASTE ONTO his tongue, swallowing the sludge before he could taste it. Though David had never gnawed on a packing pellet, he reckoned this was the equivalent flavor.

The view of the massive Plant Pipeline stretching down the center of the bottom half of Pantheon Solutions Tower sunk David's stomach. Even from thirty feet away, he could make out the details of the thickets of green leaves and intertwining vines coating the floral tube. Tropical flowers decorated the mammoth beam, adding a playful beauty to the bizarre structure. A series of large, flat lamps wrapped around the humongous pillar, providing nourishing light to the leaves.

David inspected the blank, white tube in his hand and then peeked at the vibrant flowery pipe. He squirted more gray goop into his mouth, scowling as he swirled the glop between his teeth.

The wide window spanned like a movie theater screen, allowing David to look across at the vast upper-midlevel ring he temporarily called home. His was the only visible room; huge, curved steel plates covered the other decks. David assumed the biggest casing hid the hangar he and Eric entered. Square lamps lined the ring partition separating the workstation rungs from the circular ceiling overhead.

"There's gotta be a factory floor somewhere in this funhouse," David said, gulping down another bland helping. "We had plenty to work with on the production level. These human turnips helped me build the new MegaCore, so surely, they'd know where all the parts get made."

David placed his lunch-tube on the gold-plated floor. He peered with a suspicious eye at the giant, sleek brown support pillars positioned around the building's near-hollow interior—he knew the color of rust when he saw it. Circular walkways lined the inner levels of the tower's base, each occupied with fit people occupying various workstations. Each earth-toned rung buzzed with smartly dressed men and women, typing away while sitting in cubicles and monitoring stand-up desks.

None of the model employees looked at the busy city street outside the large, billboard-sized windows. Glass encircled the first twenty floors of the tower, giving the outside world insight into the offices' fantastical design. The sun's gleam across rush hour traffic and neighboring skyscrapers served as David's only way to tell time.

David squinted as he took a quizzical look at the chiseled busybodies at their stations. He grew more skeptical with each agonizingly slow second.

"All these beautiful people sending emails, making copies, and working on spreadsheets," he muttered. "No phones, though. Not much of a customer service department, eh? Guess the lesser models can't talk."

"Activate mirror."

The window transitioned into a mirror, reflecting David's stunned face staring back at him. Chelsea and Dahlia stood at the other side of the empty room.

"Are you enjoying your nutrients tube, Mr. Boxworth?" Chelsea said, smiling with her lights beaming, yet with no one behind the wheel.

David steadied himself on the gold-colored wall as he got to his feet.

"I had a cot," he said. "One I'd steal naps in during the MegaCore's construction. If I'm spending my nights in here, it'd be nice to have a place to rest my noggin. And you're gonna need to put a chamber pot or something in here. That gray stuff goes right through a man."

The women blinked in unison—even their matching sage-gray smart suits must have came from the same closet.

"All your amenities will be taken care of," Dahlia said—at least, the one David thought was Dahlia.

"After your appointment, of course," Chelsea added.

"Appointment?" David said, bewildered.

He reviewed his charcoal slacks and black v-neck in the mirror. He decided his shoes could use a shine, and his five o'clock shadow was working overtime.

"Who needs to see me? Who would even know I'm here?"

"If you'll come with us, please," Chelsea said.

David followed them out of the hollowed room, eager to leave the memories of the lab it once was. A tall man, square-chinned and sporting a six-pack underneath a tight white button-collar shirt, passed them as they strolled through the corridor. David gave him a curious look, but the man flashed a perfect smile and then went about his way.

"What's the retirement plan like here?" David asked, making conversation with Chelsea and Dahlia's backs. "Better than mine, I guess. I'm keeping in perspective the realistic-ness of whatever my son is going to do."

The duo led in silence, walking along a curved path. A raven-haired woman passed them—instead of being a world-famous supermodel, she held a manila folder against her sharp orange jacket. She, like all the workers in the building, was stunning. Less so for their physical qualities, but in a jarring way that left David in a stunned stupor as he obediently followed his handlers.

"Not to imply that I don't have any faith in Eric," David said, resuming his one-way conversation. "I don't expect him to be able to do anything anytime soon. And in the meantime, well, frankly, I think my stay here—however long—will not be too dissimilar to what it would be even if I weren't a secret Pantheon prisoner."

They walked along the bend until they came to a white door at the end of the hallway.

"What I mean is, captive or contractor, I'm fairly certain my daily routine wouldn't change. But outlook is everything, right?"

Chelsea placed her palm on the door's blank surface. The entry opened, and he followed the twins inside an ivory-colored room with a bluish glow, but David couldn't see any visible light source. Ahead of them, a row of women worked at a monitoring station. They wore sleek, thin virtual reality headsets that wrapped around their eyes. They made little spirit fingers, indicating they were toggling through some augmented reality interface.

"I know Eric will figure out a way to crumble this

empire. How he does that without risking everything—I have no idea. Stop me if I'm babbling. It's this curse of gab, you see—"

"Eric has been taken from school," Dahlia said. "He's been sedated and will be revived once Mr. Maddox needs him."

"Taken?" David said, not taking his eyes from the back of Dahlia's blonde hair.

"Eric has been most cooperative!"

Chelsea led David past the VR ladies; David ignored them as they ignored reality itself.

"I want to talk to my son."

"Cellular service will be temporarily unavailable while in the revitalization chamber," Chelsea said.

Disc-like drones buzzed above their heads while fat tubes on the surrounding walls blinked with multicolored lights. David ducked when a meandering disc got too familiar with his hair.

"What do you mean Eric is cooperating?"

A short stroll took them to a large viewing panel—a series of white poles raised from the floor, adjusting to David's height.

"Place your hand over these funny little rods, and you'll be able to speak with him," Chelsea explained.

"With whom?"

An empty, grayish-silver area waited beyond the window.

"This is the size of my bedroom back at the Boxworth Dreamineering building," David said under his breath. "I never thought of myself as the homesick type, but..."

Skinny cords slivered up and down the chamber's honeycomb-patterned walls.

"He sustained injuries during the power transference," Dahlia said. "So, he is being cared for here until he is ready to be moved to his stasis pod."

"Who, Chelsea-Dahlia-whoever? What is this?"

"It is a state-of-the-art recovery system," Chelsea said. "We call it the 'Rejuvenation Station!'"

"Listen," David said, taking a beat to suppress the storm within. "I understand my situation—I could somehow escape and run to the cops, opening that can of worms. They'd investigate me, maybe throw in the big house for the Dreadnaught incident at the high school dance: endangering minors, and not to mention me being cool with one of my son's many abductions—the works."

Dahlia waved her hand over a rod, which ejected a thin plastic strip.

"You'll need to sign this," she said. "It's an NDA. That means 'non-disclosure—'"

"I know what it means! What do you care about legality, anyway?"

David frowned at the transparent document. A backlit, flat holographic projection lay over it. He wiggled his fingers through the intangible image, and the chipper blonde nodded in approval. The digital scribble he made on the screen would not pass for any form of written language, but the gorgeous concierge accepted it. Dahlia re-inserted the strip into the pole.

"All these crossed-T's and dotted-I's," David said. "For what? If I leave the authorities out of this, I'm at Pantheon Solutions' mercy. No one will even notice I'm gone!"

"He'll be with you shortly!" Chelsea said.

David watched the unnaturally upbeat women make their exit with raised eyebrows. Shaking his head, David redirected his forlorn gaze to the large glass pane in front of him. He pondered what made this station different from the other pods the syntho-replicant-clone-whatever-people recharged in. Whichever name Baron preferred to call his artificial employees didn't matter. There was no confirmation that these were, in fact, bio-manipulated humans, but that didn't matter either.

If Eric doesn't find a way to expose Barry, then we're doomed—and I'm the one who told him to go on like nothing was out of the ordinary.

A motion in the corner of David's eye caught his attention. A thick gyre of wires and a pair of mechanical arms lowered a man on the other side of the glass. Half-nude, a chrome casing thankfully covered the man's midsection. A separate steel sheathe wrapped around his legs from the knee-down. David watched as the silver arms positioned the body upright as if he were a cotton-stuffed doll. Eel-like cords slid off the man's face, revealing Baron Maddox. Electrodes decorated his face, and translucent tubes ran through his nose. Through it all, though, Baron's blue eyes sparked with life. His cheeks puffed—a gray and black respirator covered his mouth.

Despite the smorgasbord of various gray matter he'd ingested throughout the day, an empty pit sat in David's stomach. He didn't quite know how to react to seeing his colleague/boss/captor this way, or any of this for that matter. David could feel hints of emotions but self-censored any reaction. The VR women to his left made it even more awkward, but they seemed oblivious. David placed his hand over the pole on his right, which emitted a neon blue light once it sensed his warmth.

"Well, this is weird," David said.

"Hello, David," Baron said, his voice pumping through speakers built into the cream-colored walls.

Realizing his mouth hung open like a fish, David

shut his trap. He planted his loafers shoulder-width apart, then placed a hand on his hips.

"I need to file a formal complaint," David said. "You and your loose cannon superhero team are responsible for damaging my building. Tore a big hole right through the wall."

"The pursuit of Cybertooth spiraled out of control. As Truther, it is my duty to protect this city and its people. The damage to your home is a regrettable and gross misuse of the Super Society's sheer firepower. However, I take solace in knowing that no one was badly harmed."

The genuine concern in Baron's voice dug into David's heart like a rusty shovel. Scatterbrained thoughts scurried in confusion, but his mind settled on a strand of coherency.

"What's the plan here, Barry? Once you're cleared for action, you get Eliza's powers? And then you... fly around the city until you somehow end up ruling the world?"

After a spell of quiet awkwardness, David offered a much-needed icebreaker.

"Flying is amazing, don't get me wrong, but it's dove-hunting season, know what I mean? But, hey, I worry for Eric, too, ya know? Some nincompoop throws a well-aimed rock, and the flying parade is over."

"You confine your imagination to such tiny spaces," Baron said. "Your focus should be on completing the next task I assign you."

"So, I'm not just a well-fed inmate?"

"Your conscription is to the greater interest of Pantheon Solutions. Your life and lineage are mine alone."

David stared daggers through the glass separating them.

"I know you think you're doing what's right, Bar'. In your warped mind, you think you're keeping Eric safe. You have him in your pocket 'til it's time to use him up. You'll throw him away as soon as you find a new toy."

"Your son has fared remarkably well, all things considered. The tribulations at the Gilroy estate; the attack at the funeral—Eric is truly gifted."

Baron shifted his head, moving it up a tad, then tilting—his eyes never broke from David's. The mouthguard covered Baron's lips, making his words that much eerier. The unnatural creases and wrinkles cracking Baron's skin didn't help either.

"I sincerely hope I do not have to kill him."

Baron's steely gaze pierced through the partition and into David's—a chill followed, prancing up David's spine. David frowned, stretching his cheeks into jowls as he fought a quick, silent battle against intimidation. He cut the fear at the knees, ready to return fire.

"I don't admit to jealousy a lot," David said. "But I wish I had a quarter of the confidence it takes to say the crazy stuff you come up with. Guess I'd need to be mind-bogglingly wealthy, eh?"

"Only after you acquire monetary wealth do you truly see what it means to be rich."

"Cute, you get that off of a fortune cookie?"

"I wish you could see how alike we are, David."

"Yeah, you're right," David said. "We both want to be the smartest guys in any room. We need big, showy demonstrations of our genius. And we want our kids to see us for that, not as parents."

Baron took a while before blinking. The strange women engrossed in their VR setup grew quieter, to the point of soundlessness. They sat stiff and unmoving. David shot them a glance, then aimed his stern eyes back at Baron.

"There's a big difference between us," David said. "And it's not just my lack of greenbacks—it's the fact that I won't do absolutely whatever it takes to get said greenbacks. When I'm against the wall, I lose my nerve and won't cut any throats."

The coils holding Baron adjusted, the movement flowing like a wave through his arms and shoulders. The multicolored tendrils slid, repositioning Baron's head in subtle, fluidic motions. David felt himself take a half-step backward as Baron's pupils bored into his spirit. David shook it off and stepped closer to the glass. He placed his palm on the rod, locking eyes with Baron.

"If I had the spine for it," David said, "well, I suppose I'd have the cash to afford the same clarity as you, Barry.

"There's a saying, 'birds born in a cage think flying is an illness.'"

"Do you have a desk calendar with daily inspirational quotes or something?"

"Upon our first 'official' meeting," Baron said, "Eric appeared to be under the impression that he was born with clipped wings. He still fears his nature."

"He's a sensitive kid. But he's shown me that he's got a big set of drones. Can we arrive at a point to this soon? I'm really busy staring at the big plant thing running down your psycho-office building."

"What would you do with superpowers?" Baron asked. "Would you grow a spine then?"

David took two steps back, sliding his hand from the rod's slick surface.

"Wha-what?"

"Your MegaCore fueled my transcendence," Baron said. "Be it happenstance or pure luck that brought Eric to me, his emergence accelerated my agenda."

David cocked an eye.

"Again—what?"

"Once I saw your power battery, I knew I had the means to bring fate to reality."

David lowered his palm so that the rod's sensors detected the minimum amount of flesh.

"You were always going to replicate Eliza's power," David said as if afraid to speak above a whisper. "I already know all about that."

Baron floated, seemingly weightless in the arms of his apparatus. He waited, giving David only silence.

"You really like to twist the knife, huh?" David said with a sigh. "Sure, fine, I practically gift-wrapped a way for you to steal my wife's secret power—boy, there's a sentence. And, oh yeah, I handed over my flying boy to you just to sweeten the deal."

The women removed their VR headsets, uncovering their cookie-cutter beauty. The trio left without a word. But creepy as they were, David did not want them to go—he did not want to be left alone with Baron.

"I basically paved my own path to being your prisoner," David said. "And you're rubbing it in."

"I'm offering you a chance at freedom. I can give you the ability to fly."

"And get so sick I age fifty years in a day? Pass."

"Bend the bars of that cage you keep your imagination in, just a little, David. You have no valid proof of concept, I understand. But when I achieve my zenith, I will not offer this again."

David placed a loafer closer to the Baron's chamber. He took a tiny step once more, approaching the window. The cords pushed Baron toward the glass. They stood mere inches apart.

"I could share Eliza's gift?"

"Your wife's essence will be needed for so much more."

"She had enough juice to power you, but she might be damaged goods now?" David said through stiff lips, unwilling to display any emotion.

"I am a living trial, yes. To ensure you acquire the full ability, yours would come from a different source."

"Eric," David said so quietly he wondered if Baron heard him.

The slow nod from Baron confirmed that whatever microphone was sending David's voice to the cell worked just fine.

"Do not temper your breaths," Baron said, indicating that the speakers on his side also functioned at a high level. "Let it all out."

"He'd still have power left? Is that how it works?"

"You would find that out after the transference. You would see many things more clearly from above. Your wife could not have known of her power, and your son doesn't even want it. Soar like you were always meant to, David."

David's fingers slid off the rod's smooth glass surface. He looked down at nothing in particular, tonguing his upper teeth. Possibilities trampled through his mind, spreading in endless directions. David placed his palm back on the rod, firmly and flat.

"Eric didn't get much from me in the genes department," he said. "Except for a receding hairline, that is. The superpower was all his mom. I can't compete with that, but you know what Eric has that is pure Boxworth blood? That thing about leaving throats intact."

"You may reconsider once you see me in flight."

"I may not be able to fly away," David said, standing straight. "But I will walk away."

"Then you're of only one use to me. I will summon you for the next transference. In the meantime, enjoy looking up at all that you could've been."

The wires retracted, pulling Baron with them, up and out of sight. The absence of any type of guard unnerved David.

Whatever surveillance cameras are in here aren't in obvious places, he thought, scanning for anything resembling a lens. *I'm their prisoner yet I'm left unattended. But something tells me this isn't exactly a minimum-security prison.*

He tapped at the rod's touchscreen.

"Let's see what I can get away with," David whispered while navigating the simplistic menu screen. "Pretty basic send-receive controls, but maybe there's a directory."

A few swipes later, and he hit the jackpot.

"Hello, beautiful."

A button labeled "BOXWORTH" waited at the bottom of a contact list.

"None of what I installed during the MegaCore's construction got deleted. A bit of luck after all. Okay, BRAIN, hope you're awake."

He tapped the circular icon, and it led to a file named "Boxworth Remote Automated Interactive Network."

"BRAIN, do you copy?" David said, raising his voice just above a whisper. "I need you to send the Ultranaut suit again."

Text appeared in the window: "Unable to comply."

"Huh?" David said, dumbfounded. "BRAIN, where is the Ultranaut suit?"

"Boxworth Dreamineering," the voiceless text stated.

"Baron stored it back home, eh? BRAIN, I need

you to run the exfiltration and extraction program. Get me out of here!"

"Unable to comply. Access restricted from this location. Nice try, David."

The room grew even quieter. David backed away from the rod, eyes fixated on the message. His breaths came in waves, strong and heavy, then strained and short. He swiveled, retracing his steps back to his holding cell.

The empty corridors felt like they stretched for miles, and each of David's footsteps carried lead anchors. Reality crashed down upon his shoulders as he forced himself to walk. He realized why no one escorted him.

"I'm sorry, Eric," David said, then willingly trudged back to his gilded cage.

Chapter Eighteen: *CONTROL*

ERIC

Whush-whush-whush. The sound entered Eric's ears first, followed by gusts of cool air blowing over his face.

"Where am I?" he asked aloud in a soft, groggy voice.

Through the slits between the fingers of his gloved hand, Eric saw the slow-spinning white blades of a large industrial-sized ceiling fan—it was in front of his face and getting closer. Panic jolted him like a thousand energy drinks hitting him all at once. Fear wriggled Eric's body, which felt weightless yet dragged upward at the same time.

"Hey, what's going on?!" Eric said, desperate to hold onto anything.

He stayed careful not to extend his arm for fear of having it maimed by the nearing metal fan blades. Shooting his eyes in every direction, Eric realized he was wearing his superhero costume. Confusion clouded his thoughts, making it difficult to focus on anything other than being sucked into the fan.

"No, no, no!" he yelled.

The air pushed against his closed eyelids. Eric's

breathing slowed as the relief of stopping washed over him. Still, he remained afraid to open his eyes. He willed himself lower until he felt the hard floor on his back.

"Huh?" he blurted, flashing his eyes open. "Where's my anti-grav backpack?"

Eric floated upright, hovering over the entryway threshold of what appeared to be an empty hangar. The massive open entrance gave way to the sea of cement outside. Two Infini-Jets occupied the vast runway. Farther out, endless green plains surrounded the area.

"It's still light out," Eric observed.

Feeling the imprint of his phone bulging from within the side pocket of his pant leg, he let out a relieved sigh. Unbuttoning the flap, he peeked inside at the screen hiding inside his pouch.

"It's only been a couple of hours. Maybe nothing's happened yet."

Soothed, Eric allowed gravity to guide his dark blue boots to the gray floor.

Eric floated into the center of a wide-open space meant to be filled by an enormous aircraft. A tiny grid twinkled from the rafters.

Mr. Maddox! Eric thought.

Baron stood, perched at least twenty feet high, doing his best vampire impression—he shrouded himself with a black cloak that hung over his feet. Baron's unmasked face remained partially hidden behind a steel beam on the left wall. He held onto a metal support rod connected to the crisscrossed metal girders lining the curved ceiling. Baron's free arm raised his T-gauntlet to his face.

Uh oh. He's in his Truther outfit. Despite us both wearing our super-suits, this probably isn't a team meeting, especially since no other Society member is here.

"You're standing exactly where she stood."

"Who stood here?" Eric asked.

The golden gauntlet sparkled once more. A blue-tinted hologram projected from it, playing two-dimensional footage of Eliza. She wore a button-up lab suit with a "VISITOR" placard hung around her neck. Men in lab coats surrounded her, busy setting up for the fateful experiment.

"Mom..."

The story of how this hangar was the setting of the doomed Dreadnaught demonstration echoed off every wall. Eric knew the grim details too well. The hologram flickered into nothingness. Eric breathed in the warm air from outside.

Shake it off, Eric. Don't fall for whatever trick this is.

A draft whispered through Baron's black cape, ruffling its golden underside.

"Mr. Maddox, I don't know what's happening right now, but please tell me you didn't undress and dress me yourself."

"Drones handled your transport from the pod," Baron said. "As well as your costume change. You're going to need your protective uniform."

"So, you, uh, forget my backpack but remember to get a new cape?"

"Improved durability and weight distribution, plus it looks absolutely stunning," Baron said, admiring how the light gleamed off his cape's textured material. "I should've replaced the white cloak long ago."

Baron shuffled his cape. Eric raised his brow, noticing there was no visible platform for Baron to stand on.

"New neural pathways have formed within my

brain," Baron said. "Still, I find myself succumbing to nostalgia."

"What're we doing here, Mr. Maddox?"

"I wanted you to see this place. This was the setting for your mother's secret origin."

"You better not have done anything to my mom!"

Eric's fists tightened; he could feel the gloves' reinforced leather stretch at the seams.

"Eliza never got a say in her fate."

Baron saying her name cut into Eric's eardrums like a knife. Lividity swelled within him, causing Eric to levitate higher.

"I present this opportunity to you, her son," Baron said. "One last chance to decide—to join me."

"Join you?!" Eric said. "You make artificial people! You keep criminals in pods! You're crazy!"

"Those villains were brought to justice."

"Yeah, right! Like the police even know. You just experiment on them!"

"Among other things," Baron said through thin lips.

He coughed as if holding back the rising anger.

"The authorities know that Pantheon detains them for research, but..."

Baron exhaled a heavy sigh.

"The important thing here is—"

"No," Eric interjected. "The only thing that matters is that I'm gonna tell everyone about how you blackmailed the original Super Society! Everybody will know about your insane plan to steal my mom's powers!"

"I understand you have much confusion," Baron said. "Perhaps it's better if I show you."

He swung his arm, carrying his cape like a flag. Like an apparition, he floated in place, casting frenzied eyes at Eric.

"Mr. Maddox, you can...?"

He hovered over Eric, reveling in defying gravity.

"Yes! Yes!" Baron yelled. "Just as I imagined!"

Eric backed away.

"My body has finally recovered from the transference process!" Baron said, releasing his cape from his grip. "The purity of this strength... Unequaled potential!"

Eric's head shook as he flew over the threshold and into the open air.

"I spent hours indoctrinating myself with a hypothetical discipline," Baron said while lowering. "I mastered an art of motion that was based purely on theoretical deductions. I knew how to fly before it was even proven possible!"

"This can't be real!" Eric said, halting.

Baron floated before him, the flowing winds blooming the golden underside of his cape.

"You want real?" Baron said with a spreading smile. "Okay, let's get real!"

A commotion stirred equipment crates stacked in the corner. The blue-tinted chrome anti-grav backpack flew over to Eric's hands.

"I had a feeling you'd need to see further demonstration," Baron said.

"Whoa!" Eric said, with his jaw unhinged. "It can actually fly? By itself?!"

Eric strapped on his backpack, keeping a keen eye on Baron.

Huh. Still feels like there's nothing in it. What's the deal?

"You... You-you-you have magnetism powers?"

"Telekinesis," Baron corrected. "But you were not far off!"

"I'll stop you!"

"Ah, now that's where you're not even close!"

"S'gotta be fake!" Eric said between quick breaths.

"Seriously, Eric, are you really playing the fake-power card?"

"Where's my dad? I swear if you hurt him...!"

"David is in a safe location," Baron said, stroking his mustache. "You do know I can threaten more than one person to get you to do what I want, right?"

Whoosh! Eric flinched as Baron's cape whipped by his chin.

"Fly with me!" Baron said.

He boosted himself skyward, and Eric followed. The black cape flapped uncontrollably, but Eric saw enough of Baron's back to confirm he was not wearing an actual working anti-grav backpack—or anything that would grant him flying abilities. From what Eric could tell, there was nothing unusual about the Truther outfit itself—it was the unmasked wearer that Eric couldn't wrap his head around.

"Here! Right here!" Baron yelled over whistling winds as he slowed to a halt.

Eric still wasn't crazy about heights despite the highs he'd flown to. He guessed they floated somewhere between two to three thousand feet. Far below, the desolate grassy fields surrounding the hangar sprawled for miles.

"Where? Here? Why?" Eric shouted back. "And those are just my opening questions! Trust me; I got a million more."

"I'm thinking we start here, but, of course, we branch out above the city! Right over downtown!" Baron said.

The airborne duo slowly circled one another.

"A kingdom in the sky!" Baron declared.

His jubilant smile bared teeth and tongue; his eyes widened despite the unforgiving courses of air.

"I had machinations of expanding my empire, but I must credit you, Eric, for inspiring me to think bigger, so much bigger!"

Baron flew even higher, but Eric did not follow.

"It may take some time," Baron said. "But the means to produce floating fortresses are at my fingertips now! Only those chosen by me will be granted access to my castles in the clouds!"

"Mr. Maddox!" Eric yelled. "I don't understand! What're you saying?!"

He zoomed over to Eric.

"I'm saying, if the meek shall inherit the earth, then let them have it! We are destined for far greater things!"

Stunned, Eric backed away through the strong gusts pushing against him.

"You really did it, didn't you?" Eric asked. "You kept me asleep while you stole my mom's power!"

"The grand design of your existence eludes me for now, but not only have I confirmed that you belong to a very real race of superior humans, but I have also joined your ranks!"

Eric trailed Baron as he shot across the open sky.

"I want to see my mom! Take me to her!"

"Your mother's incident was unfortunate," Baron bellowed over the furious winds. "But her sacrifice has allowed me to soar among the heavens!"

Eric flew alongside him, trying to sort his thoughts.

"Does my dad have powers, too?!"

"David?"

Baron regurgitated a deep, mocking laugh.

"He was instrumental in powering my upgrade, but nothing more! Mr. Icarus, you must focus on the big picture!"

Eric stopped and watched Baron zip ahead, looping in vertical and horizontal circles. Baron spun, showing off a dazzling display of aerial expertise that not even Eric had achieved—all without the aid of a special device.

"Mr. Maddox bounced back from the transference in a big way," Eric said, too low for anyone else to hear over the wild winds. "So, he can fly for, like, half a day or something, and he's already way more advanced than me?"

The black-and-white blur that was Baron decelerated, slowing before Eric. They stood suspended in the air like two specks in the endless sky.

"I spent years crafting impossible skills," Baron explained. "You've validated so much of my research; you have no idea!"

Baron's sinister look tainted the serenity of open sky over the miles of uninterrupted grassland.

"I had to wait for so long, hold so many things in place until I achieved the unthinkable, but here I am! We are one and the same now! Eric, you are capable of unforeseen astonishment—you just don't understand your powers."

"Understatement of the century! I'm still stuck on how it all even works—how apparently you can just copy-paste my flying abilities!"

"It's all in your head."

Baron twisted, then sped off again. Eric struggled to keep up as they headed toward the city skyscrapers. Eric fought to match Baron's velocity, stretching his arms behind as he saw what Baron had done. He willed himself to go quicker, but the distance grew between them.

How is he so fast?

Baron slowed to soar alongside Eric. Baron tapped his temple.

"Mind over matter, Mr. Icarus."

"Don't tell me you can read my thoughts," Eric said as they drew nearer to the cityscape. "Listen, I'm fourteen, so there's gonna be some racy stuff in my head—"

"Not telepathy. Telekinesis," Baron shouted over the loud ruffling of his cape. "You—we—can control objects! Your body is an object, something you manipulate."

Their acceleration shook Eric's bones, and he worried he wouldn't be able to take much more. The patchwork quilt of green and brown below gave way to cement and steel as they crossed into the city, jetting over the tangled web of highways and tunnels.

"Your ignorance limits your massive potential!" Baron said.

He veered lower but kept high enough to whiz past the top floors and rooftops of the city's tallest spires. The surrounding buildings' windows' glinting flares warped as streaks of light as they quickly passed. The activity from the pedestrians and markets below blended into blurry streams in Eric's periphery.

Eric shadowed Baron as he descended even lower, closer to the traffic-laden streets.

"Flight is just the beginning!" Baron said, peering over his shoulder to look at Eric.

They pivoted in a new direction. Exhilaration swirled with the fear of uncertainty within the confines of Eric's skull. He thought of how cool it must've looked for anyone who may have seen a pair of superheroes torpedoing through the sky. He also considered the danger.

The Kell Bridge sat in the distance toward the east.

Eric spotted the park he could never remember the name of and the row of fast-food joints he'd frequently visit (and credited his physique to)—Eric recognized the areas they flew over.

"Why are we going to my school?" Eric shouted.

"We're not. We're leaving it!"

Navigating behind Baron, Eric noticed the big yellow school bus they tailed. Flying parallel to the road, they followed the bus as it rode through the sleepy suburban neighborhoods and merged onto the harried freeway. The late afternoon traffic flowed during the calm before the rush hour storm. For the moment, the flyers stayed elevated enough not to attract attention. After some squinting, the numbering on the side of the long vehicle became legible.

"Mr. Maddox! This is my bus!"

The bus took an exit, and they followed from above. They maintained their distance as the bus turned into a congested city street on the edge of the business district.

"The time has come to put your attributes to the test," Baron announced.

"Test?"

After a brief red light, the bus continued its course deeper into downtown, and they flew after it. Soaring between skyscrapers and over the busy intersections, Eric got an eagle-eye view of his familiar bus route.

First stop, Central Square, right on schedule, Eric thought as a lump formed in his throat.

From on high, Eric noticed the area formed the shape of a literal square.

Way too closed in for comfort!

The business district's central hub took up an expansive chunk of real estate, but the overlapping buildings and stations made it a claustrophobic place.

Blinking signs, marquee-mounted stock tickers, and the dense flocks of people coming and going all looked so small—and vulnerable.

"I need to know the extent of your abilities," Baron said. "It's what I've been measuring this entire time."

As the bus entered the slower lane, Eric and Baron matched its sluggish pace. People on the sidewalks snapped pics with their phones. The tiny flashes speckled like erratic fireflies.

The jig is up. Took them long enough to notice, Eric thought.

They were never hiding, but this exposure felt invasive.

"The future is flying," Baron proclaimed. "The world belongs to us now. The powerless temporarily outnumber us, but in time we will create a real pantheon of elites."

His eyes pierced into Eric's.

"The age of ordinary is over. Gifting those deserving of these capabilities will ensure that only the strong survive. You're the key to all of this, Eric Icarus. But I did not absorb the equivalency of your specific talents. We still need to see if maximum power skipped a generation."

Baron reached a scary level of intensity. The more he creased his brow, an unnatural number of wrinkles and folds etched into his forehead. He snarled, spreading the crinkly spiderweb on his face.

"What does this have to do with a school bus full of kids?"

"Extreme duress may activate superpowers," Baron said. "Let's get extreme, shall we?"

Baron outstretched his hand, widening his fingers. He lifted his arm, and the bus levitated as it passed a corner café. Eric's jaw dropped as the engine churned and the wheels spun, unable to gain traction mid-air. Vehicles across multiple lanes screeched to a halt. Disregarding their safety—or maybe not realizing the danger they were in—droves of people clumped together to awe at the spectacular happening. Eric's eyes bounced from multiple angles, trying in vain to decide where he should go or what he should do.

Baron's wrist's gentle motion repositioned the large vehicle across from them, approximately twenty feet away. Baron pulsated with sheer concentration. The trapped kids inside screamed. Their hands pressed against the windows. Eric knew most of the students on board—yet a stranger to their unfamiliar terrorized faces.

"I believe you, alright?!" Eric shouted, frantic with fear. "You can move stuff with your mind. I get it! Now, please just let them down!"

"This is about what you can do," Baron said.

Sweat dripped down his forehead.

"Eric, your body is young and robust, but if you're going to be the source of molecular reconstruction for an entirely new species of humans, I kinda need to know what I'm dealing with."

Baron's hand closed into a fist, and the bus lifted even higher. Sirens and shouting wailed beneath their feet.

"If you wanna test me, then test me, only me!" Eric yelled. "We can have a big power party, but I won't let you enslave anybody!"

"Who said anything about enslaving people?" Baron said, then stalled. "...You're not wrong, but I'd never refer to it as that. I prefer the term 'societal reassignment.'"

His fist loosened, and the bus dropped.

Eric's heart stopped as he futilely reached out.

The bus plopped to the street below. The onlookers scattered; their wonder turned to horror.

"Noooooo!!!!!" Eric shouted.

Seconds before crashing, the bus stopped. It raised slightly, then lifted again, quicker and several feet into the air. Eric's breath took a few beats to return to him. Under his mustache, Baron smirked. The scene below exploded into chaos; people pushed and trampled each other to escape.

The emergency exit on the rear of the bus wobbled on its hinges. The steel screeched; Baron grunted. Like magic, an invisible hand ripped off the backdoor. The mental force flung the door into the side of a nearby building. Eric sped to the back, getting a closer look at panicked students climbing over the seats to reach the front of the bus. Eric gasped at the sight of his Super Society comrades within. Out of costume, their secret identity-selves were just as at risk as the other civilians.

"Everybody, come to the front!" Yvette yelled near the unseen driver.

"Hold on!" Eric said under frightened yelps.

Tiffany and her girl crew spilled over each other to get to safety. Designer handbags flopped against the dark green seats.

"I can't access the network!" Tiffany said, tapping her phone like crazy. "The Super Society app isn't working!"

"I can't die!" Melvin shouted.

His hairy arms parted his way through the girls, followed by his shirt's red and blue dragon stretching over his belly.

"I'm DM-ing a game tonight!"

"Is that what you're really worried about right now?!" Tiffany said, eyes wide and her lip curled.

"It's the culmination of months of campaign

sessions!" Melvin said before getting shoved back into the huddle.

"Nobody's dying!" Eric said, trying to hide his own shakiness. "I'm pretty sure nobody's dying! Look, I don't know how, but I'm gonna save all of you!"

Amid the cluster, one kid fought to get to the back.

There's always a crazy one, Eric thought, hoping this classmate wouldn't tumble out the open backdoor.

When a blonde ponytail whipped into view, he breathed a sigh of relief.

"Get behind me!" Jaycee ordered.

Despite being dressed in a sky-blue top and yellow capris, she commanded the busload of hysterical high schoolers the same as if she were in her Powerhouse guise. She straightened her bookbag straps after squeezing by another girl.

"Eric!" she exclaimed, reaching the edge. "Who's doing this?!"

Her eyes bulged.

"Dad?!"

Eric looked over his shoulder to see Baron give a friendly wave.

"Hi, sweetheart!" he said. "How was school today?"

"People can see you!" she shouted.

"I want the whole world to see me!" Baron yelled back.

"Eric, you gotta do something!"

"Duh!" Eric said, wavering his hands in frustration.

Jaycee trembled unnaturally. Her arms spread as if someone pulled her strings.

"What the—?" she said.

She flapped her arms as she lost balance, then her feet left the bus floor. An invisible force took Jaycee from the bus, hovering her over the street. Panic ignited every nerve in Eric's body.

"Jaycee!"

The immaterial grip moved her away from the bus several feet above the gathering police cars and firetrucks. Her limbs quivered like she was doing an awkward dance.

"Mr. Maddox!" Eric called out. "Drop her right now!"

"Eric!" she yelled.

She glared at him with her arms stretched in an "are you serious?" pose.

"Don't drop her!" Eric corrected. "Let her go! No! I mean, stop this!"

"Young Mr. Icarus, we haven't completed your final assessment," Baron said from his floating spot. "This is a classic experiment. It's called 'save the many or save the girl!'"

Baron spread his arms, brushing his hands back. His psionic grasp relinquished them, plucking the bus and Jaycee from the air.

"No!" Eric screamed.

Without hesitation, Eric dove to Jaycee, scooping her in his arms. His momentum sent him toward the falling vehicle. On the ground, people scrambled for safety while cars collided in attempts to escape disaster. Crying, honking, and the smashing crunch of metal on metal dominated the atmosphere. The seconds ticked away as Eric carried Jaycee in a desperate tailspin, speeding toward the plummeting bus.

"Eric!" he heard Jaycee yell.

"I can't! I can't! I ca—!"

The dropping bus's yellow roof filled his vision. The street below closed in—he was too late. Jaycee's presence prevented Eric from fainting. Instead, he closed his eyes, battling to keep from crying.

"Eric," Jaycee whispered.

"I'm so sorry."

"No, Eric, it stopped!" Jaycee said, exasperated with relief.

He opened his eyes, blinking away the tears to see the bus make a soft landing. The kids bolted from the bus and rejoiced to be onto the safe surface. Civilians aimed a sea of smart devices at Eric. News cameras from clusters of media teams surrounded the crowded area.

Even holding Jaycee close, Eric couldn't bring himself to look her in the eye.

"I shouldn't have skipped lunch," he mumbled out.

She buried her nose into the shoulder strap of her backpack for a moment, then came back up for air.

"Eric, I'm..."

"Do not resent yourself for this, Mr. Icarus," Baron said, descending toward them. "You rescued who you could. I am, however, disappointed that this did not spark an awakening within you."

Red and blue emergency lights from helicopters and little white drones blinked in the distance. Whatever attention Baron craved, he got it in spades.

"Jaycee, what is it?" Eric said, mustering up the courage to face her.

"It brings me great solace, though," Baron continued, "to know that, despite this apparent setback..."

"What were you going to say?" Eric probed, paying no mind to the madman.

"...I have a faithful steward to carry on my legacy."

"You think I'll join you? You're crazy!" Eric said.

He looked back at Jaycee.

"No offense, but your dad's crazy."

"Oh, Eric," Baron said. "I wasn't talking about

you."

In a sudden jerk, Baron mentally ripped Jaycee from Eric. Eric cursed his delayed reflexes for letting her slip away. Baron lured Jaycee over to him as if in a tractor beam.

"Eric, I'm sorry," Jaycee said.

He watched as Baron grabbed hold of Jaycee and carried her away. An intangible wave of pressure plowed through Eric. After his body spiraled, Eric wiggled the dizziness from his senses. Baron and Jaycee were gone.

Cars pulled over to allow police and fire vehicles access to the area.

"Eric Icarus!" someone shouted. "Do something! Go get the Super Society!"

Worried faces gazed up in anticipation of his next move. Fans called for Extra, Supercut, and Go-Go. Their alter egos grouped near a small convenience store, behind the crowd. A spooked clerk reversed an "open" sign to "closed" behind a dapple of ad banners on the shop's window.

A wall of police officers kept the antsy onlookers at bay. Tiffany waved Eric over to follow her and the others into an alley around the corner. They gathered by a large green dumpster between two brick walls. The trash's sour fumes wrestled with Eric's nostrils, but he was grateful for what little privacy they had.

"Eric! Please tell us you know what's happening here!" Yvette said as Eric landed by them.

Her shirt read "Property of Dawson University Athletic Dept." It made Yvette look that much older than her ninth-grader companions.

"Mr. Maddox is Truther, and he's got powers now!" Eric spouted.

"Baron Maddox?" Tiffany asked, bewildered. "As

in, our big corporate boss-daddy, Baron Maddox?"

Tiffany's shaking head wiggled her big golden hoop earrings.

"Naw," Melvin griped. "Don't tell me all this time we were takin' orders from a business tycoon!"

"He's gonna conduct his psycho-experiment on Jaycee!" Eric said. "You all need to suit up! Yvette, can you run Melvin and Tiffany to Pantheon Tower?"

"Would I be taking the bus if I had my speed-enhancers?" she said, placing her hands on her hips. "The Super Society is on hiatus, remember? Besides, our HQ has been off-limits—just like our gear."

"I know exactly where your costumes are!" Eric said, taking his phone out. "I'll text you where the secret sewing room is."

As his thumbs went into overdrive composing the group message, Eric noticed Tiffany tapping away at her phone.

"Sorry-not-sorry to ghost you, Eric," she said, sliding her index finger off her screen. "But I just took care of our ride."

The smooth purr of an engine drowned out the ambiance of the nearby crowd. Sunlight streaked off the honey-colored hood of an even smoother car as it pulled up to the foot of the alley. The convertible's milk-white roof was up, catching Eric off guard. The door swung open.

"Got here as soon as I could!" Kev said, stepping out.

"Yeah, you did!" Melvin said, astonished.

"I was in the area—just wrapped up some volunteer work," Kev explained. "I read to sick children at the hospital."

"Of course, you do," Eric said, protruding his tongue into his bottom lip.

I'm sure the kids appreciated you wearing your bright red tracksuit, Eric thought, exposing sarcasm in a twisted smirk. *Showoff.*

"Shotgun!" Melvin declared while hurrying past Tiffany.

Kev turned to sit behind the wheel. A large, embroidered college logo stretched across the back of his jacket.

"Another future Dawson U student, huh?" Yvette said as she rushed to the car. "After this is over, we gotta lot to talk about!"

"We can discuss how great 'Kev' is after we stop Mr. Maddox, okay?!" Eric said, rising above them.

Even then, saying the guy's abbreviated nickname felt gross on Eric's tongue.

You can be jealous later, Eric! he scolded himself. *Get your head in the game!*

As Tiffany and Yvette piled into the backseat, Eric positioned his body in front of the windshield.

"Floor it to Pantheon Tower!" Tiffany ordered.

"One last thing, guys," Eric said. "Back at the dance, I said we weren't friends. I never apologized for that. I'm sorry."

"Don't sweat it," Melvin said, poking his head out the passenger side window. "We stick together, no matter what!"

Eric cracked a weak smile before flying into danger.

Chapter Nineteen: *SKYWARD*

ERIC

ERIC DIDN'T NEED A SIGN telling him to fly to
Pantheon Tower—the building's roof shined
like a beacon. The bluish-white spotlight grew
brighter the nearer he got. It beamed upward from
the large square black barricade atop the tower. Eric
had no doubt this is where Baron took Jaycee after he
kidnapped her.

Eric hovered over the gigantic opening, covering
his eyes with his gloved hand to block out the brightness
of the epicenter. The border's humongous dark plates
unfolded, exposing the wide illuminated ring encased
within. Floating over the perimeter surrounding the big
circle inside, Eric couldn't believe what he witnessed:
an elongated golden tube in the middle of a circular row
of slightly smaller dull gray vertical cases. The big gold
beam dwarfed the steel pods at roughly eight feet.

He lowered to the gridded floor, floating to a safe
distance from the strange assemblage of pods. The air
smelled odd and tasted even odder. It reminded Eric of
the old folks' home where he first met Judge Justice, but
enough of the open air swept in to dispel the sourness.

The beaming light shot from the top of the enormous goldenrod. The brightness bounced off the surrounding black walls. Blueish-pink energy coursed through the translucent tubing at the base of the giant round structure.

It's the MegaCore on steroids! Eric thought.

He scanned the engine's curved base's upper lining, where its domed ceiling had retracted into itself. As Eric stood below the umbrella of the central rod's intense light, it became easier to see the bizarre environment, but he still shielded his brow with his hand. The ominous hum of the giant device did little to comfort his nerves.

"I'm glad you're here willingly, Eric," Baron said.

Eric's one-time mentor emerged from the penumbra behind one of the smooth, featureless metal pods. Baron's cape flowed behind him like a majestic war banner.

"I know at this point, nothing should shock me anymore," Eric said, frazzled as he arched his head, absorbing the surreal scenery. "But heck the what? I mean, what the—I mean, are you serious with this super-weird cyber-Stonehenge stuff?!"

"This is the site where reality is forever altered. What we do today shall live in myth and lore for—"

"Where's Jaycee?!"

"Eric," she said. "Everything will be okay, but you have to trust me."

Jaycee appeared behind her father, next to the pod's reflective exterior. She hung her hand onto the strap of her backpack.

"Run, Jaycee!" Eric yelled, lifting off the floor.

"Eric, listen to me!" she shouted, halting him. "My dad told me everything! I know you don't understand, but he has to do all this! Everybody will get powers! It's going to be amazing!"

"Not everyone!"

"That's correct, young Mr. Icarus," Baron said, putting his arm around Jaycee's shoulder. "But those who are fortunate to share your gifts will be trained to use them properly."

"Jaycee, you were there!" Eric pleaded. "He was gonna kill everybody on that bus!"

"Please don't make me choose between you and my dad, Eric."

"You were born with phenomenal abilities," Baron said, hovering in front of Jaycee. "But your will is weak. I lack the time or patience to cure you of your conditional handicap."

Eric flew into the inner circle of pods, staring in awe at his warped reflection on the central tube's shiny golden surface.

"As clearly evidenced from the energy overload manifestation—the light show above us," Baron said, pointing up. "The new MegaCore is primed for activation."

A pod to Eric's left swung open.

"I would be most pleased if you put up no further resistance," Baron said.

Eric stopped to check out the drab gray interior cushioning and the compressed terminal and monitors lining the inner door.

"For us to begin, you must be inside the containment unit."

"You can forget about me getting back into one of those things!" Eric said, pointing at the pod.

"From your transitioned DNA, I estimate I will be able to transform the inaugural hundred of my newly powered populace," Baron explained. "If your body survives the transferences, we'll continue. If not,

I will move onto a more advanced replication process involving post-powered subjects."

Baron glided closer. Eric held out his hands, ready to defend himself.

"If your body withers and fails, not to worry, you will be preserved. For research purposes. Now, get in the pod."

"Solid evil master plan monologue, Mr. Maddox," Eric said, puffing his chest. "But it's over. The other members of the Super Society are on their way right now."

"Oh, you mean them?"

Transparent panels unsealed themselves on the three pods behind the central golden beam.

"I snatched them up shortly before you arrived. They didn't make it past the lobby."

Eric looked in horror to see Yvette, Tiffany, and Melvin inside their respective tombs, hanging their heads low. They stood in what appeared to be deep sedation.

"It's unorthodox even for me, but they'll do nicely should we need a backup supply of raw matter to keep the engine running."

They're just fuel to him, Eric thought. *And I'm next!*

Still waiting on the outer rim of the ring of pods, Jaycee took a deep breath. Her eyes met Eric's—her face begged for him not to interfere.

"Don't," she mouthed.

"I have to," he whispered.

Eric sprang upward, flying fists-first in a semicircle, building up steam for a downward strike. An immaterial force seized every one of his atoms, jumbling his guts. The incorporeal power thrust Eric back down. Eric felt himself be pushed into the waiting crypt-like pod. His back slammed into the padding, and an unseen source shut the door. Discombobulated, Eric squirmed in his upright cell.

Sectional keyboards lay backlit with orange light, as were the various other screens and instruments covering every inch of the chrome coffin's interior. A lift pushed Eric's feet up, accommodating for his shorter height. The blank steel in front of his face split into two rectangles and slid open, revealing a clear viewing panel. Eric's breathing quickened, fogging up the glass.

Close by the central tube, Jaycee approached Baron, who held out a confident fist—his control over objects seemed to be getting stronger. Eric couldn't translate what she mouthed, but her face was apologetic. She patted the air as if to tell Eric to stay put. Stuck to his sides, Eric's arms had no room to move. He pushed, but there was simply not enough space to put up a fight.

"Calm yourself," Baron said through the pod's speakers. "Time is of the essence, so we will bypass any further genetic testing. The machine will take from you what is needed."

The central beam twinkled, then spread tiny squares across itself. A rectangular entryway appeared, and Baron guided Jaycee inside. The doorway closed, reforming its golden outer shell. Her face was visible via the remaining small square window. She looked over at Eric with saddened eyes but not from sorrow. Eric would know pity anywhere.

The luminescent glow from above shimmered across the glass of his viewing panel. Between reflected embers of light, Baron placed his hand on the surface of Jaycee's pod.

"My guesses are educated, but they are still guesses," Baron said via the sound system in Eric's chamber. "You should have plenty of your original genetic material leftover. But in case the transmutation renders you powerless, find relief in knowing that if no one else obtains your powers, the one who did get them is the most deserving among all others."

Eric watched him smile at Jaycee. It curdled his stomach to see her smile back from within her pod.

"I had such high hopes for you, boy," Baron said, turning his attention to Eric. "Even so, the Boxworths have secured their place in the domination of common, primitive Homo sapiens. I owe each of you my thanks."

"Each of us?"

As the words exited his mouth, Eric noticed there was no microphone. He shivered at the thought of being silenced.

The pod directly across from Eric's unveiled a windowpane of its own. David stood inside.

"Dad!"

Eric's outburst had nowhere to go and bounced back into his ears like a sledgehammer.

David unleashed a silent scream. His drooping eyes looked like he combatted sedation. Baron tapped at his wrist gauntlet, allowing David's audio to stream into Eric's pod.

"Please! Barry, let him go, plea—!"

Drawled as they were, his words carried a feverish, panicky pitch.

Another tap to Baron's T-gauntlet cut off David's audio.

"Soon enough, the world and beyond shall be my stage," Baron boasted. "For now, it is my splendid privilege to perform for my private audience. Even though some won't be awake for it."

He thumbed behind him, motioning to the comatose Super Society members.

"And one shall never reawaken."

Muted from behind the glass, David begged, frantic as he shook his head. Eric desperately tried to decode what his father was yelling. "Don't," "look," and "her" were the only discernible words.

The shell to Eric's right uncovered its viewing panel. He looked back at his father—David wept. Eric felt the threat of weeping scratch behind his eyeballs. Eric knew not to, but he looked again to see who it stood inside the husk.

"Mom!"

Her closed eyes looked soft as if in a peaceful dream. Her milk-white skin stood out in the pod's dull gray interior. She stood, lifeless like a photograph, frozen in time. The overhead light streaked across the surface of her viewing glass.

"It was truly an honor to be the recipient of her otherworldly abilities," Baron said.

He sounded like a distorted thought echoing from underneath Eric's pounding eardrums. Eric's breaths came in sharp, little cuts. Cold sweat dripped down his forehead, pooling with the growing tears spilling from his eyes. Then, he no longer felt the thin edges of his lungs.

"I-I can't breathe," Eric sputtered. "I can't. I can't..."

He couldn't blink away the stinging tears from his eyelids. He wanted to see Jaycee, but at the same time, he didn't. He needed his father now more than ever but also needed David to leave and never come back.

"You inherited not only her gifts," Baron said, "but the opportunity to contribute to the next phase of human life."

Tiny electrical fires ignited in Eric's tendons, warning him that his weakness was starting. Eric's nerves tensed tighter the longer his body remained still. Being trapped in the tight space made it impossible to levitate even a millimeter. The pain burned, but the budding rage in his stomach bordered on volcanic.

"The time has come!" Baron declared. "David, if you will, please, follow the operational instructions displayed on your monitor."

Eric focused just enough to see his father shaking his head, "no."

"Fine," Baron said with a sigh. "I'll do it myself."

He twirled his fingers, causing a shift in the hum heard in Eric's pod's speakers.

"Warning! Operation sequence commenced. Unauthorized personnel prohibited. Warning!" a recording blasted.

David's voice recording on the announcement didn't make it easier for Eric's breath to return to him. Beyond the translucent tubing encircling the MegaCore's base, orange light emitted from hidden auxiliary lamps.

"Baron!" Valerie shouted, startling Baron.

The sight of Jaycee's mom brought Eric a measure of relief, which allowed him to focus. Baron did not look so welcoming.

Valerie stood aghast just outside the perimeter of the circle of stasis pods, barely within Eric's vision. Dressed in a light blue button-collar top with black slacks, Eric's teacher appeared to have come straight from school—and looked very out of place.

"Valerie?! What're you doing here?!" Baron said, growling.

"Seeing my ex-husband kidnap our daughter on the news had something to do with it! But I never expected..."

She gestured around the room.

"This."

Jaycee shook her head from behind her pod's panel.

"Media coverage was the intention," Baron said. "I meant, what are you doing right here?!"

"The light on the roof was a tipoff. Plus, I know my way around the building," she stated, snapping herself out of a confused daze. "Are you regretting those secret late-night tours you used to take me on?"

"The only thing I don't regret from our union is about to receive incredible power!"

He turned, his cape swinging behind him.

"Warning! Operation sequence commenced. Unauthorized personnel prohibited. Warning!"

Baron aimed his palm at Jaycee.

"Very well!" he yelled. "You shall bear witness to our lineage's ascension above the petty squabbles of mere mortals! Behold as our daughter rises to higher planes where she shall join divine company! I was saving that speech for Jaycee's graduation, but oh well!"

BANG!

The golden pod's door rattled and then launched from its reflective frame. It smashed into Baron, shooting him across the room like a shiny bullet, narrowly dodging Valerie. The *clunk* of his body slamming against the wall rang inside Eric's cell.

The sparkling edges of the central golden tube's doorframe jittered with mismatched grid patterns. Jaycee stepped out, clenching her metal-covered fists. The tech glistened, strapped across her school day outfit. The bionic arm braces connected down her sides glinted in the brilliant light, as did her belt attachment. She bolted from the exposed hatch.

"Jennifer?!"

"Not now, Mom!" Jaycee said, rushing over to Eric's pod.

He heard a shrill crunch—his door tore off. With Jaycee's strength-enhancing arm-casings, Jaycee tossed the thick metal slab down to the floor.

"You weren't the only one who brought their costume!" she said, tugging at her backpack strap.

Eric collapsed into her metal arms, one silver and the other gold, warm with power.

"Jaycee, it's her, it's her," he said, gasping for air. "I didn't save her. I-I-I-!"

"I swear I didn't know my dad would go this far!" Jaycee said, trying to get him to his feet. "I thought I knew what he was gonna do, but—I really messed this up, Eric!"

"My mom, Jaycee!" Eric spat out, sobbing. "She's... she's...!"

Stumbling, Eric reached over to his mother's tomb. Jaycee turned him to face her.

"Listen to me! I can take care of the others, but my dad won't stay down long! You're the only one who can stop him!"

"How?" he asked, grunting in pain from being stationary. "He's too strong!"

"Your mom may not have known she was passing down superpowers to you, but I know she'd be so proud of what you've done with them!"

"I haven't done anything! I've let so many people down," he said, casting his eyes down. "I let my mom down. Again."

"You wanna make it up to her? Go save everyone in this city. Go save the world!"

He stared at her as a tear spilled down his cheek. "What if I—?"

"Eric, you have done so much more than

anybody—or yourself—thought you could," Jaycee said. "You see what's hard, what's dangerous, and you do it anyway! You're a superhero!"

Eric wiped the welling tears away and sniffed.

"I wish saying I'm good enough didn't hurt so much."

Clang!

The golden door landed a few feet from them. Valerie hunched over, covering her head. Eric glanced over his shoulder to see Baron stomping toward them, wearing a crooked scowl across his lips. Eric's anger rose, as did his body. He propelled himself like a heat-seeking missile, colliding with Baron. They pushed each other skyward, taking their battle to the clouds.

Chapter Twenty: *NOSEDIVE*

ERIC

Eric rode out the storm, climbing onto the little golden T's on the shoulders of Baron's Truther costume. The man's black-gloved hands gripped Eric's blue leather shoulder straps, equally unrelenting while they breached the sky. The light from Pantheon Tower dropped beneath them, as did the rest of New St. Cloud City.

Don't let go. Don't let him win. Don't die.

The instructions Eric provided himself were simple enough, but the results varied in execution.

"I could've trained you!" Baron shouted. "You would've never conceived of unleashing your potential if not for me!"

"I did learn one thing from all of this!" Eric yelled back. "What goes up must come down!"

Eric launched a reinforced kneepad into Baron's gut. The fraction of a second the strike granted him was ample time for Eric to slither behind his aerial opponent. He grabbed hold of the ebony cape. Eric flipped over the textured material to its golden underside and wrapped Baron's head underneath.

He struggled, but Baron's disorientation was enough for Eric to steer him like a wild bull. Eric willed his body to spearhead back down while pulling the cloak over his enemy's face. They plunged deep enough to dodge the tops of skyscrapers. Flipping his arms up, Baron escaped his cape. An unsettling psionic force hurled Eric's body away, flinging him toward the glass wall of a building.

Pleeeease don't die!

Disoriented, Eric struggled to gain control as he torpedoed toward the glistening tower at breakneck speed. He closed his eyes, preparing for impact—and the worst. When the crash didn't come, Eric opened his eyes and found himself looking at his reflection in the window.

I did it!

He didn't have long to dwell on his accomplishment as he knew Baron shot straight toward him. Eric launched himself against the glass surface, but his aimless jettison sent him on a collision course with a nearby platform.

His dark blue boots skittered over the gravel surface of a high rise's broad deck. Eric's momentum stutter-stepped him past a freaked-out cleaning woman behind a window. His bobbing motion saw shaky images of the woman holding a spray bottle— it dropped as did her jaw. Eric skipped across the concrete.

"Sorry!" he blurted before gliding to the next the building.

Landing on the stone parapet of a shorter apartment complex, Eric took a breath and a look behind him. Steady in his pursuit, Baron burrowed closer. Several construction vehicles camped around an old, rundown hotel a few blocks ahead. Parked on a heap of rubble, a yellow truck with a long, erected crane positioned a big dust-covered wrecking ball that dangled from its thick metal chain. Eric raced to the demolition zone while taking quick mental notes of the surrounding structures and the civilian occupants.

"Way too many toys for Baron to play with," Eric muttered.

The workers and tenants from the neighboring establishments fled as Baron stormed the sky.

"And way too many casualties waiting to happen!"

Swooping over the debris-strewn ground, Eric swiped up a grooved rebar rod, launching it at Baron. A bright laser blasted from Baron's T-gauntlet, plucking the metal stick away.

"Hey, you need me alive!" Eric shouted while picking up a hefty chunk of concrete.

He chucked it at Baron, but another pulse of energy obliterated it.

"I got plenty of mileage with your mother being at death's door," Baron said. "So, I think you can stand to take a few bumps and bruises!"

Baron unloaded a rapid series of laser fire. Eric dodged and weaved, letting the shots sear into a parked jeep by the sidewalk a couple of yards away.

"I do love showing off," Baron said. "But I don't have all day."

"Big talk! Just wait until the army gets here!"

"Let them come," Baron said, sneering.

Baron gritted his teeth as he mentally propelled the dark brown two-seater jeep upward, catapulting it at Eric.

With a diagonal swoosh, Eric evaded the crashing car.

SMASH!

Steel crumpled, and glass splintered. Eric hunched

over to avoid jagged chips on the windshield as he reached into his pants pocket.

"You won't deny me my destiny!" Baron roared.

Fast-paced heavy metal music thundered from Eric's phone speaker. He held up his device while headbanging.

"Sorry, I can't hear you!" Eric yelled over a shredding guitar solo. "Can you repeat that?"

Baron's balled fists shook with frustration. He descended upon Eric.

"You won't deny me my destiny!"

"Thought that's what you said!" Eric quipped.

With lightning-quick reflexes, Eric unstrapped his metal backpack.

The phone dropped as Eric whacked Baron in the face with the pack. Eric swiped his phone, stopping the song's playback as Baron reeled in pain.

"I see that in order to finalize your defeat, I'm going to have to be more creative," Baron said, rubbing his sore jaw. "Drone Squadron Omega, activate!"

Eric slid on his backpack in mid-flight, zooming up and away. A flurry of white spherical drones dropped in front of him, forcing Eric to hit the brakes. He spiked above them only to see three larger drones lowering down. Blue dots swirled across the smooth, blank surfaces of the orbs. The bigger trio's dots blinked before opening their "faces."

Smooth slats of curved metal retracted, revealing a sextet of futuristic gun barrels. Each drone exposed its inner turrets. Blue light sparked from inside the short black cannons.

"Drones—return to base," Baron instructed. "Target: David Boxworth. Lethal force authorized."

"No!" Eric shouted.

"One way or the other," Baron said. "You're doing

what I want."

Circling back, Eric led the chase to where they started.

He could be bluffing about Dad, but I can't take that chance!

Eric zipped beyond the drones.

"Gotta get back to Pantheon Tower!" Eric said to himself while flying at full speed.

Baron flew, hot on his heels.

"I'd like it if I didn't have to knock you out, Eric!" Baron's voice yelled from behind him. "Honestly, I just want to see the look on your face! I want you to be fully aware when your essence is ripped away from you!"

After a quick trip, Pantheon Tower stood below Eric. The roof beamed, alive with light, attracting Eric like a moth to a flame.

Zap! Zap! Zap!

Neon yellow laser beams rained down on Eric. He covered his head with his forearms, unsure if the volley came from the drones or Baron's blasters. Another round of energy bolts forced Eric down. He dove far enough to reach the building's base.

After a shaky landing on the concrete, Eric looked up to see a large golden lightning bolt pointed to the sky in the middle of a round fountain. The drones emerged; their faces resealed. They formed a curved line of blank balls to restrict access to the marble steps leading to the building's entrance. Despite the horde of curious people on the street, no one could get near the Pantheon Solutions corporate art statue—the upward-pointing lightning bolt stood as an island unto itself. Chatter from the excited watchers entered Eric's ears.

The tower's rounded, smooth edges showcased the lower stories' view of the gigantic plant pipeline housed within. Farther up, a series of looping windows sparkled in the sunlight. It looked so different from the ground. Craning his neck, Eric gasped as the emanating light stream atop the building abruptly shut off.

"Stand back, citizens!" Baron said in his deep Truther voice. "I'll handle this!"

Eric rubbed his eyes with trembling hands. He blinked away the confusion as he stood on wobbly legs. The crowd erupted as Baron descended.

"Baron Maddox is Truther? No way!"

"Truther's gone crazy!"

"He's gonna kill Eric Icarus!"

"How do we know the kid isn't the evil one? How much do we know about him?"

Men, women, and children from all walks of life cheered or chanted—they weren't sure how to react. Grouped at the base of the tall tower and out into the street, it became clear that they were oblivious to the danger.

Baron stuck out each arm with quick, rigid bursts. His fingers extended like a claw. Eric felt a pulverizing force strike his torso, blasting him away. Jolted, an immaterial force shoved him into a structure across the street.

A wide opening. Cars. A parking garage? Shadows.

The landing's impact dashed away the notion of recognizing where he'd been hurled. The shock sent Eric into darkness.

JAYCEE

The mirrored elevator doors slid open, and Jaycee led her worried mother and a groggy David into a well-lit hallway.

"That thing is shut off, correct? Valerie asked as they rushed down the empty corridor. "Just because you turned out the light doesn't necessarily mean—"

"The MmmmegaCore is deactivated," David slurred.

The man looked like a business casual mental patient with his V-neck collar askew and shuffling in his dark gray slacks.

"But we shhhould still go back and at least install a password or something!"

"What kind of gas did you say were doused in?" Valerie asked.

The residential suite of Pantheon Tower had once been Jaycee's home, but at that moment, the orange-hued walls felt foreign. Nevertheless, she pushed herself to carry on like she was on any other mission as Powerhouse.

"Follow me!" Jaycee ordered. "We can take the super-secret superhero elevator!"

"What about your, eh, teammates?" Valerie said, struggling to keep up with her daughter's brisk pace. "And don't think we aren't going to discuss this whole you being a costumed crime-fighter thing! And I knew you were Powerhouse this entire time!"

"Did not."

"I'm your mother. Of course, I knew."

"Suuuure, Mom," Jaycee mocked as they turned a corner. "Look, I—I dunno what I can do for the other Super Society members right now!"

Frustrated, she shook her steel-encased fist.

"I should just rip off the doors to their pods like I did Eric's!" Jaycee said, seething. "I freed you that way easily enough, Mr. B!"

"Me and Eric were awake—barely, in my case,"

he reminded. "We dunno what the risks are if we prematurely remove them from whatever cryo-sleep deal they're in. Believe me—I wanna tear open all the pods, too."

"David, your, well, Eric's…" Valerie fumbled with her words, rattling Jaycee—hearing her mother so unsure was alien to her. "We will go back for Eliza."

"Just…" he said, trailing off into a haze. "Just gemme to Eric."

Down the hall, a familiar peppy blonde woman stepped out of an open door.

"Well, there you all are!" Chelsea said while walking to meet them. "I've been trying to hunt you down!"

She giggled.

"Uh, I don't think we want this lady looking for us," David muttered.

"We're smack dab in the middle of a bit of a sticky situation outside the tower," the gleeful woman said while holding them up midway through the hall. "Nothing that you should be alarmed about, but just as a precaution, it's best if I get you somewhere out of the way until this hullabaloo blows over!"

"Your concern for our wellbeing is appreciated," Valerie said. "But we'll be fine. We know the way out."

"Ooooo—afraid that's a no-can-do," Chelsea said, squinting in disappointment. "The present kerfuffle has the building under a complete lockdown."

She put her hand on Jaycee's metal-cased shoulder.

"It's standard protocol, sweetie," Chelsea stated, keeping her eyes on Valerie. "Trust me. It's much more secure here than your, ahem, current, temporary living arrangement."

"That does it!"

Valerie swung a right hook and decked the unsuspecting woman, knocking Chelsea to the floor.

"I've been wanting to do that!" Valerie said, exhaling a satisfied breath.

"Whoa, Mom!" Jaycee said, mouth agape. "Keep that up, and you'll need your own superhero costume!"

A mob of model employees strode up the corridor. The heavy sound of their unison footsteps echoed off the walls. Chiseled jaws, perfect hairdos, and stylish outfits stormed toward them.

"This is safer?!" David exclaimed as he began backing away.

"Detaining you three will be safer for Pantheon, yes, indeed!" the downed blonde said.

"I can take 'em!" Jaycee announced, raising her steel fists before she was tugged away by her mother.

With Valerie taking charge, Jaycee and David followed her back the way they came. Jaycee looked over her shoulder—Chelsea had joined her seemingly mindless brethren in the chase. Dahlia emerged from behind her, doubling their trouble.

"Who put the Terminator Twins in charge?" Jaycee remarked.

The prowling pack walked quiet yet steadfast. Jaycee ran past Valerie to have the first crack at whoever may have been waiting for them.

To her surprise, nothing or no one occupied the small junction of elevators. On the opposite wall hung a flat Pantheon Solutions lightning logo made of sleek silver metal, which Jaycee used to think was cool. That instant, however, she was not as big of a fan. Beyond the line of lifts led to another lengthy hallway. The trio stopped at the first in the row of golden doors. Their reflections appeared on the shiny surfaces.

"I'm gonna pull rank as the smartest guy here and

say it's a bad idea to take the elevators," David said, earning a peeved look from Valerie. "If they even work with the place going on lockdown."

A new batch of cover girls and hunky guys came marching down the opposite hall like it was a runway. They surrounded Jaycee, Valerie, and David.

"Anybody else getting a 'Night of the Living Dead' vibe?" David said.

The girl stepped in front of the adults and flexed her bionic muscles.

"If I gotta make these beautiful people a little less beautiful, then that's what I'll do!"

David and Valerie pressed their backs against the elevator doors as Jaycee stood in front of them, putting her cyber-dukes up. The hordes on either side grew in number. The models didn't run, but it wouldn't take long before they swarmed.

"There are too many of them!" Jaycee said, blinking like crazy. "Weeeee might be flushed."

"Quick! In here!" a voice called from a service door.

They followed the voice to a cracked opening across from them, splitting the big lightning logo. The door retracted deeper into the wall, revealing the entry like a magic trick.

"Not even I knew about this secret door!" Jaycee said while she, Valerie, and David headed straight for it.

The door slid shut. They found themselves in a short, dimly lit passage. As she crossed through, Jaycee's eyes bugged out at all the huge, white pipes winding up and down the deceptively large area. Access ladders connected to little walkways with matching red guardrails. Bulky generators and other metal units sat below wheels, levers, and control panels.

"Hurry now," Yvette urged.

Jaycee turned to see her, along with Melvin and Tiffany, standing by a massive tube on the other end of the floor.

"Guys!" Jaycee said, elated.

She raced over to her comrades. Jaycee went in to hug Yvette but remembered her overpowered arm braces and rescinded.

"How'd you escape?" Jaycee asked.

"Not sure," Yvette said, shrugging. "We woke up after you punched your way out of the ginormous gold pod."

"You must've short-circuited the system," Melvin added. "We were all still pretty out of it. When I saw the army of assistants going loco, I thought this has to be a dream!"

"How'd you know about the top-secret, um, boiler room?" David asked, eyeing his surroundings.

"Yvette's been here since she was, like, twelve," Tiffany said. "Not getting adopted has given her plenty of time to explore."

Jaycee joined Melvin in giving her an appalled look.

"What?" Tiffany said, flipping her fiery red hair back. "I didn't say it was a bad thing."

Whup! Whup! The herd outside pounded on the thick door.

"There isn't much time," Yvette said. "Over there is an exit."

She pointed to a stone-gray door on the other end of the room.

"It leads to the lower decks and outta here!"

"What are the odds we don't run into more model employees?" Valerie asked. "What on earth has possessed them?"

"Let's just say the Plant Pipeline isn't just for show," Yvette said, hanging her head as if ashamed of what she knew.

"Say what about the plants?" Jaycee asked, wiggling her head in confusion.

"Spores," Yvette clarified. "The plants are artificial, like just about everything around here. That overgrown pipe releases tiny little seeds or whatnot that control all the worker bees."

"That's ingenious!"

They all stared at David.

"Don't get me wrong," he said. "It's a diabolical, mad scientist thing to do, but, man, I wish I thought of it first!"

"Look, I was never supposed to find out," Yvette continued. "But it's true. If you're here long enough, you hear things. No one swore me to secrecy or anything; I just..."

Her eyes cast down, deep with sorrow.

"Jaycee, Ms. Cooper, everybody—I'm sorry I never said anything. I was scared. I just didn't want to seem ungrateful for your... For Mr. Maddox..."

Jaycee placed a hand on her shoulder, careful not to apply super-strength.

"Believe me," Jaycee said, shifting her eyes to her mother. "I know all about not wanting to let my dad down."

"Pantheon Tower is in emergency mode," Yvette said. "The hive will stop at nothing to contain what they're programmed to think is a threat."

"All the more reason we need to leave," Valerie said. "I hope you all understand that Baron will be exposed as the mad despot that he is."

Jaycee frowned at that, but she knew Valerie was right. Every bulb in the confined space lit, blinking red.

"Emergency lockdown has been initiated," a recording of Chelsea's pleasant-sounding voice announced. "All personnel and visitors, please report to the designated safe zones. Pantheon Solutions thanks you for your cooperation."

"Auto-locks will be engaged," Yvette said while rummaging through her pants pocket. "You're gonna need this to get anywhere."

She produced a white keycard with the Pantheon lightning logo printed on it.

"This'll override anything. It's how we got in here," Yvette said, handing it to Valerie. "Super Society field commander duties aren't without their perks."

David wore a perplexed look of slit eyes and scrunched lips.

"Man, I must've gotten sprayed with stronger knockout gas than you all," he said, puffing out a whistling sigh. "You guys bounced back quick. Makes sense, though, since you're Go-Go! And Extra! And Supercut!"

David pointed at each of them with a shaky finger and a dopey grin.

"Guess we shouldn't bother with the decoy holograms, huh?" Melvin said.

"Do you still hate superheroes, Mr. B?" Jaycee said.

"Let's just say I have a lot to make up for."

Whup! Whup! Whup! The banging on the access hatch was growing stronger and louder.

"This party is about to get a lot less private!" Tiffany said.

"We can hold them off!" Yvette said, motioning for the exit.

"What are you saying exactly?" Valerie asked.

"She's sayin'," Melvin said, "while y'all get

yerselves out of this building, the least we can do is give ya a head start!"

"No way!" Jaycee said. "We can't leave you!"

"We came here to suit up," Yvette said.

A slow smile formed on her face.

"And that's what we're gonna do!"

Valerie led Jaycee and David behind a heightened bulkhead. Yvette lined up with Tiffany and Melvin. They faced the closed entry. The increasing thumps forewarned it wouldn't stay that way for long.

"Masks on!" Yvette shouted.

Jaycee ran past a series of fire extinguishers and electrical boxes on her way. Valerie rushed ahead to insert the card into a slot above the door handle. A little green light flashed, and they hurried down a pale peach-colored set of stairs.

"We're going back for everybody as soon as we end all this!"

"We will, Jennifer," her mother assured. "No one could stop you if they tried, anyway."

They halted at a door with a label marking an entrance to an operations ring. Quick with the key, Valerie opened the door. A quartet of attacking models waited for them on the other side. David and Valerie pushed away a stunning redhead and her studly partner. Jaycee grabbed the remaining pair of women with long black hair and short skirts. She tossed them against the wall of the promenade.

Red alert lamps flickered along the curved ceiling, casting an eerie, blinking glow. While maintaining pouty lips, the ginger woman and hunky dude silently reached for Valerie and David. Jaycee watched as David and Valerie dodged the grabbing attempt and pulled the replicants over. David and Valerie used their momentum to send the models crashing into the hard, red-toned wall. The models slumped into unconsciousness.

"It's so predictably disturbing that these represent Baron's vision of perfection," Valerie bemoaned.

"Hey, he married you," David said. "I mean, there's a compliment in there somewhere, right?"

She sneered.

"Iss the knockout gas talking," he explained, shrugging.

"Emergency lockdown has been initiated," the recording replayed. "All personnel and visitors, please report to the designated safe zones. Pantheon Solutions thanks you for your cooperation."

Jaycee peered over the clear guardrail. The worker rings extended down ten stories. Smartly dressed hotties flooded every floor. The gargantuan plant pipeline stretched down the middle—a sight just a few hours before would've taken Jaycee's breath away. It morphed into a monolithic monument of her father's tyrannical ambition.

Clomp. Clomp. Clomp. Sounds of synchronistic footsteps warned of more opposition coming. A platoon of zombified staffers marched along the bend, zeroing in on them.

"Stairs!" Valerie commanded. "Back to the stairs!"

They made a beeline back for the stairwell, but a pair of fierce fashionistas burst through the door. Jaycee sent them back into the stairwell with a powered push. Echoing footsteps meant reinforcements were on the way.

"Over here!" David yelled.

Jaycee and Valerie ran behind David as he approached a docking station a few feet past the doorway from where they had entered. He stepped through the dock's open gate and into the ivory-colored cushioned seat of a golden transport. Valerie hesitated, sizing up the compact floating car.

"Can we trust anything automated?"

"Notta lotta choices right now, but thissa good plan," David spewed in a daze.

"I'm driving," Valerie said.

She helped Jaycee into the space between her and David. Valerie tapped at the touchpad on the dashboard. The gilded glider unhooked itself from the small port. The models and their hive-minded mates spilled out of the stairs. They teemed by the dock. As the shiny little cab zoomed off, lunging them over the transparent guard walls.

Jaycee's stomach lurched as her mother nosedived the hovercraft. Round drones zipped up—their usual tiny blue dots switched to an angry red as they collected into a wall in front of them. Valerie pressed the little forward icon on the console screen. They crashed through the ball-barricade, scattering the little white orbs.

"I must be hallucinating," David said. "'Cause it looks like an army of clones down there!"

Jaycee lifted herself to see above the dashboard—swathes of models covered the bottom floor.

"You aren't imagining things," Valerie confirmed.

Valerie pulled up, shifting Jaycee's organs once more. The trio's golden ride sat, hovering a few feet from the humongous flowery rod. On every ring surrounding them, gorgeous models crammed themselves up the railings.

A loud mechanical whirring erupted from far behind them. Sounds of giant rotors spinning grew louder. The reverberations of huge chunks of metal churning got closer. Large plates of silver-toned steel expanded in a grid, shielding the vast windows encircling the wide tower.

"Lockdown phase two initiated," Chelsea's recorded voice boomed over an array of speakers.

"We're trapped!" Valerie said, gasping.

The semicircle of metal coverings closed around them. Daylight narrowed with each guarded window. Jaycee looked straight ahead at the enormous column of glass.

"I have an idea!" she said. "Floor it, mom! Straight ahead!"

She clenched her steel fist. The knuckles on her golden hand beamed a bright green, indicating it maxed out at full power.

"I most certainly will not!" Valerie exclaimed. "The glass is too thick! This is preposterous!"

"Trust me, mom!' Jaycee said, readying her hands. "I've done this before! Well, I ran through a smaller window at a baseball game, but this is still pretty close!"

The big metal plates spread over more windows. Valerie held her breath and punched it. David gurgled out something profane as their flying car darted toward the glass. Jaycee climbed up and shot herself like a supercharged missile.

CRACK!

The window cut into dense shards of glass as Jaycee exploded through the pane. Behind her, Valerie and David slipped through the broken hole. Jaycee's momentum carried her out through the glass, but within seconds she slowed, drifting downward into gravity's clutches. The golden car swooped in, catching her right before she went into a freefall.

They veered right, riding away from the tower to safety. The neighboring skyscrapers blurred as they descended.

Plink! Clank! Skruuuuunch!

Pantheon Tower's exterior shielding strained to cover the splintered exit. A quick peek verified that the gaping hole stayed open.

"I just broke dad's building! O-M-Geeeeeeee!" Jaycee wailed as the transport plunged to the concrete.

Chapter Twenty-One: *ASCENSION*

JAYCEE

THE MASS OF PEOPLE CROWDING the base of Pantheon Tower poured into the street. As their craft landed on the road a safe distance away from the herd, Jaycee pushed up between David and Valerie. Cop cars blocked traffic, clearing the lane, but it left them without cover.

Baron levitated in front of the marble steps that led to the building's glistening facade. Sheets of metal stood behind the clear entrance doors. Shards of broken glass littered the entrance area. A semicircle of little white drones blocked the perimeter. None of the onlookers dared approach Baron.

"Jennifer," Valerie said without taking her eyes off the swarm of bystanders who gawked right back. "You may want to put on your mask."

"I don't think that's gonna matter," she said, removing shrapnel piece-by-piece from her busted arm casings.

Valerie gasped at the heap of mangled and dented power braces on the cab's hood. Valerie's eyes bulged at the twisted coils and bent coverings.

"Are you okay?!"

"I'm fine," Jaycee said with a frown. "Can't say the same for my strength-enhancers. The glass was too thick. I should've listened to you, mom."

"I'm very happy you disobeyed me," Valerie said. "This one and only time, though!"

Jaycee stuffed the scraps into her bookbag when Baron rose higher, sending a wave of shouts and murmuring throughout the audience. Beyond the ocean of onlookers, Jaycee saw news teams arriving behind police and other emergency vehicles. People ogled from open windows scaling as far as Jaycee could see of the next-door high rises. She never paid much mind to the neighboring office buildings—they were dull workplaces, unlike the majestic spire in the middle of the lengthy street. However, Jaycee became hyperaware of all the potential collateral damage at that moment.

She did a double take when she caught Kev's face in the crowd.

"Kev, what're you doing?" Jaycee whispered. "Get out of here!"

His anxious face matched those around him encamped by the tower's entrance. Baron stared at Jaycee from afar. His face twinged. Jaycee knew her father's angry faces, but this was outrage on steroids.

"Do you all see the destruction caused by lies?" he asked the congregation surrounding him.

"What're the odds he's not talking about us?" David asked, sliding down in the car seat.

"In the face of uncertainty, the people still flock to me," Baron yelled. "Despite the risk, the mystery has captured their imagination. It is not merely intrigue that gravitates these citizens here now. No, it is their pure adoration of me."

Jaycee followed Baron's eye line. He seemed to be speaking to someone in or around the stacked parking garage across the street.

"As Baron Maddox, I improved the quality of life itself, thus molding society," Baron went on. "As Truther, their beloved protector, I provided a symbol of hope while vanquishing the young, upstart betrayer."

Pat-pat-pat-PAT-PAT-PAT!

Rapid-fire footsteps grew louder. A streak of motion shot out from the gaping hole Jaycee had punched through. The blur raced ten stories down the front of Pantheon Tower. It snapped the mass's attention from Baron—his ruffling mustache indicated he wasn't happy about sharing the spotlight.

WHOOM!

A sonic shockwave shook the pavement. All but Baron lost their footing. Steadying herself on the cab's door, Jaycee flashed a big grin at her teammates. They landed in full gear a mere handful of feet away from the main doors. Had they touched down a yard to their right, they would've been skewered by the pointy lightning bolt statue sticking out from its round, babbling fountain base. The costumed trio clutched onto each other like a big, colorful ball. Applause spread like wildfire.

"Speaking of upstarts," Baron said, twisting to face them.

"Super Society reporting for duty," Yvette said in her all-business superhero voice as Go-Go.

Her dark curly hair wiggled as she settled, which couldn't have been easy with Tiffany and Melvin tucked under her arms.

"We know how to make an entrance, don't we?" Extra said, struggling to compose herself on wobbly legs. "Which was uber-impressive considering how much, ahem, extra weight Go-Go had to carry."

She straightened her Extra mask and then nodded to Melvin, who pulled up the trousers of his Supercut uniform.

"Yer a riot," he said, leaning over with his hands on his knees.

He heaved, taking in as much air as he could.

"How many of you did it take to come up with that, Extra?" Supercut asked with a curled lip.

"Why don't you tell all these people the truth, Truther?" Go-Go yelled. "Or are we not doing the secret identity thing anymore?"

"Secret identities," Baron bellowed as if annoyed at the notion.

He buoyed in place with a wall of concerned faces behind him.

"Protected, hidden lives. I dedicated my life to unraveling mysteries, but I, too, concealed who I really am. When people think of me, they think of honesty. But I'm just a liar like all of you."

Jaycee climbed onto the hood of the parked craft to get a better vantage. She peered over the river of bodies in front of them.

"I need to join them. I have to help my team!"

"Get down! He'll see you!" David hissed.

The bunched-up people kept their distance from the confrontation but stirred more and more.

"Take your masks off!" a belligerent voice hollered from the crowd.

"There's no need for that," Baron said. "My files containing the Society's real names are encrypted, so you needn't worry about anyone leaking the info. Soon enough, that data will be pointless anyway."

"Eric, you can show yourself any time now..." Jaycee said under her breath.

Her teammates stood on one side by the building entrance. Baron floated across from them by the edge of the street—while being cheered on by a massive audience. The standoff staged itself like a pay-per-view bout. The spacious entrance area made for a perfect battleground: the ivory-colored steps leading up to the wide white-top walkway allowed ample room for a fight. The news cameras ensured they would appear on screens everywhere.

I should be in the arena, not in the cheap seats! Jaycee thought.

"Let's talk about usefulness," Baron said, pointing at the threesome. "Specifically yours."

Extra and Supercut stepped forward, but Go-Go sped in front of them. She held out her steel-braced arm to still them.

"I am the arbiter of fate," Baron declared. "And I deem you unworthy."

"Excuse me?" Extra blurted. "We got axed because you decided to free the mustache? Unreal! Even after we all agreed to your stupid 'no superhero social media rule.' I sacrificed so many potential followers because of you!"

"Your willingness to serve was why you were selected to begin with."

"Is everybody hearing this?" Go-Go said to the crowd. "We were just puppets to you?!"

"You were seekers, and as such, you performed your duties with exemplary skill. Your search bore no fruit, and though that is no fault of your own, your roles are no longer required."

"Searching?" Supercut asked. "You mean looking for bad guys?"

"You weren't aware of it, but every patrol, every vanquished wrongdoer, was a part of an ongoing quest to discover the existence of superior humans."

Baron flew forward and then quickly stopped. Jaycee's heart skipped a beat.

"I can't just sit on the sidelines!" she said, tapping her sneaker on the hood.

Valerie hoisted herself up onto the dashboard.

"We should be getting as far away from here as possible!" Valerie insisted. "He isn't focused on us—that's our advantage to leave!"

"Go if you want," Jaycee said. "But I'm not wasting the element of surprise."

She took off, dodging Valerie's outstretched arm. She plowed through the crowd, navigating between bodies like a pinball. Her nostrils flared at the musty mix of cologne, perfume, and sweat. Pushing her way closer to the front of the pack, Jaycee planted her feet to secure her ringside view.

Baron flung his cape as he turned to face the mass. Across from Jaycee's spot, police burrowed their way through to the frontline, barking orders for everyone to keep back.

"You are witnessing guided evolution!" Baron shouted. "Now that I've acquired the means to harness true power, I am finally ready to reshape existence as we know it!"

"Okay, you're the baddest man in the land; that's cool," Go-Go said.

She motioned for Extra and Supercut to stay behind her.

"But you just made the villain list. And everybody knows what the Super Society does to villains."

"The great charade is over," Baron announced.

News helicopters and various drones lowered, clouding the sky.

"I was not born with these abilities," Baron

stated. "But now that I possess them, I am the only one fit to judge who may join me in realizing a greater civilization—a true super society."

"Get ready to attack on my mark!" Go-Go commanded.

"Don't care what ya did to yerself, bud," Supercut grumbled, popping his claws. "Yer goin' down!"

He charged after Baron, slicing the air in a berserker rage.

"Supercut, stop!" Go-Go pleaded, barely heard over the raucous roars from the audience.

Go-Go took a kneeling stance, ready to run. Baron lifted his arm. Thick, jagged pieces of glass arose with it, enveloping her.

"Too slow, Go-Go," Baron said with a smirk.

More sharp shards formed, trapping the speedster within a spherical glass cell. Light glinted from the transparent, loose daggers. Go-Go kept her limbs close, unwilling to risk being cut by the uneven edges of the fragments swirling around her.

Extra ran to the opposite side of Baron.

Tiffany is flanking the bad guy, just like we've practiced, Jaycee thought. *Guess she paid attention in at least a few training sessions.*

Supercut halted underneath Baron. He gestured with his claws for Baron to come down to his level.

"Unbelievable as it seems," Baron said, looking down his nose at the boy. "You all pose as potential opposition for me. Therefore, you must be eliminated."

"Eliminate this, big man!" the hairy hero said, swiping at the bottom of Baron's black boots.

"You ever wonder why I gave you such useless equipment? Did you ever stop and think that I legitimately thought the way to fight crime is with little finger-blades?"

Don't listen to him, Melvin! Jaycee thought as she squeezed through a pair of businesswomen's large tote bags.

She stopped cold when a white drone flew in front of her. It was the last in the barricade of balls that stretched along the bend, helping to keep the crowd at bay. Red dots popped up on the orb before her. Jaycee stiffened, unsure of her next move.

The drone floated closer. Its red dots began blinking. Darting her eyes, Jaycee spotted the pair of big brown leather bags behind her. Snatching them wasn't as quick as she thought.

Are they packing concrete computers in these things?!

Jaycee pulled the hefty bags together with their owners still attached, striking the drone. The ball wiggled in place—the red dots scrambled over its face, then faded and fell. The round drone rolled into the crowd. The startled women looked like they were going to jump out of their pantsuits.

"Sorry, ladies!" Jaycee said, dashing off.

Keeping a shaky eye on the action as she ran, Jaycee could tell Baron's words had cut deep into Melvin. He lowered his claws, visibly dejected. Jaycee shook her head but pressed on, not letting the distraction go to waste.

"Hold on, Yvette," she said to herself, hoofing it to the tower's main entrance. "I'm coming!"

"Supercut!" Extra called out from the other side of Baron.

The boy simply gazed at his finger-blades as if seeing them for the first time.

"Look at yourself," Baron said. "You'd have to make a serious upgrade just to be called cannon fodder. But, still, that's what you are."

"Hey, father of the year," Extra said, marching up to him. "I'm the only one allowed to roast Supercut like that!"

She tapped a button on the pink button in the middle of the metal "X" across her chest. Copies of herself materialized around her.

"One tiny nanite won't do much..." Extra said, kneeling to jab the ground.

Her mirror-image projections' fists phased through the painted pavement.

"...but a swarm of them in each fist packs a punch."

She struck again, and the duplicates' fists pounded the ground with a solid *pang*.

"Wanna know what ten at that same time feels like?"

In unison, the duplicated divas raised their orange-gloved fists. Applause and hollering surged from the audience.

They should've sold tickets! Jaycee thought as she raced her way up.

"I know all about the illusion of 'hard light,'" Baron said. "I invented it, didn't I? I created all of your little toys!"

Extra jumped, and her twins followed.

"Don't!" Go-Go warned from within her glass cage.

The Extras leaped, but with a wave of Baron's arm, the identical girls careened through the air. The doubles disappeared, leaving the real Extra to crash solo onto the ground next to the fountain.

"No!" Supercut shouted.

He swiped his blades at Baron, but his stubby arms could not reach. Baron rolled his eyes at the stocky boy's blind attack. With a flick of his wrist, an invisible force hurled Supercut across the ground. He crashed down near Go-Go.

Adrenaline carried Jaycee past the wall of people and up the stairs to the tower's base. The shards around Go-Go spiked like a pulsating muscle, causing Jaycee to skid to a halt.

"Jaycee!" Go-Go said, shocked. "Get out of here!"

"Dad!" Jaycee screamed. "This whole taking over the world thing has got to stop!"

Baron patted the air, trying in vain to calm the crowd's "oohing" and "aahing."

"Sweetheart, you should stop seeing this as a 'taking over the world' thing and more of an 'I'm doing humanity a favor' thing."

"How can you do this to the team?!" Jaycee yelled. "You practically raised them as your own!"

"Out of necessity. It's not my fault that no one wanted to adopt them."

Through the distorted flickering of the floating glass, Jaycee could see Go-Go's jaw drop. A second later, she stiffened her lips. Even under a mask and behind a razor-sharp barrier, it was clear Go-Go was done hiding.

"Truther—Mr. Maddox!" Go-Go shouted. "As long as we're just letting it all hang out, no matter how badly I wanted to impress you, you're not my father. But my teammates—the Super Society—they're my family!"

A furious howl erupted from her lungs as she burst through the glass. Jaycee shielded her face from the exploding slivers. Go-Go fired herself at Baron like a cannonball.

"Think of your family," Baron said.

Go-Go stopped cold underneath Baron. Jaycee could only see Go-Go's back, but the bleeding scars on her arms were evident. Jaycee blinked in disbelief. The crowd's discordant murmuring echoed her confusion. Extra and Supercut's levitating bodies answered why the speedster hit the brakes. Go-Go looked back, heaving up and down with each heavy breath.

"Don't hurt them!" Jaycee warned. "I may not have any armor on, but I won't sit back and let you do this!"

"Armor? I am beyond reliance on such contraptions," Baron said. "Gadgets have their place, though—my place. I am reclaiming my property."

Baron closed his fingers like he was squeezing blood from a torn-out heart and yanked back without looking. The metal attachments lining Go-Go's costume ripped away. An invisible hand threw the braces by the doors behind Jaycee. Go-Go stumbled onto her knees with the sleeves and leggings of her tunic shredded— save for her mask.

Baron clenched his fist. The steel casings around Supercut's fingers flew off with no mercy shown to the bones they had encased. Supercut shrieked in agony as his index fingers cracked and bent in unnatural angles under his wrinkled gloves. He fell to his back. A flick of Baron's wrist tossed the daggers over to the main entrance doors.

Extra yelped as her armor stripped itself from her. Piece by piece, the steel flew off, collecting itself with the scrap heap. The redhead tumbled, then rolled over in a lifeless slump.

Extra and Supercut lay unconscious on either side of Jaycee. Ahead, Go-Go fell flat on her back. Jaycee waited for the strategies to appear to her. No actions played out in her mind, nor did any flashes of inspiration come. Despite the volume of people present, Jaycee felt like it was just her and her father, staring each other down.

"Jaycee, I'm not mad," Baron said. "Just disappointed."

Baron scooped up air, pulling at nothing. The

alarmed crowd ignored the cops' demands for order.

"A warm, friendly face will give these people solace," Baron said. "Few, if any here, will join my elite race of superiors. Do not worry, though; I shall ease their passing."

He widened his grin.

"I just flash a smile, and they know I bring them respite from terror."

Crouching over Supercut, Jaycee inspected his fingers.

"These are some nasty-looking sprains! You're lucky nothing's broken!"

"I don't feel very lucky," he said, eyes glazed on the precipice of passing out.

Jaycee rushed to Extra. She remained unconscious.

"Not good," Jaycee said. "She's too exposed!"

"I'll take care of her," Supercut said, crawling over.

Jaycee shook her head, but he wasn't stopping.

"Just go check on Go-Go!" Supercut said.

Without hesitation, Jaycee took off. Go-Go leaned on her elbow, grimacing. Her scratched arms bled on the ivory-colored ground. She, like the crowd in front of her, focused on Baron. Onlookers formed a curious barricade separating Jaycee from her floating father. Baron gestured, and a few remaining security orbs buzzed off. Baron stood over the people, hovering above the middle of the street.

"When an animal bares its fangs," Baron yelled, "it's bracing for a fight, growling out a warning."

Go-Go waved for Jaycee to stay back, but she sped ahead regardless. Jaycee burrowed her way through the thicket of people, but without her arm attachments, she could no longer simply brush them aside.

"Present yourself, boy!" Baron demanded, further

bewildering Jaycee as to who he was referring to. "Display for the people if you'll smile and take it or reveal just how much of a wounded creature you really are."

Squeezing through rubberneckers, Jaycee made it to the other end.

"Well, come on, then, Mr. Icarus," Baron said, low and with a snarl. "Show me your teeth!"

The crowd shouted in shock.

"Whoa!"

"It's him!"

"I thought he was dead!"

Eric Icarus emerged from the wide, darkened entrance of the parking garage. His blue costume appeared intact, but his eyes were closed. As his body lifted past the outer levels of the white-painted parking structure, his messy hair wavered in the breeze.

"Eric!" Jaycee called out, unwittingly joining a chorus of concerned voices.

The boy hung limp as Baron willed Eric to lay facedown on a sidewalk in the middle of the boisterous audience. Slowly, Eric's limbs flailed like he was drowning in molasses. The excited crowd gave space and did not attempt to touch him, seemingly at Baron's unspoken command. Even the drones moved back.

"I knew you were weak, boy," Baron said, floating above him from a short distance. "But this is getting embarrassing."

Eric trembled, his chest barely leaving the concrete.

"What are you doing...?" Baron said, gazing at his hands, looking utterly confused and visibly angry.

Fixated on Eric's struggle, Baron didn't appear to notice Jaycee standing a dozen feet away in the crowd. The sight of Baron terrified her. His manic eyes, his wild glower—it was a side of him she had never seen before, a side he somehow managed to hide from the world.

Eric's muscles pulled tight, with a vein throbbing on his forehead. His body lifted slightly, then again, higher, until he floated several feet up.

"Come on, Eric," Jaycee whispered.

Eric lowered his head as his body lifted. Parking meters on the sidewalk behind him wiggled. To Eric's right, a forest green-coated metal waste container shook. Across the street, at the tower's base, the glass shards rose as a cloud of shimmering fragments.

The scene quieted for just a moment.

Eric's body lifted higher—his face grimaced, a mask of sudden determination. Jaycee had never seen him this way. He hovered across from Baron. She watched as their eyes met like two prizefighters in the final, exhausting round.

"At last, we witness the ascension of Eric Icarus," Baron said with an approving nod. "Congratulations on unlocking this achievement. Pity, it's too little, too late!"

An intangible vice clamped into Jaycee's ribs. A mental force drew her skyward, raising her up, up, and higher still. She looked down to the street below. Gasps and shouts erupted from underneath her as dozens of fingers and cameras pointed in her direction. Jaycee had no idea where David and Valerie were, but their absence relieved her—they weren't here to join in the punishment.

"Eric, your insurrection has shown you to be beyond untrustworthy," Baron yelled.

Dark veins coursed down Baron's forehead like erratic spiderwebs.

"But how fortuitous it is to know," Baron said,

"you'll be bequeathing your full power to Jaycee!"

Her glimpses of Eric came in strobing flashes. From what Jaycee could tell, Eric looked poised to act but would not—or perhaps could not. The invisible clamp tightened its crushing grip around her ribs. Jaycee grunted—the pain was like nothing she'd ever felt. What added to the torment was that her father afflicted it.

"I made you what I needed you to be!" Baron shouted. "You're not a real hero! Tell me this, boy— what is proving me wrong worth to you?! Is it worth her?!"

A million little hands grabbed Jaycee's insides. She screamed—a sickly, shrill sound she didn't know she could make. Yet, despite it all, she kept her eyes open.

The air around her seemed to vibrate. At first, Jaycee thought it was her father's doing, but Baron's concentration appeared to be teetering, and he looked around in wonder.

Jaycee saw it first, but only because of her aerial view. Centered in the fountain in front of Pantheon Tower, the ten-foot golden lightning bolt wiggled. It reminded Jaycee of a loose tooth at the cusp of freedom.

Finally, her father took notice.

SNAP!

Something yanked the bolt from its circular metal base—it ejected itself from the spilling fountain. It shot upward then straight into Baron's back.

As her father hurled her across the street, Jaycee fell.

"Dad!" Jaycee yelled.

An unseen cloud softened her landing. She hoped that her father provided the padding—or that he somehow protected himself in the same way.

No, no, no! Please be alive. Please be alright!
When she touched down, Jaycee immediately took off into a sprint, desperate to get to her father. Scattered chatter from the onlookers rattled in her ears.

Eric lowered to the foot of the tall opening of the parking garage. He floated above where Baron lay prone with his cape tangled and strewn by his side. Eric's chest heaved with deep breaths as he wordlessly raised his right arm—the lightning bolt rose with it.

"I can't believe it," Jaycee said. "Eric Boxworth can move things with his mind!"

"It's Eric Icarus," he said back with a smile, which startled her—she didn't think he'd be able to hear her.

Crowd members backed away as Eric flew forward a short distance to be closer to Baron. He lay facedown on the road. With a mental command, Eric aimed the pointy end of the bolt at Baron. Eric's gloved hand constricted into a fist. Lividity curled his lips and creased his brow.

Jaycee ran toward Eric.

"Don't do it, Eric!" Jaycee pleaded.

He punched down, striking the bolt down toward Baron. Jaycee stumbled as she felt the air leave her body.

The pointed sculpture hit the pavement with a thunderous crash and then toppled over, away from Baron's unmoving frame. Jaycee regained her footing and saw that Eric apparently guided the statue away from her father, sparing him. Eric descended to his former leader. After staring down at the broken Baron for what felt like an eternity, Eric finally looked up. Apologetic sadness washed over the anger on his face.

The onlookers crowded back around; some even applauded, though most buzzed with baffled murmuring. Jaycee ignored the background sounds of first responders holding back reporters and civilians. She took cautious steps forward. Drones zipped over her head.

"Eric, I—"

Before she could get the words out, Baron sprang to his feet. A psionic forced shoved cops and citizens. Baron punched the air, pushing Eric over Jaycee's head. Baron's fist loosened, then motioned for something to his right to come. Jaycee felt herself stumble backward into a cluster of well-dressed businessmen. Something stirred beyond the crowd's freaked-out faces.

Now would be a good time for the Super Society to rally, she thought, hoping her friends were coming in like the calvary.

In an instant, she discovered her wish had only half come true.

Metal apparatuses extended and spun en route to Baron's floating frame. The cybernetic instruments formed into their distinctive shapes: Go-Go's speed-enhancing silver leg braces snapped over Baron's thighs and shins. Supercut's chrome sheathes wrapped around his forearms, settling over the T-gauntlets. Extra's X-shaped chest piece conformed to his size. Baron twitched as the machines assimilated and linked together as a gestalt over his Truther costume.

"I could end all this just by a flick of my wrist," Baron said. "But I like having options."

Chapter Twenty-Two: *RISE*

ERIC

BARON ADORNED HIMSELF IN THE Super Society's bones, leaving a sick feeling twisting in Eric's gut. Pinkish light flashed from the emblem on the Extra chest armor. A dozen floating Baron duplicates popped up, surrounding Eric. The copies moved behind and in front of the original, camouflaging what or who was real. Sirens wailed in the distance.

"Hear that? More police are coming to take you away!" Eric said. "I can't promise I'll visit you in prison, but I'll be sure to write!"

"If the cops are coming, then I'll need more of me to sign autographs!"

A plethora of doubles appeared at a rapid pace, blocking Eric's view. The synchronous smiles on the many Barons seemed welcoming of the arriving authorities.

"Exploiting this city's love of superheroes is the whole point of the costumes," the Baron horde said all at once. "Eric, I know this is your 'year one,' but come on, get your head in the game!"

Eric swung at the encroaching replicates, but their

holographic images merely flickered. Fists struck from all around, jabbing Eric's ribs and stomach. He wheezed from the pain as the full circle assault jerked him around. For intangible projections, the Baron holograms hit hard.

The legion of twins swung their arms down as one, pulling Eric with them.

"Recess is over!" they shouted in hideous harmony. "You still have work to do!"

Baron raised his cyber-enhancer-laced arms like a bear about to maul its prey. The projections spread their arms, echoing each other like an infinite void. Synapses in Eric's brain ordered him to move, but a sudden impact shook his senses before the electrical signals could process.

The hologram doubles vanished, replaced by a world of shapeless blurs. Streetlights became green trails, people rendered into ghostly afterimages, and cars appeared as amorphous blobs. Pure speed yanked Eric's organs and fibers without mercy. Baron's pumping legs vibrated Eric's torso like an automatic earthquake. Eric shoved, but the might of the man's strength pulled him in face-to-face. At top speed, they pushed and pulled like high-powered magnets.

"Your little growth spurt doesn't make you stronger than me!" Baron spat out.

Up way too close and personal, Eric got a vivid look at how reddened Baron's face had become. Pulsating black veins cracked across his sweaty skin. It looked like they were about to explode.

"You're sick!" Eric said. "I don't think you can handle the power! It wasn't meant for you!"

As he shifted their path, cutting through the wind, Baron's will overpowered Eric's. Baron countered everything Eric tried to think into happening.

Navigating around buildings in milliseconds and zooming over streets, they sped into a familiar area. Eric punched at Baron's chest. Unfazed, Baron faced forward.

A blink later, Baron released Eric from the incalculably fast ride.

"The only problem with the super-speed armor is that it's ground-based," a singular Baron said. "I'll have to reconfigure that for flying."

Eric collapsed onto the street. His lungs threatened to hyperventilate upon seeing the Boxworth Building dead ahead.

"You know what I'm starting to realize, Eric?! When I first blew a hole through your home, I should've finished the job!"

"Oh, no-no-no-no!" Eric sputtered.

"Oh, yes!" Baron said with a sinister laugh.

The building's boxy pale concrete frame clashed with the near-black metal square panels covering the first floor's side. The metal patches did little to conceal the jagged edges of the damage from the Cybertooth battle—an event that felt like it happened a lifetime ago. As he found his footing on the sidewalk, Eric noticed the light traffic on the road. Intermittent cars and trucks passed, but the abrupt appearance of a duo of unmasked superheroes turned the heads of passersby.

"Do you want the narrative to be that you surrendered willingly...?" Baron asked.

Fikt!

Eric's eyebrows perked at the sight of Supercut's signature finger blade popping out from the index finger of Baron's right hand.

"Or the other way?" Baron said.

The razor-sharp metal edge inched to the sky-blue up arrow symbol in the middle of Eric's chest straps.

Still shaky from the quick trip, Eric's spaghetti legs buckled.

"I don't feel so hot!" he blurted.

Eric put his hands on his stomach and took an uneven step closer to Baron.

"Eh? What are you—?" Baron asked.

"I think I'm gonna barf!"

Eric lunged forward with full cheeks. Baron recoiled, turning his head to avoid a potential puke splash. Eric grabbed the man's arm and pushed up, sending the blade across Baron's face.

"Yeeeowwwwwarrgh!" Baron yelped in agony, pushing Eric off.

Stumbling backward, Eric showed no sign of losing his lunch. Baron bent over, grunted, and clutched his face. Silence washed over the onlookers. Heavy heaving came from the hunching man. It could've been five seconds or five minutes; time had abandoned them for the moment.

Baron whipped his cape up in a dramatic wave, unveiling a crimson streak smeared across his otherwise bare upper lip.

"My mustache!"

His livid cry sent shudders throughout the growing audience, including Eric. Like a battering ram, Baron collided with Eric.

CRASH!

Eric smashed through the Boxworth Building wall, hitting the floor hard. He had put up a telekinetic cushion to lessen the impact, but the hyper-charged entry left Eric wobbly. With his heart racing, and his periphery a jumbled mess, Eric blinked his way back to reality.

It had been weeks since he'd been back home— it looked relatively the same save for knocked-over workstations and carts. Sunlight flowed through the re-opened wall, spreading brightness over the spacious operations floor of the Boxworth residence. Outside the gouged gap, the large steel pieces had been tossed like they were made of tin. The metal sheets lay flat on the edge of the sidewalk.

Mr. Maddox must've moved the panels just in time, Eric thought, scanning the room. *But where is he?*

Hacking coughs came from behind Eric. He turned and saw Baron hovering in front of the original MegaCore. Though the engine dwarfed in size compared to its successor, it still took up most of the colossal stage it sat on. Its domed top stood still, dull from inactivity.

"Such humble beginnings," Baron grumbled.

Spastic convulsions crawled across his body. He coughed once more, this time with a stomach-turning watery sound.

Eric levitated but did not match Baron's height.

"What're we doing here, Mr. Maddox? You want the grand tour?"

"I have very little interest in your quaint domain," he rasped. "I only wish to destroy it."

Eric floated forward but stopped at Baron's outstretched hand.

"I do not make excuses for my grandiose nature," Baron said. "Saying that, this still could've been a straightforward exchange. Then you went and proved yourself to be quite the threat. That—that, you insufferable twit—made me mad."

Tools around Eric floated. Powered-down drones rose.

"Now, I will take everything away from you. I will make you hurt, Mr. Icarus."

Sparks exploded from a nearby terminal. Cords dangling from the ceiling whipped like violent snakes. A bank of monitors hurled backward, breaking as the screens smacked into a corner. Clunky drones crashed into each other.

The Ultranaut warsuit lifted like a corpse rising from the grave from behind a pile of rubble and loose machinery parts.

"I'm sure you'd agree that Ultranaut stay here, at your home," Baron said. "It was no trouble transporting it. Though calling it anything but Dreadnaught will never feel right."

The hollow armor positioned itself behind Baron, then rose above him. The metal husk hovered lifelessly, befitting its deathly symbolism.

"Poetic, no?" Baron said through his bloody grin. "The same instrument of your mother's devastation is present for your demise."

Through welling tears, Eric glared at Ultranaut. It hung, staring back like an abyss. Motionless, it emanated sorrow like the grim reminder of doom it was. Baron laughed as Eric looked down.

Eric stretched his fingers out like claws. He closed his eyes.

"The Boxworth Building will be removed like the stain it is, but do not fret," Baron said. "You will find great comfort in the pod I have waiting for you back at Pantheon Tower!"

"Shut up for a second!"

"What?!"

"I have to, like, concentrate," Eric said, wiggling his fingers. "I have to kind of mentally search for a switch, a button to push telekinetically, or something to..."

"Wait," Baron said, cocking an eyebrow. "You're

not doing what I think you're doing, are you?"

"Depends..." Eric said, closing his hand into a fist. "Is it this?"

Ultranaut's chartreuse helmet lit up with activation. Its arm jerked up, aiming a wrist-mounted cannon at Baron. As Baron turned, laser fire blasted him in the chest.

"Gahhhh!" he screamed as he slammed face-first to the floor.

Eric collapsed as his concentration broke, severing his telekinetic control over Ultranaut. The armor crashed onto the floor behind Baron with a loud *chank*! Slow to get up, Eric heaved in the air as he stared at the fallen warsuit. He wiped away a tear, scowling. Manipulating the robot that killed his mother sickened him. Eric puffed his cheeks, holding back bile for real this time.

Even not physically touching that thing is still horrible, he thought. *It's over, though... At least it's done.*

A rumbling quaked throughout the vast room. The shaking grew more intense. The wailing whine of metal support beams twisting, and bending sliced like nails on a chalkboard. The foundation broke down all around them.

Baron levitated to his feet. Blood ran down his face and onto the golden T on his chest.

"Innovative to the bitter end," Baron said, spitting blood. "Your mother would be proud."

Eric balled his fists and hunched over, readying to plow into Baron.

"Brute force?" Baron asked between coughs. "Have you learned nothing from this experience?! I mean, seriously! You've gained new powers, I'm wrecking your home, and your plan is what exactly? Knock me over?"

"Well…"

"And not even with a statue this time? Which, in case you forgot, I got up from! The Ultranaut thing was a nice attempt, but even that wasn't good enough. No, your big idea is to send your tiny knuckles and try to give me a teeny, little punch? Egad, boy, what is the strategy here?"

"My strategy is that I really hope this works!" Eric said. "BRAIN! Activate the MegaCore!"

The translucent dome lit up, emitting a deep hum. The tubing wrapped around the thick base flashed to life with pulsating purple-blue energy. The brightness beamed into a big, brilliant white spotlight. The hum grew into a roar.

"This pathetic prototype is a toy compared to my new and improved model!" Baron shouted over the *whoom-whoom* beats of the MegaCore's rhythmic hum. "What could you possibly hope to accomplish by turning it on—?!"

Baron's chest sunk into itself, and his arching back crumpled his body into a fetal position. He gurgled out an unintelligible string of syllables. Eric backed away, exiting the building through the broken gape. Hurtling heavy crates, keyboards, and other chunks of equipment filled the interior of the base level of the Boxworth Building. The objects spiraled like a furious hurricane.

A guttural scream erupted from inside. Eric flew over the neighboring trees and other shrubberies to view the surge from a safer distance. Light flickered out of the cave-like entrance like a wild rave. The engine's booming waved through Eric's chest like a bombastic bass groove. The illumination spread into a vast, singular flash. Eric covered his eyes.

BOOM!

The humming stopped. The light faded. Falling devices and other things *clanked* onto the floor. Tenants from nearby buildings called out, but their voices grew fainter and fainter.

JAYCEE

"Can't this thing go any faster?!" Jaycee asked, tapping the dashboard monitor for anything that would increase their acceleration.

Their head start had put them in front of the mob of curious pedestrians, and the bottlenecking four-lane traffic stalled any motorized followers. Still, the golden cab moved much too slowly for Jaycee's liking.

"From what I can tell, this thing was only meant for very short-range transport," David said, pecking at the console monitor. "It's a fancy shuttle designed to make you feel poor, not a getaway car!"

Facing the rear, Jaycee saw a swarm of people fighting to get a glimpse of the chaos headed in their direction.

"They're gaining on us!"

"Jennifer," Valerie said, turning around in the front seat to scan Jaycee, looking for any imperfection. "You have to rest!"

"I'm fine, Mom! Really!"

"I don't care what new powers he has," Valerie said. "I'm going to kill—!"

"No!" David screamed.

He jammed the breaks, bringing them to a haphazard halt. For a moment, he simply sat, blinking, his mouth slightly ajar. The east-facing wall of the Boxworth Building bore a giant gash. Computer parts, drone shells, and several handheld devices littered the nearby grassy area—along with the large steel sidings which had been used as temporary barricades.

Valerie reached, resting a hand on his shoulder. David shrugged it off, opening the door and stepping out into destruction. Jaycee and Valerie exited the vehicle and approached the gaping hole but kept their distance.

"Oh, come on!" David yelled, falling to his knees.

He grabbed a rock off the ground, launching it at the damaged building. From inside, shadows stirred.

"Uh, Mr. Boxworth," Jaycee said, eyeing the creeping motion. "You may wanna back up..."

A darkened form stepped into the light.

"Dad," Jaycee whispered.

Baron shambled out and bent over, his cloak hiding his body. With his head down, Baron took stuttered steps. David crab-walked away before making an awkward transition to his feet.

Baron's frail form shook, and he seemed to have aged several decades in the span of what must have been an hour if that long. Seeing her father so weak jarred Jaycee.

"Baron, what...?" Valerie started to ask, but her voice trailed off as though lost.

"The MegaCore was active," David stated while peering into the operations floor. "I can tell—I—I can see the data on a couple of screens in there, well, cracked screens, but, but—"

A trembling hand shot up from under Baron's cape. He straightened his posture, revealing his bloodied and pale face. His widened eyes bore a maniacal glare, but it looked like life had been drained from him.

Baron coughed, spraying a red mist from his mouth. Blood seeped into the crevices of his teeth.

"You... will not... deny my... destiny!"

He stumbled to the ground, first to his knees, then flat on his back. Brushing her mother aside, Jaycee rushed over. She placed a trepidatious hand on the textured sleeve of Baron's tunic. He lay still as a corpse. The crimson mask splattered across Baron's lips and chin made her fear the worst.

Oh, no! she thought.

She closed her eyes, and the tidal wave of weeping taunted her throat and puffed out her cheeks. Tears pooled in her eyes.

Baron let out a shallow breath. Jaycee exhaled a gust of air.

"Hard to tell, but..." David said from deeper inside the building.

He banged on the corner of a tablet until it displayed the info he wanted.

"I think the MegaCore—this one, the original—absorbed Baron's, uh, ah, essence, for lack of a better word."

"Did your machine remove his... powers?" Valerie asked, hesitating.

Baron's arm lifted, jolting Jaycee. He squeezed the air—something moved behind David's feet.

"David, watch out!" Valerie cried.

David hiked up his knees in a startled little dance and scampered outside.

Responsi-Bulldog's small, struggling mechanized body hobbled into the sunlight.

"Looks like someone left some poopy in the yard. Wasn't me! Ha. Ha. Woof. Woof."

The artificial canine trotted beside David. Baron

collapsed. Jaycee released the floodgates. She bawled over her father—her former hero.

"Oh my—everyone, look up!" Valerie said.

Jaycee wiped away tears and heeded her mother's calling. Above the tallest tree in the greenery area, Eric hovered. Jaycee made a rough estimation that he flew twenty-five feet in the air—and rising. He had won but looked so defeated.

"Eric!" Jaycee shouted, running underneath his position. "It's over; come down!"

"I can't," he said. "It hurts."

"You don't have to touch the ground! You can just float. Please, just come back down!"

"Jaycee," Eric said, pulling farther upward. "We knew I'd get to a point where I'd have to stay higher and higher eventually. This is eventually."

Raising more, Eric became a dark blue speck in the air.

"Eric!" David called out. "You've done so much more than me or anyone—or yourself—thought you could! I get it now; I really do!"

"It doesn't make up for..." Eric said before trailing off. "For what happened. For Mom."

David joined Jaycee, positioning himself directly under Eric.

"You feel guilty about your mother, but you shouldn't!" David yelled, his voice rife with emotion. "It was an accident—my accident, not yours. You didn't do anything wrong!"

"I pushed her away!" Eric yelled back.

His voice got harder to hear the higher he rose.

"These powers should've gone to someone else!" Eric said. "Someone who..."

David put his face in his hands.

"I was too busy selfishly wallowing in my pain to

do anything about yours, Eric."

"What is it?" Jaycee asked, frantic. "What's going on? Eric's powers are like my dad's, so what's the problem?"

"Some genius I am. It's so obvious now," David said, lowering his hands and revealing his watering eyes. "It was never a weakness. It's a mental block! You subconsciously won't allow yourself to come down!"

The crying claimed David.

"Forgive me! Forgive yourself!"

A crowd found them, and the mass of nearby concerned citizens formed a circle around Jaycee, Valerie, and David. Drones and helicopters blipped by, appearing as specks on the horizon.

"What's taking them so long?!" Jaycee said, frantic. "All the flying robot things in this city, and none of them are here when we need them!"

Firetrucks, ambulances, and police vehicles honked to clear the way. Among the beeping cars sat Kev's, top-down and carrying Go-Go, Supercut, and Extra.

Behind the wheel, Kev's face tensed—his eyebrows raised so high they could've left his head. Chauffeuring battered and beaten superheroes and experiencing the rest of the day's mania had left him shaken. Jaycee wondered if she should tell Kev that he was secretly giving a ride to their mutual friends, Yvette, Melvin, and Tiffany—or if they simply informed him on the way.

They're here. That's all that should matter, Jaycee thought as a hot tear streaked down her cheek. *But what can they do? What can any of us do?*

"Forgive yourself!" David screamed once more with tears flowing down his face, but his son flew too high.

Eric Icarus floated up into the clouds until he disappeared.

Chapter Twenty-Three: *CLOUD*

JAYCEE

JAYCEE COULD ONLY SEE HER forehead in the reflection of the glass viewing panel. It was positioned to be eye-level with an adult, but when she stepped a little closer to the pod—standing on her tippy-toes—Baron's slumbering face came into view. The screen attached just underneath the rectangular pane displayed his vitals: the high level of sedatives pumping into Baron's brain guaranteed it'd be a long, long sleepy time for this would-be conqueror. Drugged or not, standing in front of his stasis chamber gave Jaycee the creeps.

"Why wasn't what we had good enough for you?" she whispered.

Footsteps startled her.

"So, it looks like I'll be hanging around Pantheon Tower a little longer than expected today."

Mr. B? Jaycee thought, alarmed.

Jaycee scanned the row of pods on either side of her but saw no sign of David.

"Meetings with attorneys and investigators, buncha boring formality stuff."

David emerged from behind the last pod on the left, speaking into his phone.

"Big, rich corporate guys have popped out of thin air, all with their eyes on what to do with Baron's business. They want to keep me around to discuss a consulting position."

This level is off-limits. I can't be seen here! Jaycee thought, hiding behind Baron's chrome pod.

"There's a ton of tech talk left to be done," David said. "The executives' pitch contained words like 'patents' and 'compensation.'"

Jaycee made a cautious move, careful to stay hidden behind her father's chamber. She peeked around its curved edge. David stopped in front of the pod next to Baron's. Jaycee tensed, freezing her muscles, and wishing she could turn into a ghost. She peeked at the vertical cell across from them, behind where David stood. It was dim, but she could still read the pod's nameplate: "EXTENDO."

Oh, that just makes this way more fun, Jaycee thought, pushing away grim memories.

More rows of pods stood behind Jaycee. She feared for a moment that she would have to navigate her way to freedom through the shrouded maze.

As a nervous twitch, David tugged at the collar of his black V-neck.

Who is he talking to? Jaycee wondered.

"They might just be covering their collective heinies, but, uh..." David said.

He paced up to Baron's pod. Jaycee crouched down, hoping the faintly lit room would provide enough shadow to cover her.

This is so flushed! The last thing I need is to explain what I'm doing here.

"I think me liking it here isn't the craziest thing

that's happened recently," David said.

She braved a glance. David stared at Baron's unconscious face.

"I at least gotta take in this moment before they kick me out for sneaking into levels I'm not supposed to be on," he said, softening his voice. "If I'm caught, I'll just say I got doused with more knockout gas, and I'm a little loopy."

He gave a light chuckle while looking at the room's corners.

Checking for security cameras, Jaycee thought. *He's just as paranoid about being here as I am. Well, lucky for both of us, this room isn't under surveillance. Fat chance that'll last long, though.*

"Oh, and I'll make sure they preserve your mom here. It's weird, but maybe something good can come from this."

Jaycee leaned against the side of the pod. She exhaled in a long, controlled breath, careful not to make a sound.

You're right, Mr. B. It is super weird.

"Maybe we can find out if there are other people like your mom. And if there are, I hope they're a lot like you."

He sighed.

"It's late and it's been an, ah, unpredictable day, and—look, I know about your, um, current cloudy condition, but, hey, lemme drive you home later. It's a dad thing. Bye, Eric."

Jaycee held her breath to keep from choking on air. After a beep, David tapped a button to disconnect the call. He lingered on Baron.

"At least I'm not as crazy as you," he said.

Jaycee's panicked lungs betrayed her. Jaycee sputtered out a breath. Her eyes met his.

"Ms. Maddox?!" David said. "What're you doing here? I mean, what I'm doing here is, um…"

"How about we settle for an 'I won't tell if you won't tell' kind of deal?"

She stood up and stepped beside him. Looking down at her sky-blue top and pink shorts, Jaycee wondered how she was able to hide for as long as she did.

"Deal," he said. "But I'm pretty sure we're both here for the same reason."

They both gazed at Baron.

"I wish I could've just talked to him," Jaycee said, forlorn. "Maybe I could've done something. Soon enough, this whole building will be crawling with investigators. With all the 'model employees' locked in these stasis pods, this place will be a science circus. Who knows when I'll get another chance to just…"

"Face him?" David answered for her. "I've been holding onto the idea of a second chance for years now. Even when hope is right in front of me, it still feels so far away."

"What do you mean?"

"Let's just say I'm not thrilled with who they put Baron's pod next to."

He tapped a button on the pod to the right of her father's. The metal panel retracted, revealing Eliza's comatose face underneath the glass. A lump formed in Jaycee's throat.

"Eric will get a chance to see her again," Jaycee said. "I just know it."

"I've been calling him," he revealed. "Leaving him messages. He doesn't answer, of course. I dunno, it's stupid, but I kind of just like doing it."

He strolled down the aisle of faceless pods. The back of his head wiggled as if shaking off the dungeon's creepiness.

"I came here looking for my dad," Jaycee said. "But, uh... I'm glad I found you, Mr. B."

He stopped.

"Me, too, Ms. Maddox," David said, looking back with a weak smile. "Me, too."

• • •

"HE FLEW TOO CLOSE TO THE SUN!"

Jaycee scrolled to the next headline.

"TEEN HERO MISSING AFTER BATTLE WITH BILLIONAIRE"

She swiped down to read another.

"ERIC ICARUS FEARED—"

She turned her phone away, unwilling to finish reading the last part of the sentence. The fancy hotel's busy lobby left Jaycee unnoticed, standing with her mother near the vestibule. Through the glass of the revolving entrance doors, Jaycee saw the street outside come alive with out-of-towners going on their big evening out.

Busy night for a Thursday, she thought. *Busy day for a lifetime.*

It was getting late; she thought she ought to go home and try to sleep. Even though she had a lethargic dampener weighing down her brain, Jaycee knew that rest wouldn't come to her no matter how hard she tried.

David walked up from the entryway, brushing past a couple dressed for a swanky date night. Sparkly jewelry festooned the affluent woman while her partner exuded class in a sleek black suit and tie. David shuffled along, out of place in his wrinkled t-shirt that looked straight out of a Pantheon custodial locker. A large Pantheon lightning logo on the front of his top completed the lost and found look.

He approached Jaycee and Valerie. He opened his mouth to speak when Duncan swarmed over, wedging himself between them. The snooty concierge's speed-walk wiggled his little shiny nametag.

"May I show you to your room, sir?" Duncan offered. "I understand you are a brand-new guest here in our hotel."

"Oh, I'm already checked in, but, man, this is some quick customer service, huh?" David said in a drowsy drawl.

No way he could sleep either, apparently, Jaycee thought.

"More like he wants to get out of the way before the rich folk see you," Jaycee said.

"Always a pleasure to see you, Miss Maddox," Duncan huffed, squinting his eye at Jaycee. "For those, ahem, unfamiliar with such a big, clean place, finding your way around can be quite the maze."

"He'll be quite alright, Duncan," Valerie butted in, coming to the rescue. "I can take it from here."

"Very well, Ms. Cooper," Duncan acknowledged, flashing an insincere grin before returning to the check-in counter.

"You don't have to do any of this, Valerie," David said. "I could've stayed at Pantheon. I have meetings scheduled there anyway. Or I could've just stayed at the Boxworth Building. I'll tell the repair crew to keep it down. It'll be fine."

"Please, you don't even have any bags with you. This is the least I can do," Valerie said with a warm smile.

Who is this woman? Jaycee pondered, sizing her mother up as if first meeting her.

"Trust me," Valerie continued, "exploiting

everyone's overly apologetic willingness to bend over backward for me is one of the few things I can enjoy during this…"

She looked away.

"Now I'm apologizing," Valerie said, sighing. "I keep talking about myself. I feel like an imbecile—"

"Don't sweat it," David said. "I could use a break from thinking about myself and, well, everything. Besides, I like seeing you flex your muscles."

Her mother's smile got a little bigger. Jaycee felt her stomach turn.

"I'll let you try to get some sleep," Valerie said. "And I can do more than take advantage of the perks my, er, status grants me. If you need to discuss things, I'm available."

"Believe me, if I get wind of anything, I'll call you."

Valerie paused. Her brief silence made Jaycee realize how loud the comers and goers were in the background, as well as the nonstop ringing and answering of phones.

"If you ever want to meet outside of a hotel lobby…" Valerie started before her cheeks flushed with red. "That would be very acceptable."

Valerie's eyelids fluttered as if she had an unwanted epiphany.

"Absolutely take your time," Valerie said, flustered. "I mean, you're in a time of grief, and it was highly inappropriate of me to suggest—!"

"It's a date," David said, rescuing her.

"What's going on here?" Jaycee said with a spiked eyebrow. "Are you two…?"

"Saying goodnight," Valerie stated.

"You're, just, what, going to bed?!" Jaycee said in disbelief. "Am I gonna have to lead the search party myself, or what?! Fine, you go to sleep; I'm gonna go look for—"

"It's only been a few hours," David said. "He'll come back when he's ready."

"The first few hours are the most crucial, Mr. B!"

"Drones are still scanning," he assured. "Aircraft radar didn't detect anything, but the satellite feeds are constantly updated."

"Are you kidding me? In this city? We have smartphones, smart drones—heck, there're probably nanites in our toothpaste! Anything could scramble their signals! Come on!"

"Jennifer," Valerie said. "Everything that can be done is being done."

She slid her arm around Jaycee.

"And if everything isn't good enough, we'll do more," Valerie said.

Valerie fidgeted then placed her hand in her pants pocket.

"Well, we just wanted to see that you're settling in," she said, easing back into her usual stark demeanor. "Talk soon, David."

He gave a gentle wave as he made his way to the elevator at the back of the lobby.

"Be right back, Mom," Jaycee said, pocketing her phone.

She strode at a brisk pace that would make Duncan jealous. In no time, she walked beside David.

"I didn't wanna bring this up in front of my mom," Jaycee said, careful to keep her voice down. "But I need to know what's up with this whole you knowing everybody's secret identities thing."

"What I—and your mom—know," he said, matching her tone as he kept walking. "Isn't something you or any of the other super-kids need to worry about."

Jaycee's grimace didn't display confidence.

"Hey, I honor all my deals," David said, winking. "Especially the 'I won't tell if you won't tell' kind."

"I'm sorry to bother you," a kind voice said.

They both looked up and saw a brunette girl in an orange floral frock. She appeared to be about Jaycee's age.

"I just wanted to say how sorry we all are."

"Oh, I, eh, appreciate that," David said with a curled lip.

"What your son did today was fantastic."

"Yeah," David said, uneasy. "I'm proud of him."

"Eric has paved the way for a lot of people who want to follow in his footsteps."

"He's a role model, for sure," Jaycee said, not knowing where to go with this encounter.

David sidestepped his way to the glossy doors of the elevator.

"My name is Rebecca, by the way," the girl said to David. "Your wife probably never spoke about my father or the others."

He looked away, ignoring her, but Rebecca followed him.

"My father used to be one of Eliza's caretakers when she was very young."

David stopped dead in his tracks.

"What?"

"It was only for a short time, and she was only a child," Rebecca said.

Jaycee didn't know what to say. Part of her thought the girl was a crazy fan. Another part knew better.

She can't know about Eric's mom. There's no way.

"You've probably read a lot about my family and me," David said, annoyed. "Sometimes, I think the freedom of the press is a little too free. Look, I'm sure you mean well, but I've got to be going."

"Eric will be okay," Rebecca said, watching David tap at the "up" button. "He'll fly his way back down to earth."

Jaycee's eyes bugged out, but David brushed off the odd comment. He stepped into the lift.

"People like us always do," Rebecca said.

David raised his eyebrows, confused, as the doors closed.

"Jennifer, we must be going," Valerie said from behind Jaycee.

"What'd you say your name was?" Jaycee asked Rebecca.

She resisted the urge to paw at the girl just to confirm she was real and not a hallucination.

"Now, Jennifer!"

"In a minute!" Jaycee snapped back through gritted teeth.

Valerie placed her hands on her hips, oozing with impatience. Jaycee turned around only to see that Rebecca had vanished.

· · ·

The full moon's reflected sunlight did little to illuminate the dark sky. Jaycee pressed her face against her bedroom window, desperate to catch a sighting of a boy soaring through the nighttime clouds.

Come on, Peter Pan. Neverland isn't so great.

"Jennifer Claire."

Her mother's voice startled her. Jaycee wondered how long she had been sitting at the window. Jaycee slid off the sill and scanned her room. Her pink bedsheets were neatly pulled up to her matching pillows. Her bookbag was arranged neatly by her uncluttered desk. She had already changed into her sky-blue sleep shirt and matching shorts. Jaycee reasoned that her things were orderly enough to pass the warden's inspection.

"It's late. You should sleep," Valerie said.

Jaycee made no effort to hide her surprise as she sat on her bed—she expected a scolding. Standing in the white-framed doorway, Valerie clasped her hands together, putting out an unusually warm vibe. Since she still wore her business casual attire from earlier, Jaycee knew her mother hadn't completely thawed.

"Tomorrow, I'd like it if you resumed your studies. Learning doesn't stop just because it's almost summer break. But I understand if you don't think you're up to it."

"Uh, okay," Jaycee said, further puzzled.

"What? I'm not allowed to go a little easy on you? After all of this—"

"It's late, and I should get some sleep," Jaycee interjected.

She crawled into bed, facing away from Valerie.

"I just don't want to add any more stress," her mother said. "There will be enough of that as is. I want you to know I'm on your side through all the superhero business."

"Good to know. Snoring now."

"Pantheon's executives and shareholders wish to handle this as internally as possible, but there will be an investigation."

"My secret identity will still be a secret," Jaycee said. "No one can access the encrypted Super Society files anyway. They'd have to talk to Dad, and he's not gonna..."

Mentioning him made her feel sick.

"Everything about Baron Maddox is complicated. I'm here if you want to talk—"

"He was power-hungry and went crazy!" Jaycee snapped, sitting straight up. "What's so complicated about that?! I don't want to talk about him! I'm going to bed!"

Jaycee lay back down, gazing at the ceiling. Her mother lingered for a moment before closing the door. Jaycee grabbed her phone from her nightstand. A tap later and her messages to Eric displayed. She stared at the previous exchanges, waving her thumb in little circles over the touchpad's keyboard. She selected a female zombie emoji and hit send. Jaycee sighed at the thought of her digital ghoul being ghosted.

Feeling moronic about wasting her time with a text, she put her pink-cased phone back on the stand. She reached up to switch off her pink lamp, dousing the room in darkness save for a unicorn-shaped nightlight. Pulling up her covers as she rolled over, Jaycee shut her eyes and took a deep breath. Consciousness drifted away.

"Note to self," she said, half-asleep. "After school tomorrow, go to Pantheon... Snag some state-of-the-art surveillance tech... Or get super-speed gear like Go-Go's... Lead the search on my own if no one else will."

Too tired to move, she gave into slumber.

• • •

"Kev is, like, such a good tutor! Def making him my exclusive study buddy, if you know what I mean," Tiffany said.

"It's good you've lined up a tutor," Valerie said from behind her desk, disrupting Tiffany's boasting to her minions. "At the rate you're at, you're going to need one for summer school. No talking.”

From a few rows over, Jaycee smirked at Tiffany, who rolled her eyes as she turned to face forward in her chair. Tiffany glanced back and smiled a sad smile. Jaycee returned in kind. They had settled into their routines but at least now had found common ground, grim as it was.

Jaycee ignored the test paper on her desk, slipping her attention to the window next to her. She reckoned it ought to be against the law to keep kids inside the school on such a sunny day. Gazing at the fluffy white clouds, she daydreamed about what it would be like to live so high up. She grinned at the idea of being so free and above all the nonsense down on earth. She caught herself dreaming about him again.

“Miss Maddox—Jennifer!”

Her mother’s voice shook her back to reality.

“An incomplete means a zero grade,” Valerie said. “If you think I’m going to take it easy on you, you are sorely mistaken, young lady.”

Jaycee stretched her lips into a crooked frown, scoffing at the concept of her mother being chill for more than one second.

“It’s highly irregular that after yesterday’s, ahem, excitement, you all are allowed to take the final today—frankly, it’s been a week full of unexpected distractions,” Valerie said. “But these are unprecedented times. Just because it’s a Friday, don’t rush through the exam. I hope that you all used what time you had to study.”

Jaycee knew her mother was talking about her. Ignoring her, Jaycee stole a glance at the clouds once more and smiled.

Bang!

Jaycee whipped her head in the direction of the

now wide-open door, her heart leaping into her throat.

"Sorry-sorry-sorry!" she heard coming from the doorway.

The hope to see Eric float through the door lasted a millisecond, but it was long enough to disorient her. Jaycee's head cleared as she heard Melvin's sneakers squeaking on the way to the empty seat next to her. He shot her a nervous grin as he sat.

"Melvin, so nice of you to join us in taking the final exam," Valerie said, feigning courtesy.

"He won't be tardy again, Ms. Cooper," Yvette said from the door.

She gave a half-wave to Jaycee.

"It's the last day of school. Think you're up for the challenge, Melvin?" Valerie mocked.

She nodded at Yvette as she left.

With his bandaged fingers, Melvin took his pencil and notebook out of his backpack. He slid his smartphone from his shorts pocket to peek at his messages.

"No phones!"

"Yes, Ms. Cooper!"

The boy let out a little snarl. Jaycee put her palm over her mouth to suppress a laughing fit.

"Couldn't find a ride?" Jaycee whispered. "You needed Go-Go to run you here?"

"Doncha think we woulda got here a lil' quicker if she had her workin' boots on?" Melvin whispered back. "As if all superhero business isn't on lockdown for the time being anyway."

"Lockdown, schmockdown. As soon as I get new power enhancers, I'll show all of you how to be a real hero!"

"No talking!" Valerie scolded. "Considering recent events, I'm willing to give the so-called 'Pantheon Pals' some leniency, but I'm warning you two!"

"Sorry, Ms. Cooper!" Melvin said before quieting his voice back down. "How are you, by the way? Are you good?"

Jaycee thought about her answer.

"I'll get there," she said in a soft voice.

He sent her a polite grin, but it faded into a saddened look that only someone with the weight of the world on their shoulders would have.

"We shoulda known or done somethin' sooner."

"Hey, if I didn't know, no one could've," she whispered. "The Society sticks together, right?"

He darted his eyes to Tiffany, who snuck a peek back long enough to flash a smile.

"That's right," Melvin said quietly. "That goes for every member."

He nodded at the window. Jaycee looked at the open sky.

"Every member," she said, smiling.

"Okay, that does it!" Valerie snapped. "Principal's office, both of you! Now!"

Melvin's jaw dropped. Jaycee's eyelids fluttered.

"But Mom!"

ERIC

The sun hurt Eric's eyes as he opened them, so he cast them down to the clouds below. Beds of fluffy white puffs swirled together far beneath his feet. Blasts of wind shook the grogginess right out of him.

Oh no! I must've passed out! he thought. *No telling where I've drifted.*

He reached into one of his belt pockets and retrieved a folded pair of dark blue sunglasses. His fingers shook, but he was careful not to drop them. He wrapped the shades over his eyes. Sleek and smooth, they matched his costume.

I didn't bring any snacks, but apparently Mr. Maddox remembered to pack eyewear in my costume. Which is good because otherwise, this would've, ya know, really sucked.

With his vision protected, Eric gazed at the endless sky above him. He felt his body lift higher as if being pulled by a magnet.

"Next stop, outer space," he said into the forceful winds.

He took out his phone from his pants pocket. The message and voicemail notifications displayed double digits, something he was unaccustomed to seeing.

"'Hey, everyone, thanks for reaching out,'" Eric said with chattering teeth. "'Sorry I didn't call back, but a few hundred feet ago, something started blocking my service. I'd try to figure it out if I wasn't too busy using all the willpower I have left to concentrate on not blowing away in the wind. It's no biggie. We've all been there, right?'"

Eric noticed the low battery level—and the time.

"Friday? It's been a whole day?!" he said in disbelief.

He imagined the other kids at school, excited about summer break. He thought of his teammates and felt a flush of sorrow.

"I know you won't think it's long enough, but... Call off the search, Jaycee."

Eric carefully inserted his phone back into his pocket, like he was handling a fragile antique. Eric considered how his personal effects would be discovered; hidden treasures to be looted off his lifeless body. His trembling fingers withdrew the thumb drive from a pocket on his belt. The small plastic metal stick slipped from his hand. The wind stole the little case; Eric watched through squinted eyes as the thumb drive vanished as a blip in the vast sky.

Hugging his torso, with his knees bent, Eric sunk his chin into his chest. Furious gusts of air pummeled his body and whipped through his hair. Eric's face grew colder—fierce winds bit at his ears. The gradual ascent made for a grueling ordeal, worsened by his crippling inability to move in any other direction. Pangs of hunger strangled his belly. With an outstretched hand, Eric reached down for nothing. Or maybe it was anything, whatever sense of control there was to be had. His arm wavered in the bluster as he recoiled back into himself.

"I don't know why I can't... I don't know, I just don't know," Eric said aloud, nearly unable to hear himself. "I'm so sorry, Mom."

He told himself to go back to sleep. As he closed his eyelids, he saw... something. It blurred far away, bright and hovering. The orange-ish object moved closer to him. It was no thing—this was a person. Eric raised the sunglasses to see with his own eyes— whoever it was glided with ease.

It was a girl. She looked like she could've been one of his classmates—if the school uniform was an orange jumpsuit with black straps and a face-covering that looked like a futuristic gasmask. Sunlight streaked across its smooth surface.

"There you are, Eric Icarus," she called out.

I'm dreaming.

"My name is Rebecca," the girl said.

Eric figured her voice projected from a speaker

device on her mask. She wore no anti-grav device that he could see.

"Okay, now I know I'm dreaming," he said.

Rebecca floated nearer, providing a better look at her face beneath her transparent mask.

"And I'm dreaming about an angel?"

She smiled with a casualness that betrayed the intensity of the extreme elevation and uncontrollable airflow around them.

"I'm dead, right? Eric asked.

"Nope," Rebecca said. "I've come to take you home."

"Which home? I technically have two. One is basically destroyed, and the other, well, it's a palace of weirdness that always felt strange—"

"Not that home."

She pointed up, and his face followed. In the distance, even higher still, a cluster of clouds seemed to move at will, dispersing into the atmosphere. The wisps dissolved, revealing a shimmering silver city in the sky. Eric blinked, not believing his eyes. Spires shone in the sunlight, and domed structures sparkled, with glass and metal twinkling like a crystal castle. Its towers stretched above and below the rim encircling the city. Eric squinted, struggling to glimpse what looked like people flying in and around the massive metropolis.

"This home," Rebecca said. "Your real home."

ABOUT THE AUTHOR

As an author drawn to superhero sci-fi aimed at young adult readers, Jon McBrine adds a unique spin on coming-of-age stories - by adding superpowers, snarky villains, and big robot fights. Focused on pure fun and adventure, Jon also showcases the people under the mask (and spandex).

Jon works in the Dallas area as an author, graphic designer, illustrator, and comic book aficionado. He combines these different fields of work to build interesting projects that capture humor, intrigue, and authentic emotion. His ever-evolving career trajectory keeps his sense of wonder alive—and his coffee cup full.

ALSO AVAILABLE

UNSECRET IDENTITY:
ERIC ICARUS - BOOK ONE

Tech mogul Baron Maddox takes superpowered Eric under his wing and transforms him into Eric Icarus, the newest—and maskless—addition to the Super Society, legendary defenders of the city. Equipped with his trusty decoy anti-gravity backpack, Eric is able to pose as just another costumed crusader without becoming a lab rat. Overnight, Eric finds himself catapulted into a world of action, adventure, and suspense, as he battles villains and saves the day with his incredible flying ability. Eric's inventor father keeps a wary eye on him, remembering all too well the shadow that Baron Maddox once cast over their lives.

jonmcbrine.com

ALSO AVAILABLE

ERIC ICARUS
MYTHOS

AVENGE HER

AVENGE HER

On the day of a weapons demonstration of an advanced set of cybernetic armor, fame-craving scientist David Boxworth expects his invention to set him for life. After a disastrous accident, David's life spirals into darkness, leaving him questioning his city's heroes and taking fate into his own hands.

jonmcbrine.com

ALSO AVAILABLE

THE SUPERVILLAIN'S OATH

Teenage sidekick Sidebar has been training under Judge Justice, the leader of the Super Society, and is itching for action. Sidebar gets more than he bargained for when he is face-to-face with one of the team's deadliest villains. Separated only by a pane of glass, the young superhero must look evil in its eye - or, in the case of the case of the dangerous villain Hotwire, an eerie faceless abyss. Can the heroes foil the criminal mastermind's chaotic scheme, or will the city's greatest defenders go to an extreme they must keep hidden for generations to come?

jonmcbrine.com

www.ingramcontent.com/pod-product-compliance
Lightning Source LLC
Chambersburg PA
CBHW071750110726
47908CB00006B/1752